James H. Kelly

REBELLION

First and Always: Rebellion

"I AM A SOLDIER, FIRST AND ALWAYS"

THE DISTINGUISHED CAREER OF WINFIELD SCOTT HANCOCK

A NOVEL

VOLUME I: REBELLION

James Harold Kelly

First and Always: Rebellion

"I am a Soldier, First and Always" The Distinguished Career of Winfield Scott Hancock, Volume I: Rebellion is a work of historical fiction, and is the first of two volumes in the Winfield Scott Hancock series. Known persons and events appear throughout this novel and are included to tell Hancock's story. They are not intended to change the fictional nature of the book. In all other respects, any resemblance to persons living or dead is entirely coincidental.

ISBN 9781700045003

Cover Photograph by the Author: "The Confederate Line" Gettysburg National Battlefield, Pennsylvania

For Linda Marie

First and Always: Rebellion

TABLE OF CONTENTS

LIST OF MAPS

James H. Kelly

FORWARD

He drew the smell of the battlefield deep into his lungs and his consciousness. The sensation was at the far edges of his memory after fifteen years, and now it came rushing back. In the distance, gun smoke and the faint sounds of men in conflict rode on the wind. He recalled the strange mix of warfare's excitement and horror, where most soldiers lived, and felt it building within him.

Many adversaries were his long-time friends, or at least acquaintances, with similar backgrounds and training. Some were West Point classmates who had served with him in places like Chapultepec and Churubusco or on the Western Frontier. Their shared battlefield experience now set aside as they swore to bring surrender or death to each other – it did not matter which. He believed the Confederates to be traitors to the nation, the Constitution and the oath they swore upon graduation from the United States Military Academy.

Winfield Scott Hancock, West Point Class of 1844, felt the weight of the stars on his epaulets as he stood before his regiments in line of battle. Hancock scanned the open area near the Confederate strongpoints that ran between the York and James Rivers. Hancock's brigade swept through the left of the undefended Confederate line and stood alone, preparing to attack. Longstreet's Rebels readied themselves in the strongpoint, unsure who the soldiers were on the small plain. Colonel Amasa Cobb, commanding the 5th Wisconsin, stood with Hancock watching the enemy's strongpoint activity.

"Cobb, they appear to be curious or confused as to who we are. Let's tell them." They raised the National colors on the redoubt's highest point as the artillery began its deadly fire. The Confederates would never forget the name Hancock.

PART ONE. THE SOLDIER

CHAPTER 1
THE PATH FORWARD

"Wait for me!" John yelled, as his fifteen-year-old twin brothers, Hilary and Winfield, ran through the tree line marking the edge of their grandfather's farm. The vibrant colors of the trees, a mixture of deep greens, and the smell of the summer season was refreshing. John, five years younger, continued to sprint in a vain attempt to catch his older siblings.

"Winfield, slow down," once more a cry to reach the boys as much a call to be one of them. The brothers slowed to a walk as they approached the house and let John catch up.

They loved living in the rural Pennsylvania countryside. The area between Philadelphia and Valley Forge held Norristown for the last three decades. Along the banks of the Schuylkill River, the rolling hills of Montgomery County provided the perfect setting for the Hancock boys to learn, explore, and dream of future adventures.

The three boys caught their breath and entered the house loudly, as most boys do. Benjamin was waiting in the parlor.

Benjamin Franklin Hancock, following his father's example, gave his sons well-respected names. Winfield Scott, inspired by some unforeseen connection to history since the end of the war with Great Britain, only a short decade ago, or perhaps an accolade to the great chieftain and national hero. Hilary, named after a former mayor of

Philadelphia, and young John Hancock, a founding father. Their names were familiar to everyone in Norristown. The twins were not identical, and their characters were further apart. They resembled their father – fair complexion, tall, athletic, and handsome young men with boundless energy.

Benjamin and his wife, Elizabeth Hoxworth, were native Pennsylvanians and descendants of several generations of farmers and patriots who served in the American Revolution. The Hancocks settled in Norristown, where Benjamin taught school while studying law. Admitted to the Montgomery County Bar Association, he established his law practice in town. Always active, he was a deacon in the Norristown Baptist Church and participated in municipal government as Justice of the Peace. Elizabeth ran a small business creating and selling women's hats from their home. Over time, the family became prominent and established themselves as notable contributors to the Norristown community.

The boys thrived in the town setting. Hilary and Winfield initially attended the private Norristown Academy, where Benjamin was a trustee. He was also a member of the Norristown School Board, working to establish the state's free school system. The Hancocks believed it set a better example for other parents to enrol the twins in the Norristown Public School, and the boys excelled. Winfield's public speaking skills were second nature. Among the topics, Benjamin reinforced patriotism and a citizen's responsibility.

"Service to the community, and more importantly, to the nation, is of major import. You must bond with your country, community, and government through active citizenship."

The boys took turns imitating Benjamin and repeating his lines when they were alone, never realizing they were reinforcing his lessons. They learned respect for the law, reverence for God, and the principles of the newly-formed Democratic Party. Benjamin introduced the boys to politics – part of the plan to expand Winfield and Hilary's understanding of the republic. It was one more step towards the practice of the law. They listened intently to the discussions concerning the nation and of the administration, Congress, and local politics.

Winfield was developing into a person of action, and, coupled with his desire to lead, continually sought to distinguish himself.

"It's time for your studies," Benjamin loudly proclaimed, "but before we start, why don't you tell me about your trouble today?"

His gaze fell upon Winfield. The problem with small towns was news traveled fast, and bad news even more quickly.

"No trouble. There were a few boys taking advantage of a new boy. It is simply not right. I felt someone should stand up for him, and I believed that someone was me."

The incident flashed through Winfield's mind. His latest adversary was slightly taller than the fifteen-year-old Winfield and somewhat stockier. They moved slowly, steadily, circling one another as Winfield sized up this opponent. Closing the distance between them, Winfield sought an opening. There it was – a hesitation. The larger boy's eyes were darting to survey the others who had gathered around them. Striking quickly, Winfield landed a sharp blow to the larger boy's cheek. An audible sound, not a scream, just a slight recognition of pain and surprise. A second strike, this one to the midsection, causing the boy to lose his breath for an instant. The boy raised a hand, a signal the contest was over. Winfield didn't press the advantage.

"I only threw one punch to the chin of the loudest of the bullies. There may have been a second punch. I don't remember. He never even touched me, but it will not happen again. We will include any new boys in our games and the like – and it didn't take much arm twisting by me at all."

"I have heard it was a short altercation. You are aware of my feelings regarding fighting, especially by my sons. I tend to agree there are times when we must stand up for those who need help. I am satisfied your courageous display was only short-lived. Remember, I do applaud your actions, but your mother and I cannot condone ruffian behavior nor attitude from you or your brothers."

Winfield nodded, accepting his father's direction and believing he had handled the situation correctly. Satisfied, Benjamin moved on to the topic of public speaking, a necessary skill in the boys' future law careers. The brothers participated in school debates and clubs, each helping in some way to shape their ability to think critically and convey cogent arguments. Winfield was somewhat at ease speaking to groups of people. Hilary's oratory was adequate, but he needed to overcome his nerves.

Independence Day arrived as it did every year, and Norristown held an annual Fourth of July celebration, which the Hancocks always attended with the rest of the town's people. This year, in particular, Winfield was more than an attendee.

"Winfield!"

He turned on his heel as he heard his name called and faced the direction of a group of boys. They stood patiently waiting for their leader, their captain, to issue the orders of the day. He had formed a junior militia, which was regularly seen by nearly all the inhabitants of the town as they paraded through the streets. It was clear to all who observed this group who was in charge. Was it something within him that kindled the desire to lead soldiers? Was it his name, or perhaps a combination of the two? Nonetheless, Winfield stood before the novice militia company preparing for the town's Independence Day celebration. He had other things on his mind.

"No drilling today, boys. I'm off to deliver a speech in the town."

The boys laughed, then formed a line behind Winfield and the family as they headed into the center of Norristown. Foremost on his mind was his pending delivery of the Declaration before the entire town gathering for this celebration. Those who knew him recognized his public speaking ability. He was selected by his teachers to provide the address, and it was an honor, his father assured him. The boy had been skeptical at first but dutifully prepared for his presentation. The day was finally upon him.

Dignitaries and local government and business leaders were seated on the platform as a band played. Townsfolk sang patriotic songs, and civic leaders made speeches as Winfield sat patiently next to his parents, waiting for his introduction. Words tumbled in his mind.

"Please don't stumble over the words," Winfield said to himself, concerned about the slight shaking he felt in his core. A nervous feeling started to make its way to the surface, bringing with it a sense of nausea in his stomach.

"Oh, God, don't get sick. You'll never live it down."

Elizabeth noticed the slight movement of Winfield's legs, a little trembling, barely visible, and certainly not noticeable by anyone but her. She touched her husband's arm and nodded towards Winfield. Resting his hand on Winfield's shoulder for reassurance, the nervousness seemed to disappear at his father's touch. He stared down, studying the printed words in his hands. Winfield barely heard his name announced as Congressman Florence finished speaking and introduced him to the crowd. He stood and strode purposefully to the podium, recalling the instructions to project and enunciate. He was about to read a document adopted by the Second Continental Congress on this day in Philadelphia, only 63 years earlier. Benjamin's lessons rushed through the young boy's mind. He thought of the republic, and the people gathered before him and those throughout the country.

"I'll be alright."

Winfield was ready. Mind racing, scanning the large crowd, he said quietly to himself, "Thank God. Start speaking, you fool, and it will be fine."

It was loud enough for the dignitaries gathered on the platform to hear, and they chuckled. No one in the crowd had an inkling what was going on with the young man standing at the podium. Winfield thanked the assembled group and began slowly. Confidence would never be a problem for Hancock.

"When in the course of human events..."

People stirred in their seats and many who were standing shifted their stance for comfort, but heard the handsome young man, and what seemed to be his natural ability to capture everyone's attention. The warm July air was hardly noticeable as they listened, transfixed on the words and their presenter. He had a presence!

"We hold these truths to be self-evident, that all men are created equal, that they are endowed by their Creator with certain unalienable rights, that among these are Life, Liberty, and the Pursuit of Happiness."

He read through the document flawlessly. The crowd applauded, some cheered for this youngster, a future leader, and son of Norristown. Some could only speculate what the future held for this young man.

Congressman Florence approached Benjamin after Winfield's presentation. For the first time, Benjamin discussed the possibility of his son's attendance at the United States Military Academy in New York. It presented an intriguing alternative path of higher education.

CHAPTER 2
A CONGRESSMAN'S FAITH

Summer passed. Over the next few months, their sons' future was a frequent topic. Benjamin seriously contemplated a continued education for both Winfield and Hilary in the study and practice of the law.

"It is a noble profession. It will enhance one's stature within the community and may even lead to an elected office," Benjamin thought to himself.

"Lizzie, I believe the opportunity to attend West Point could serve the boy quite well. It's a good path for Winfield."

They sat quietly in the yard, surrounded by the red and yellow hues that seemed to be everywhere in the autumn foliage. The coolness of the breeze blowing across the Pennsylvania sky was invigorating and carried with it the distinct smell of fallen leaves. Elizabeth especially loved the autumn. She thought of days long past and harvesting on her father's farm. She wanted to drift off and enjoy the sunlit afternoon, but the seriousness of the conversation was getting in her way.

"They are just fifteen, Ben," Lizzie said.

"Sixteen on their next birthday and I'm speaking only of Win. I don't think Hilary would do well there. The boy isn't cut out for military life. Perhaps John, as he favors Winfield."

Elizabeth was not wholly convinced but would defer to her husband.

"When he graduates, he must serve the necessary time as an officer. Winfield would be positioned quite well to pursue a career in law. I'd love to have all the boys follow me; however, the first step is a university. Appointment to West Point is only possible through nominations by your

Congressmen or Senators – in a highly-competitive process."

Liz silently hoped Winfield might not be able to secure one of the coveted appointments. Not because of his ability, which was never an issue, but open nomination positions were scarce. Benjamin could hear the apprehension in his wife's voice.

"I will speak with some city leaders who know Winfield. We can trust their counsel."

Elizabeth understood and, nodding in agreement with her husband, said, "Please include the Reverend Bertram in your visits."

Deciding the right path was critical, Benjamin sought the counsel of the two men with whom he had close ties: the former State representative and Norristown Democratic party leader, and the pastor of their church, as Elizabeth requested. Both men had, on many occasions, spoken with and enjoyed the company of young Winfield, and thought highly of the young man. Each man valued continued education and believed West Point offered a significant advantage.

"West Point would be a great experience for Winfield, and he would do well academically," Benjamin offered in his meeting with former Congressman Sterigere.

Pausing, the former Congressman sat back in his chair, then provided Benjamin his guidance.

"The boy is a natural leader. He is articulate and, I believe, thrives on the regimentation West Point would offer. I recommend you set aside any misgivings, and we can pursue what steps are necessary for entry."

"Who would nominate Winfield if a vacancy exists?" Benjamin inquired.

"Congressman Florence, who is currently here in Norristown. I will request a meeting on your behalf, and I'm sure Florence will be supportive."

The Reverend Bertram and the Hancocks were friends since Benjamin and Elizabeth established themselves in Norristown. Pastor of the Norristown

Baptist Church, he welcomed the opportunity to discuss Winfield's education with his deacon, Benjamin.

"The United States Military Academy would provide a solid university education at the government's expense. It cannot, however, be a decision solely based on expense. Winfield would do well at the Academy, but is it the right course?"

"I must ask, what does Elizabeth feel is the correct path?" The Reverend seemed concerned.

"We are both concerned about our Christian beliefs and what, I expect, Winfield would be called upon to do as a soldier."

"I see your dilemma, Benjamin. I'm sure Elizabeth feels the same. However, service to the country as a soldier, and as an officer, is necessary. It will continue to be in the future. Winfield is a member of our congregation. I can only hope that his service includes the Christian ideals of which you speak. There is always the hope he may spread these to his soldiers and any adversary he faces while in service."

"I could lose my son on the Frontier or find that he prefers a martial life, for which he may be well-suited."

"Winfield's religious roots will serve him well as a Military Academy graduate and future officer. He may yet study the law and follow in your footsteps."

"I agree. I believe the path to West Point is the best alternative, at least for the present."

They spoke at length of service to the nation and of family. Benjamin thought through the discussion he was to have with Elizabeth and, ultimately, Winfield. He was satisfied with his decision.

Winfield waited patiently for his father. His temperament was his own, but his father shaped the political, religious, and educational foundations over the last sixteen years. Benjamin and his boys had spoken lately about university attendance and of Winfield's desire to excel, regardless of the institution. West Point, however, was something unplanned and had never before been seriously considered. An institution where leaders were shaped – not merely by the curriculum of advanced studies to be completed over four years, but by developing necessary traits to lead men, soldiers. Presently, young Winfield could see service and gallantry on some distant field where men hung on his every command. The law seemed so very far away.

When Benjamin entered the room, Winfield rose, partly out of love and respect, and partly due to the gravity this particular discussion warranted.

"Win," Benjamin began, "You, Hilary, and I have spoken before regarding the next step in your education, but hear me. You may have an opportunity shortly to study at the Military Academy. Your mother and I believe there are many places to enhance one's expertise in a chosen field, but West Point may suit your character."

Winfield had pondered, as much as a 16-year-old can, the possibility of soldiering as an adult. Only recently did he seriously consider West Point as a necessary step. The young man focused on his father's words.

"I believe you would find the Academy rigorous and challenging. You are bright and have done extremely well in all of your studies, so I don't feel the required entrance examination would be an obstacle."

Winfield leaned forward as his interest peaked. He nodded affirmatively—more than a casual nod a son gives a father when being schooled in some task, or when a father imparts his wisdom. It was an acceptance of his father's faith in Winfield's abilities. An officer, leading men and serving the nation, at least for the next few years, was intriguing.

"This requires a nomination by one of our locally-elected representatives and approval in Washington. If you are accepted, the next class would be gathering this summer, I expect."

Excitement and anticipation quickly built within young Winfield like the rush of the wind.

"So, tell me what you think."

Winfield, never at a loss for words, paused uncharacteristically, knowing well that his response may decide his future.

"Father, I believe attending West Point would be a great adventure. I may do well if, as you pointed out, I am nominated and accepted. Who must we contact to make this happen?"

"Congressman Florence," Benjamin replied. "I believe he would gladly submit your name. The Congressman is a fellow Democrat, a lawyer here in Norristown, and currently a member of the United States House of Representatives. A vacancy has recently opened in his list of nominees providing the opportunity for you to compete for Academy entrance."

"When must I interview with the Congressman, soon I hope?"

"We will meet him at his office here in Norristown. He will return to Washington in January."

They agreed West Point was the next step. Within a week, Winfield was escorted into Florence's office while Benjamin waited outside. The Congressman stepped from behind his desk, and they shook hands.

"I am very pleased to shake your hand once more, young man. It's not every day I have the chance to meet a distinguished speaker."

Winfield appeared puzzled, then understood the Congressman was present at the Independence Day rendering of the Declaration.

"I am honored to meet you once again."

"I have your record, and you have done quite well, Mr. Hancock. What interests you about the Military Academy?"

"Sir, I want to be a leader of men. West Point is famous for its ability to match academics and leadership skills. They are graduating only the very best of men. Service to my community and the nation is essential. I wish to be a graduate and a soldier serving this country."

Benjamin's coaching was paying off, and the Congressman was impressed. They continued the interview and discussed the Army, academics, and the fact that Winfield was only sixteen, but should be able to handle the rigors of the cadet life. The interview complete, Winfield walked back to his father's office with a sense of accomplishment.

Winfield and Hilary sat outside the house on the fence bordering the road. The cold winter air rushed past them, stinging their faces, breath visible with every word, but the twins enjoyed the feeling. They wrapped themselves in scarves, winter coats, and caps pulled down tightly over their heads. The boys spent much of their time outside anyway, and it seemed fresher with every breath they took.

"You have spoken with Father," Hilary said, looking down at the road. "Are you truly going to the Military Academy?"

The hurt in his voice hung on the small cloud of mist leaving his lips. They paused for a moment. The twin brothers had not spent more than a day apart since they were born. The fear of being without his brother was new to Hilary, and he was having trouble comprehending why Win would even consider West Point. Was it his own choice, or was Winfield merely going along with Father's plan?

"If I'm accepted," Win replied, "but it takes a lot to make it happen. I must be nominated, accepted, then pass a pretty hard entrance examination. I thought about this for a while, and I told Father I'd like to attend if I'm accepted."

"Do you even know anything about the place?" Hilary shot back.

"Did you know that West Point was a Continental Army location in 1778 – during the Revolutionary War? Grandfather Hoxworth told me about it. He clearly remembered being there with his regiment under General Arnold. It's located on the Hudson River about 50 miles north of New York City. They even built a Continental Army fort there."

"Thanks for the geography lesson."

Hilary enjoyed mocking his brother's new-found litany of facts.

"There's also the fact that Arnold tried to surrender the fort to the British for a huge sum of money. Grandfather was still angry over Arnold's treason and the fact the general got away."

"I'm not familiar with that and never heard Grandfather speak about it."

"President Jefferson wanted professional army officers, so he started the Academy years ago. They have very high standards for academics and discipline. It's the best engineering school in the country, but includes military studies."

"So, you want to be an engineer?" Hilary asked.

"No! It graduates more than just engineers. You graduate as an army lieutenant."

He could see from his expression Hilary already missed him.

"What happened to our plan to go to university together and study law, like Father? We would be great at it, and we could work together or open our own office. What about our plans?"

"We spoke about it more than once. This opportunity is too great to pass up. It's too bad that we cannot go together."

"Are you serious, me in the Army? I don't feel it suits me, perhaps you. You'd be excellent, and maybe John." Winfield put his arm around his brother, and they sat without talking for a while.

"Boys, come in the house. Your father is home, and dinner is ready," Elizabeth said through the doorway.

They searched one another's eyes for reassurance. Winfield could see the tears welling up in Hilary's eyes.

"I'll always be there for you, and you'll be a fine lawyer one day and represent my interests."

Hilary laughed but knew his brother would soon be gone. He wondered what it would be like to attend West Point.

First and Always: Rebellion

The next day, Benjamin and Elizabeth sat quietly at the table in his law office. She preferred Winfield remained home and pursued studies at a university, but she kept it to herself. Florence asked Benjamin to provide a personal letter to Secretary Poinsett, describing his son to help with the final decision. Benjamin, in turn, asked for his wife's help. The office was better for this sort of thing, so the boys did not disturb either parent. He broke the silence as he shifted in his chair.

"How should I describe Winfield? We've raised him, so this shouldn't be difficult."

Elizabeth knew the letter intended for the Secretary of War and Congressman Florence was part of the formal nomination to the Academy.

"Describe Winfield in terms the Nation's Army is seeking, about his physical person."

"Winfield displays leadership characteristics normally found in men older than his 16 years. He is five and one-half feet tall and well-proportioned. Winfield has a sharp mind and has no illness nor abnormality that prevents him from military service."

"Mention his academic background."

"He comprehends and writes extremely well and demonstrates an excellent grasp of mathematical concepts."

Elizabeth was becoming frustrated with Benjamin's description.

"You are a lawyer and Winfield's father. How can you find describing your son so hard? Perhaps you ought to mention his familiarity with other subjects."

"Winfield is versed in philosophy, chemistry, geography, and has studied Latin."

Benjamin thought for a moment, then added details as to his oratory skill and debates at school, both skills necessary for success at West Point. The letter complete, Elizabeth agreed and delivered it to the Congressman.

Florence was impressed and awarded him the last nomination vacancy, petitioning the Secretary of War for Winfield's appointment. In his correspondence, he stated the young man "possesses all the necessary qualifications under the rules of the department."

He sent a persuasive second letter to Secretary Poinsett in March. In his correspondence, he reiterated Winfield's significant qualifications for attendance to the Military Academy from the Congressman's district; and further, that his nomination was without objection.

The letter prompted the Secretary to approve the nomination and fill the remaining Montgomery County vacancy. Winfield received an acceptance letter for a conditional appointment to the Academy. It also included a separate requirement for Benjamin's consent and Winfield's agreement for eight years of compulsory service. The path was complete. Winfield, the boy, would very soon enter a soldier's world.

CHAPTER 3
CADET GREY TO ARMY BLUE

It was early summer when Winfield and Benjamin stepped down from the barge and onto the landing at Buttermilk Falls, New York, on the Hudson River. His father had taken the trip to West Point with his son to ensure Winfield's arrival went smoothly. More importantly, to reinforce the father-son bonds as Winfield transitioned to manhood and the military.

"Well, you have arrived, and a new chapter of your life begins."

His father found it hard to contain the excitement in his voice.

"This will be an adventure, Father. I hope I can pass the examination."

Winfield was concerned, and Benjamin noted the slight hesitation in his son's voice. He had rarely seen Winfield worried about anything. He always exuded confidence. Benjamin loved that about him.

"Winfield, you have never lacked confidence. It is one more hill to climb, and that's all. You are ready, both physically and academically; however, don't take it too lightly. You are a Hancock, and I expect you to do well. Don't dwell on the pending entrance examination. You will be fine."

They took a moment to scan the buildings on the plateau high above them. It was the grounds of the United States Military Academy. Winfield was not alone as more prospective entrants were gathering at the landing. The train ride from Philadelphia was uneventful, and the anticipation built as they drew closer to the Academy. There was small talk, mostly with a few boys also heading to the Academy. The thought of his mother and brothers seeing him off at the station still lingered. He already missed them, just as Hilary said he would.

Winfield walked through the gate carrying a small satchel of personal items and clothing. Someone was barking orders, and the group began to gather. Nothing new for Winfield, but certainly more intense than the Norristown boys' militia. Benjamin listened, then quickly moved off a few steps with the other parents who were saying farewell to their soldier-cadets. One last glance, one final handshake, and a father's embrace for the son who would be forever changed by this institution.

"Do well, son. We will see you on your first break from school."

Moving towards the gate, Benjamin refused to glance back. It was too hard for him, and it would be harder on the boy.

"Stand in line and drop whatever bag you unfortunates have dragged here with you!"

A cadet, apparently one or two years ahead of the assembled group, began bringing some order to what had been a bunch of young men milling around the landing. Winfield thought the cadet appeared every bit the military man he portrayed while noting the distinct Southern intonation, more pronounced to his Pennsylvanian ears.

"I am Cadet Sergeant McLaws, and I will be your guide for the next few days during your initial processing and entry into the United States Military Academy."

The Georgia-born McLaws loudly projected his best "command voice." His words hung in the air, only for a moment, while the new arrivals shifted their stances to see the cadet addressing them. Another cadet approached McLaws, calling him Lafayette, and handed him a roster. Winfield smiled to himself, noting the uniquely historical name and mused at his moniker, Winfield Scott.

"When I call your name, you are to respond with 'Here, Cadet Sergeant!'"

The names of a dozen prospective cadets, Winfield's included, were called rapidly.

"Face to the right and follow me."

McLaws stepped off in typical military fashion. The group, in two ranks, turned right, making their best attempt at a military formation and moved with the sergeant. The first day at West Point had begun.

New arrivals were not yet "plebes," a term for Fourth Class cadets. They were actually "appointees," signifying their recent appointment by a congressional member, but other cadets referred to them as "conditional things." All faced a rigorous entrance examination before becoming part of the cadet corps. They were grouped five to a room, wore the civilian clothes in which they arrived, and began learning military orders and drill as they prepared for the examination. The issuing of military clothing would follow after the test for those becoming members of the corps. Upper-level cadets, like McLaws, provided instruction. Winfield quickly grasped when fellow "conditionals" move he should follow. Drum rolls that signified orders and directions were not challenging to learn.

The entrance examination, given at the end of June, included subjects taught across the conventional school system. It was the first hurdle to become a cadet. Winfield passed easily, having attended the Norristown Academy and public school, as well as tutoring by his parents. Half of the one hundred conditionals failed the test. By the end of four years, the remaining cadets in Winfield's Class of 1844 would reduce their number to twenty-five, either due to the stringent academic requirements or the rigors of a military setting.

He embarked on the next phase required for entry to the Academy – the annual summer camp – living a simulated soldier's life before commencing the academic year. Not fully matured, Winfield appeared even younger, almost pre-adolescent, when standing next to prospective cadets much older and experienced; however, he was tall and athletically built. He thrived during the annual camp. He was impulsive, and maturity would require a longer time to develop fully. West Point would shape the adult, along the way producing a university graduate and newly-commissioned army officer. He was a cadet transitioning from civilian to soldier, and his excitement was hard to contain. Anticipation and apprehension fought for emotional control within young Winfield. He would don a cadet's grey uniform, joining the corps while letting go of both his civilian clothing and mindset and taking another step closer to the soldier he was to become.

"Good morning, I'm Alex Hays, and it appears we are roommates."

Winfield entered his assigned room and noted the accent was distinctly northern and extended his hand.

"I'm Win Hancock, Winfield Scott Hancock, to be precise."

"You're joking. You have the same name as 'the' army general?"

"My father's name is Benjamin Franklin Hancock; younger brother is John Hancock. How's that?"

Hancock dropped his bag and smiled. Hays broke into a hearty laugh and shook Winfield's hand.

"Well, I am very pleased to meet a distinguished member of such a distinguished, and may I say, historical family."

Winfield liked Hays immediately. Alexander Hays was also a Pennsylvanian, north of Pittsburg. Five years older than Winfield, he recognized the overwhelming impact West Point already had on his sixteen-year-old roommate. Hays resolved to shepherd the less experienced youngster until he got his feet on the ground. It would not take long.

"If you've forgotten anything, you can purchase personal items with the pay we receive each month. Academy cadets earn a small stipend of $28 per month. They will put it in an account under your name."

It was to Winfield's delight; however, he never saw the full amount. Everything a cadet needed to subsist they paid for from the stipend. Although it appeared to him to be somewhat unfair, he understood the necessity for the debiting each month and made sure he included that point in the next letter to his parents.

Seated across the room was another cadet. Winfield knew he was not a plebe and must be senior. Winfield braced, rigidly at attention, as he recently learned. Hays told him to relax.

"This is Sam Grant from Ohio. He is a second-year man."

Grant slowly inspected young Hancock, on one side, then the other, as upper-level cadets generally do. He smiled and extended his hand.

"Welcome to the United States Military Academy, Mr. Hancock. Just watch out for those demerits."

Hays and Hancock were equally anxious at the mention of demerits. Grant explained accumulating 200 in a given year was grounds for dismissal.

"Demerits can be given for all violations, large and small, running from uniform infractions to failures in judgment and are accompanied by some form of punishment. The common infractions include drinking, smoking, fighting, and, my favorite, leaving the Academy for the town without authorization."

The two new arrivals made sure they filed that particular piece of information away, but in the next four years would test the limits of the system.

Unpacking, he placed a copy of a law primer his father had given him. Benjamin requested Winfield read it several times among his other studies. Sir William Blackstone's "*Commentaries of the Laws of England*" was required reading for a career in law. In the United States, it allowed for the development of the American legal system. The curriculum also included "*Kent's Commentaries on the Constitution of the United States,*" which delighted Benjamin. Winfield's comprehension of both writings enhanced understanding, and was, by design, intended to inform new officers. He could only see his course load had increased with West Point's requirements and his father's assigned study. Winfield would handle both, although not easily.

It didn't take long for Winfield and Alex to seek extracurricular activities that would balance their daily rigor. By the end of their plebe year, the two had found their outlet.

"Let's go. We can stay out of sight using the wood line. There's a path, they say well worn, that we can follow leading to the town."

Older cadets shepherded the small band off the Academy grounds heading for a place called Benny Haven's Tavern – Hays and Hancock included. All cadets knew that drinking and leaving the Academy grounds without authorization were offenses that warranted dismissal. Benny Havens provided both infractions, but this did not deter cadets from risking all.

The winter evening was transitioning from dusk to early nightfall, when someone watching may be unsure whether cadets were making their escape or only shadows along the wooded area adjacent to the Academy. The cold chill of the New York air was not much different than Norristown, the thought crossing Winfield's mind, and snow had not fallen for some weeks. It was an advantage that allowed the stealthy troop to negotiate the Academy grounds and make for the wood line without leaving tracks – always a factor in a trip to Benny's tavern. The tavern was just over a mile away along the river in Buttermilk Falls. It had become an oasis for cadets bold enough to exercise clandestine breaks from the Academy's rigorous and regimented daily schedule. Senior classmen mentioned Benny's in low, reverent tones all the time. It was a place for good food, rum, and cider drinks, and a home away from the school for a while. Winfield, befriended by many of the upperclassmen, always seemed to be near when Benny was the subject of conversation, and he wanted the experience. It was hard to find someone at West Point for more than a year who had not heard of the "haven" for restless cadets. The problem was moving undetected into and out of the tavern without being caught by cadets on duty, or worse, faculty and staff.

On this particular night, experience won out, and the small band moved quickly off the grounds and through the town. The tavern provided music, food, and drink, and the staff ensured cadets were waited on promptly, given the short time they were able to visit the inn and begin the trek back before anyone noticed they were gone. It was a game, and the generations of cadets learned how to play it well.

"What is this drink?"

"Buttered Rum, but you should just stick to the cider, Winfield, and get something to eat."

Winfield smiled, nodded, and took another large gulp from the container of rum that came his way. Its slightly bitter-sweet taste seemed smooth to him. It didn't take long before the second drink found its mark, and Winfield felt a bit "heady."

"We must return to quarters."

Hays understood that his young friend might require slightly more assistance for the trip back. With a head nod towards Hancock, who wanted to explore various dialectic topics of conversation at a rapid-fire pace, a clear sign of the rum already consumed, the upperclassmen headed to the door. Benny and his wife wished them well and a safe return trip.

They perfected their timing based on the latest intelligence of the guards and supervisors. The group re-entered the grounds holding onto young Hancock's coat, ensuring he kept up and continually telling him in whispered tones to "be quiet." They expertly found their way back to their rooms, and bed.

Morning came, and it was still dark. Winfield was startled by the sound of Alex's loud voice.

"Get up, you fool! Get up! The first call has already sounded, and you need to move. You look unkempt, young man."

His head seemed heavy, and pain seemed to shoot through his eyes. Hancock wondered if this unwelcomed feeling always accompanied a night of drinking. For a moment, he thought he would have to hold his head upright with his hands throughout the day. More importantly, the officer of the day might recognize the signs of a cadet's unauthorized exploits, be they inside or outside the boundary of the Academy, and the ramifications would be severe.

"We made it back without incident?"

"Yes, but barely. You continued to talk when quiet movement is the secret to a tavern visit."

"Next time, I'll promise to be quiet. What did I drink?" Winfield laughed as he scrambled to get into his uniform.

"Next time, we'll leave your ass here!"

Alex seemed annoyed. Even with his head pounding, young Hancock relished the excitement of the excursion and would revisit the tavern. Alex could not help but shake his head and wonder how his young classmate might survive the next few years.

They barely made the formation. During a morning inspection, the Gods had shown their light upon Winfield as one of the senior cadets who had accompanied the group the previous evening stood before him.

"Your uniform is not to standard. Your buttons tarnished, and you are late."

The cadet officer announced the infractions loudly while another recorded the violations next to Winfield's name on the roster he carried.

The demerit count had begun. The officer had a wry smile on his face, and, examining Hancock, chuckled and moved on to the next cadet.

The experience was just enough to convince Winfield that instead of foregoing future trips to the tavern, he needed to be more careful with imbibing. He constantly heard, "Cadet Hancock, your room is out of order," or "Cadet Hancock, you are out of your quarters after the prescribed hour." Uniforms and rooms were the banes of his existence, and the demerits increased moderately.

His first two years passed in turmoil as Winfield continually sought ways to bend the rules, many times unsuccessfully. He cared little about demerits. After all, the cadets senior to him did not seem to focus their attention, nor their tempered wrath, on him as they did many of his other classmates.

"I've got to focus a bit more."

He mulled the words over in his mind. Hays had admonished him for a large number of demerits Winfield accumulated in his second year alone, dangerously close to the 200 and dismissal. Alex was alarmed.

Hays glared at his young friend and said, "You'll have to temper your attitude and make better decisions. You're just getting by in academics and are much smarter than your grades would indicate. Get serious, my friend, if you wish to continue here."

"You are right! That certainly cannot happen again, and I cannot be one of the many we see leaving each year. How would I explain that to Father and Mother? What would the town say?"

Approaching his third year, the gravity of accumulating demerits weighed heavily. He would take his friend's advice going forward.

Winfield strode past the barracks buildings and onto the open field that was the Plain. He did not often find himself alone and able to merely reflect on what had transpired over his first two years. He reviewed his schedule for the upcoming year. It included analytical geometry and calculus, surveying, and the usual French, and English. Rhetoric and history were favorites, but drawing came naturally, and he could depend on an excellent grade to help his less than stellar academic average. The schedule also included the first part of artillery basics.

The load seemed daunting, but he would somehow get through it. Thinking of his family, he sat beneath the large oak and started his next letter to his parents, laying out the curriculum he would undertake in his next year at the Academy. He always included the obligatory mention, and sometimes a question, of his law readings to appease his father. He chuckled when he did so.

The mischievous Hancock had performed well in those tasks associated with leadership and soldier skills, and was therefore designated "Cadet Sergeant." Winfield quickly scanned his class list once more as the new arrivals shuffled into the formation.

"I am Cadet Sergeant Winfield Hancock. Focus your attention on me."

The group of conditionals, having just arrived, were standing in four ranks, other cadets having placed them in their first formation.

"There will be ample time for you to meet one another later, so stop the chatter. Let me welcome you to the United States Military Academy at West Point. For the next week or two, you will be trying your very best to pass the examination phase for acceptance into the corps of cadets."

The new "conditionals" were focused on Hancock, his uniform spotless and impeccably fitted, highlighting the athletic build of the young man he was becoming.

"First, I will get you settled into rooms where you may leave your meager possessions. Listen and respond loudly with 'Here, Cadet Sergeant' when I call your name."

Summer camp of 1842 was nearing completion. Every year, the General of the Army, General Winfield Scott, came to the Academy to visit and mingle with cadets, talking about the U.S. Army and relating stories of his career. A first-year cadet always accompanied the general as his escort, and Sam Grant had the honor. During a short pause in the discussions, Grant could not resist the urge to mention that the assembled group included Winfield Scott, a very capable cadet. General Scott grinned broadly and asked, "Where is Cadet Sergeant Hancock?"

Surprised, Winfield sprang to his feet. Coming to attention, he identified himself, satisfied that he could get the words out without tripping over them.

"General Scott, Sir. I am Cadet Hancock."

He couldn't believe the most senior general in the army knew his name, and, more perplexing, what he could want. The general graciously recognized Winfield.

"Well then, young sir, I expect you have excelled at this institution. Perhaps you will do the same in your career?"

Hancock smiled broadly and hoped the general was not aware of his current standing and mediocre academic performance, as Scott continued.

"My very best regards to your father. You are not the first to share that name, but my faith is in you, Mr. Hancock. I expect that you will lead men in a manner where they will willingly follow you anywhere."

Winfield braced a bit more and answered, "Sir, thank you, and I will not let you or West Point down." Grant held in a laugh, but General Scott's premonition would ring true.

Hays' constant guidance and Winfield's growing maturity took over as the infractions dropped significantly. However, he was still the old Hancock, popular and well-liked across the corps of cadets, with a heightened sense of adventure. He became quite adept at clandestine trips to Benny's, training his many charges in the best methods to move to and from the town undetected. He was satisfied that passing on the "tradition" was just as crucial to the young cadets as were their studies.

"Winfield, it is good to see you once again." Benny was always glad to see the cadets, especially Winfield, who had made it a practice to visit the tavern often.

"Benny, I bring new charges which will carry on the tradition. Treat them well."

Hays could not help wondering about his friend.

"Had Winfield's attitude changed, or was he just better at avoiding detection by the cadet leadership? A little of both, I'd gather."

Hancock was responsible for the cadets assigned to his squad. Two cadets displayed a dislike for one another that seemed to grow with each passing month. No one knew what caused the friction, least of all Winfield. It could have been that one was rural, Southern-born, while the other was a product of Northern city life. Hancock reasoned that it might have been vastly different educational backgrounds of the two, but the two young men did not like one another. Regardless, one evening, harsh words flew as the two cadets squared off for a fight. Winfield understood the rules and the ramifications, weighing each carefully and reasoning the hatred could not continue.

"I've had enough of this nonsense. Let the two men fight if that is what they want or have words yet again. Either way, it will end here."

Hays had been aware of the situation all along but focused only on his squad.

"You could see a disciplinary board for this, Winfield. Hell, I'm curious who will come out on top."

Out of sight of the Academy leadership, the two squared off. The first blow struck, the two moved in close and clinched, as boxers do, wrestling each other and occasionally swinging wildly. Hancock watched from a few steps away, opting to keep his distance from the fight and refusing to choose one man over another.

"There must be a winner."

He didn't see the Academy duty officer rounding the building. Cadets tried to scatter, only to be ordered to halt by the officer, now glaring at Hancock.

"The three of you will follow me. I also want the names of all cadets watching this shameful display."

The board of cadets and faculty members convened within days.

"Mr. Hancock! You were on duty while the fight broke out between the two cadets?"

"Yes, Sir. They seemed to be at each other coming across the pathway between the academic buildings."

"It was your responsibility to stop the altercation. Are you aware, Mister?"

"I certainly am aware. The cadets seemed determined to carry their grievances even further. When Cadets Smithe and Gardener exchanged words near the library, I believe it best to let the confrontation take its natural course. It would be easier picking one or both of them up than getting pummeled in between the two while breaking up the fight."

Grant and Franklin, also a first-year, both hung their heads to keep from laughing during what was intended to be a solemn proceeding.

"Sir, as a result of your inaction, you will receive demerits. The board will notify you of the total number, and further punishment is warranted."

"What happens to the two cadets? Do they face dismissal?"

"Not your concern, Cadet Sergeant. You are collecting quite a few demerits. You should take care in the future."

Winfield saluted and walked from the board room.

"Well, at least the demerits were worth it. That was one hell of a fight."

Despite his best efforts to reduce infractions, it was nearly impossible to eliminate demerits. Hays was pleased that Winfield did significantly lower the number of faults in both his "second-" and "first-year" as they headed to commissioning. Infractions ranged from being late to the formation to witnessing other fights, but never for Benny's. He had perfected that break, and along the way, he had instructed many underclassmen how to do the same.

The drums beat the order to a formation. Henry Heth noticed that everything moved to the sound of the drums. He gathered his class materials and headed down the corridor with the mass of scurrying cadets to the exterior of the building. Cadets Hays and Hancock, beginning their final "First Year," stood watching the new plebes "fall in" as the corps of cadets mustered for class.

"This one has promise." It was a favorite pastime of upperclassmen to single out an unfortunate plebe and subject him to mild harassment – "devilling" in cadet parlance. Hancock could see Heth rushing by in a vain attempt to sidestep the upperclassmen and join the formation. Hays nodded in agreement and held his hand out to slow the young Heth down.

"Where are you rushing to young man? Do you not know you could easily collide with an upperclassman and thereby interfere with his planned travel, or worse yet, cause him permanent harm as he begins his 'first' year, thus depriving the Army of a fully trained officer?"

The verbal assault went on for minutes, and the refined Heth seemed unmoved by the experience. Hancock noted the calmness of the man.

"What would you say then?" Hancock yelled, glancing briefly at Hays, who stood behind Heth smiling.

Heth braced in his best position of attention, staring straight ahead, unsure of what was about to transpire and fearing he'd be late to the formation.

"Sir, I am sorry this cadet inadvertently interfered with an upperclassman's schedule."

"That doesn't answer my question! What would you say?"

Heth thought quickly, as the formation was coming together, and he did not want to be the last one in its ranks.

"Sir, I would say I'm alright; no harm was done to me, and continue on my way."

Hays nodded approvingly, and Hancock fought the urge to smile, but instead feigned anger.

"That's a bit sarcastic. What's your name, anyway?"

"Sir, Cadet Henry Heth."

Heth was unsure just how much trouble he could be in with these upperclassmen and what it would cost him so early in his West Point career.

"Sir, I simply wish to convey to the upperclassman that we both had somewhere to be quickly, and could we continue on our way."

"I have my eye on you, Mr. Heth. Get to the formation, quickly."

The two "Firsties" looked at each other and laughed.

"We need to take care of that one," they said, almost in unison.

It did not take long before Winfield led Heth and others to Benny's. Harry enjoyed the atmosphere and camaraderie, as he and Winfield became friends. They shared similar backgrounds. Harry, raised in a privileged home in Virginia, had attended private schools and was well-spoken. He had been accepted at both West Point and other major universities, highlighting the intellect within. However, like Winfield, his mischievous nature overcame the regimented Academy lifestyle. Hancock would pass Heth the torch of clandestine trips to the tavern.

In their final year, the determination of a newly-commissioned lieutenant's specialty in the Army began with a cadet's placement in his graduating class. As an engineering school of higher education, the number one graduate entered the Engineer branch. Graduating "First-year" cadets requested their preference of career branch. Coupled with the needs of the Army, the officers began their service as engineers, or perhaps artillery, dragoons, and infantry. Winfield's class standing was eighteenth of the remaining twenty-five cadets in his class and personally held an average academic record. He happily selected infantry – a branch in which he would be well-suited and excel.

Congress established the size of the Army. Upon Winfield's graduation, there were not ample spaces available to accommodate the twenty-five West Point graduates as regular army lieutenants. It was common practice to grant temporary, or brevetted, promotion to the graduating officers.

Commissioning Day arrived on the last day of June 1844. In place of the hundred or so "conditionals" who walked the Plain at West Point four years previous, now stood twenty-five young men waiting to become officers and university graduates. "Winfield Scott Hancock!" His name called, Winfield moved forward to collect his diploma and commission. The new second lieutenant searched for his family, and, finding them, was immediately embraced by Elizabeth. Benjamin extended his hand, and behind them stood young John.

"Hilary is still away at school and is unable to attend. We are so very proud of you." They were amazed to see that Winfield, a lad of five feet, five inches when he entered the academy, was over six feet tall and a strikingly handsome young man.

The Frontier

"What is next?" John asked.

"I will join the infantry, the Sixth Infantry Regiment, to be precise." Elizabeth looked quizzically at Benjamin. Although unspoken, their conversation years earlier about Winfield's service and the inherent danger rushed over her, and she held her son even tighter. The boy had grown to manhood and was a professional soldier. Tears of joy and fear mixed and rolled softly down her cheeks.

"Please don't cry, Mother. I have enough leave approved before I am to report for duty, and I'll spend it all at home. We shall enjoy our time together," Winfield said in a vain attempt to stop his Mother's tears. He hated to see her cry for any reason.

Lieutenant Hancock read his orders carefully. The journey to the far western reaches of the country was tiresome, but he finally arrived at the regiment. The commander sent him to a post in the Indian Territory, Fort Towson, on the Red River. He moved a short time later to Fort Washita, Oklahoma Territory. Assignment as an infantry officer and the excitement of duty on the Indian frontier was almost overwhelming. The Army of the Frontier was thinly spread across the territory guarding settlements and protecting the lines connecting them against hostile Indians, exploring the region, and general policing. The new lieutenant wanted to be part of it all during his posting on the "Permanent Indian Frontier." The patrols provided security for settlers while watching the indigenous tribes and newly-arrived Indians who the government resettled after forcing them west of the Mississippi.

Relations between whites and the Indians were generally calm during Hancock's assignment. The expansion of the west was gaining ground as he settled into his first year. Instances requiring intervention between Indians and settlers were rare. Instead, Winfield focused on his assigned responsibilities and continued to hone his skills as an officer and leader. Little associated with this assignment would prepare him for senior-level command, but lieutenants were assigned a myriad of tasks as they developed their leadership skills.

Hancock excelled at those assigned tasks, and his commanders noted it. The routine duty on the "Plains" provided time acclimate to life as an infantry lieutenant. They tried to keep abreast of the latest issues affecting the nation and the army, but the information was limited on the frontier.

From his first day assigned to the Infantry, Hancock began to develop his expertise in, and affinity for, rules and regulations, the administration of which enable a properly functioning military organization. He continued to read, study, and develop his professional competencies, a prerequisite instilled at West Point.

Winfield and his fellow officers followed with interest news from the rest of the country and gleaned as much as they could about the growing tension on the border between the Republic of Texas and Mexico. His sense, and that of everyone he knew currently on duty with the army, anticipated the tension escalating.

The nation had a new leader. President James K. Polk was in office, and the President had his eyes on expansion. There were rumblings of armed disputes between countries. If war were on the horizon, it would not be long before the Sixth Infantry was called. The excitement of battle contrasted the duty of policing the frontier territory. Hancock wanted to be part of the action, if it were to come – all young officers did.

CHAPTER 4
POLK'S WAR

Texas declared independence from Mexico in 1836 with the belief that it would join the Union. When its application for statehood was accepted, Texas was welcomed as the twenty-eighth state on 29 December 1845.

The Texans maintained that the Rio Grande, not the Nueces River 150 miles north, was the Republic's border. The U.S. inherited the border claim, and Mexico began talking of war. The Mexican government refused earlier U.S. offers to buy their land, and annexation handed Polk the opportunity he sought for the nation's expansion. Defeating Mexico would at once solve the border and land issue, and the country would extend to the Pacific Ocean, enhancing Asian trade. Angered Mexican government officials increased their talk of armed conflict. The President tried settling the issue diplomatically but included a show of force.

Winfield continuously followed the developing story. In his latest letter, Hilary wrote, "It appears that the Army is heading to the border."

Army officers scrambled to get the newest information, sharing and embellishing the story with each other and their excitement building at the possibility of action. Word spread rapidly through the Sixth Infantry officer's corps.

Captain Walker sat behind his desk as Lieutenants Armistead and Hancock listened to the latest headquarters dispatch announcing Brigadier General Zachary Taylor's change of command. Taylor commanded the regiment. Everyone was anxious for a word concerning the border.

"Taylor is leaving the Sixth and will command the force," Walker said flatly.

"Will we follow?" Armistead asked, with Winfield hanging on the response.

"Not yet. Taylor's building a force with troops from the South, including artillery, infantry, and dragoons. Unfortunately, we must wait, and it could be over before any action happens."

Within weeks, Hancock read the news that Taylor's force was near the Rio Grande River with several thousand troops. While probing the lines, the Mexican cavalry had ambushed a detachment of Taylor's Dragoons, and the war was on.

"We have got to get in on this action!" Winfield exclaimed as he read the latest news from Washington.

Officers across the U.S. Army, Hancock included, saw the pending conflict as an excellent opportunity. The regiment was already preparing for battle at each of their posts. There were only eight infantry regiments in the Army, each with ten companies. Winfield was confident that the Sixth Infantry would surely be on the list of regiments. Hancock was a regular army officer, and he resolved to do whatever he could to ensure that when the Sixth Infantry left for Mexico, he would be among their ranks.

Clashes on the border between Texas and Mexico filled their ranks with volunteers and the leadership with anticipation. The routine duty along the frontier gave way to action. The conflict would mean much-needed combat experience, leading men in battle, converting military lessons and theory into practice, and advancement.

There were three paths in Polk's strategic plan that would either defeat Mexico or create the conditions for a negotiated settlement that met U.S. objectives. First, Taylor would secure the border at the Rio Grande, then cross the river and conduct operations to defend cities and land areas in Northern Mexico. Second, Polk ordered the army in Fort Leavenworth, Kansas, to secure Mexican-held land in New Mexico and California, over 1,000 miles away. The U.S. had already acquired the Oregon Territory and, when Mexico ceded California, Polk would have the entire West Coast. Finally, General of the Army Winfield Scott was named commander of all operations in Mexico.

Winfield's excellent performance of duty, in his first assignment, belied his academic standing at West Point. He excelled at the tasks assigned to him and continued to refine his expertise. Two years into his first assignment, he finally received his commission as a Regular Army second lieutenant, no longer brevetted. The company commander congratulated Winfield on the commission but had plans for his sterling lieutenant.

"Lieutenant Hancock, I am assigning you to recruit duty."

The dismay was immediately evident on Winfield's face, fearing he would miss his chance in Mexico.

"You are to report to Newport Barracks, Kentucky, across the Ohio River from Cincinnati."

"Is there any way I can remain with the regiment, Sir?"

"Not even the slightest chance. Listen, the Army must recruit and expand for Mexico. Newport Barracks serves as a center for replacements and supplies. That is critical since the war has come."

Disappointed but professional, Winfield saluted and took the orders from the captain. Reporting to Newport Barracks in January 1847, he took charge of a group of sixty recruits bound for the Jefferson Barracks, Missouri, and the Sixth Infantry.

Hancock sat at his desk early in the morning. His chair was tilted back, resting its frame against the wall, front legs off the floor, and his feet propped up on the open top drawer. The cold winter morning battled the wood stove which soldiers tended to all day. The lieutenants generally arrived early for duty after morning parade, but not before the non-commissioned officers came for the day and delivered the necessary dispatches and official documents to the commander's desk, and, more importantly, made the coffee. Winfield was very comfortable as he read the newspaper, only a few days old, and drank the first coffee that the sergeant just handed him. The paper's front page contained news of the action ongoing between Texas and Mexico, and the officers had been discussing the impact on the Army and its future operations for days. Across the room was a fellow officer, Lieutenant Jordan, who also sat with feet propped up. The sound of recruits marching, under the direction of their non-commissioned officers barking commands, echoed throughout the building. Hancock would soon take charge of the detachment and lead them back to Missouri to join the Sixth Infantry.

"Jordan, General Taylor has won at Palo Alto and Monterey." With decisive victories at Palo Alto and Resaca de la Palma, in May, and Monterey, in September, Taylor had forced the Mexicans back across the Rio Grande.

Hancock sat forward, rocking the chair into an upright position.

"It says here that Taylor's position is miles into Mexico. I have to get back to the regiment before this is over."

Jordan looked up from his papers.

"Well, good luck on being released. The Sixth is not called yet, and our release may be more difficult than you know, given the increasing number of volunteers who want to join this fight with Mexico."

Winfield quickly responded with a broad smile.

"This is our chance. It is the perfect opportunity to get some real experience, practicing everything we talked about at the Academy, and in our regiments. We don't want to miss one, and I can't imagine when the next opportunity will arrive."

What the two young officers missed was that General Winfield Scott, General of the Army, was in command by order of the President. He had a new plan to compel Mexico to end this conflict, and the Sixth Infantry was to play a significant part. General Taylor's maneuver in Northern Mexico failed to force Mexico to cede its lands, prompting Scott to land at Vera Cruz. In March 1847, he landed with 12,000 troops and moved inland to capture Mexico City and bring an end to the conflict.

When he finally arrived at Jefferson Barracks, he was directed to continue to Fort Scott, Kansas. Winfield was, once more, proficient in his duties, and the recruiting branch recoiled at the thought of losing his abilities. At Fort Scott, he expected to be relieved of his recruiting responsibilities and rejoin his company. Instead, he was ordered to return to Newport Barracks. Winfield was disheartened and resolved to do whatever he could to join the fight in Mexico. He petitioned the commander.

"I wish to be relieved of duty at Fort Scott. I must rejoin my regiment."

"Orders change, lieutenant. You are to return to Newport Barracks."

It seemed the Recruiting Department, like everyone else, looked for excellence in their officers, and would go to great lengths to retain his services. He knew that further discussion was pointless and submitted an application for transfer, knowing it would not be approved. He understood the chain of command and sought to petition the colonel in command of Newport Barracks.

"I request that I be allowed to rejoin my regiment. The Sixth has been ordered to Mexico and has already begun movement. Sir, if you disapprove of this request, may I ask that you forward it with your comments to the Army?"

"Lieutenant, you are assigned here until I release you. I need officers, and you are quite adept at recruiting. However, I will forward your petition."

Hancock's nature would not allow him to sit idly by without exhausting all possibilities in reaching his goal – service in Mexico. He was exasperated and personally sent his request to the Army Adjutant General with a letter explaining that he was an officer assigned to the Sixth Infantry Regiment. He was detailed to bring recruits from Newport Barracks back to Missouri and the regiment. It worked. Lieutenant Hancock would lead a detachment of recruits to Mexico and rejoin his unit.

First and Always: Rebellion

"Attention! The detachment is present for duty, Sir."

The sergeant's voice reverberated along the platform as the detachment of soldiers snapped to the position of attention. The rail cars were ready for boarding, and the "new" soldiers stood motionless as Hancock came before the sergeant and the formation. Their eyes were fixed on the young lieutenant as he returned the sergeant's salute.

"Well done. If the recruits are prepared to board, you may do so. Ensure each man carries rations for the trip. It's a long way to New Orleans. There will be stops along the rail line but keep the soldiers together. I'll ensure we resupply, as needed. I want to check the roll by name as the soldiers are boarding. Provide the list to me when complete. Take charge, Sergeant."

When they were aboard, Hancock dropped his bag on the first bench and watched the recruits filling the rail car. He noted that the soldiers were readying themselves for duty at the front, the anticipation of what awaited them driving much of the conversation among the small groups. They settled in for the trip to the port of New Orleans and the ship that would take them to Mexico.

His small detachment arrived in Vera Cruz in July. Scott's Army, including the Sixth Infantry, had moved west along the national road and was in Puebla, preparing for the assault on the Mexican capital. Hancock wasted little time once he stepped off the ship. Within hours he was temporarily assigned to a regiment under General Franklin Pierce and his 2,500-man reinforcements.

He heard his first shots fired in anger. The enemy fire came as the column repulsed the series of attacks, and always at the ready, there was never an instance that would be considered a battle. The "zip" of a musket ball was easily distinguished but never came close enough to cause him concern. He was eager to pursue this unconventional foe but smart enough to hold his position in the line of march.

The Mexican Army was much further to the west, establishing locations around the capital, and battle awaited them.

The column was in Puebla on 6 August, and Hancock, at long last, had rejoined the regiment. The Sixth Infantry was part of General William J. Worth's division, with orders to move west on 7 August and expecting to meet Generalissimo Antonio Lopez de Santa Anna defending Mexico City. Finally, he was with his company and readied himself for battle.

CHAPTER 5
CONTRERAS, CHURUBUSCO, AND CHAPULTEPEC

They moved on Mexico City from the south. Santa Anna deployed his 30,000-man force south of the city along the Churubusco River. All that separated Scott and Santa Anna was a pre-historic lava field – the Pedregal.

Worth's division was on the move in mid-August. Marching along the main road to Mexico City that bordered the Pedregal, the units came under heavy artillery fire as they approached Churubusco. General Clarke, commanding a brigade that included the Sixth Infantry, was unable to flank the Mexicans with the Pedregal to their west and water to the east. While Clarke halted, the Mexican force, anchoring the right flank of their line, moved forward to Contreras intending to counter the Americans' advance.

The Mexicans opened with their cannons. Irish artillerymen, in service to the Mexican Army, fired the guns and rained down the explosive metal on the unprotected elements, tearing holes in the formations.

Artillery fundamentals were part of the curriculum at the Academy; however, this attack was real and deadly, with shot and shell landing in and near the regiment's position. Some shells exploded with no effect, while others shred bodies, and Hancock watched in awe as men suffered terribly. He had not seen death in battle before and found it appalling and impressive, at once. There was a calmness within him as he observed the action, even as the danger seemed to surround him.

"Take cover."

They found the low grade along the road providing adequate protection, as long as one stayed down. Soldiers attempted to scatter along the route. Intuitively, Hancock knew that the stationary guns could be outflanked and overtaken, and he immediately sought the best approach.

"Sir, we're ordered to withdraw by General Worth."

Captain Walker's courier disappeared as quickly as he had appeared. When the firing stopped, Hancock yelled down the line.

"Stay low and pull back. We'll regroup and come at the enemy again."

Once assured he could cross the Pedregal, Scott attacked with two divisions from the south. In the early morning hours of 20 August, the Mexican position was taken entirely by surprise, and the battle was over in 20 minutes.

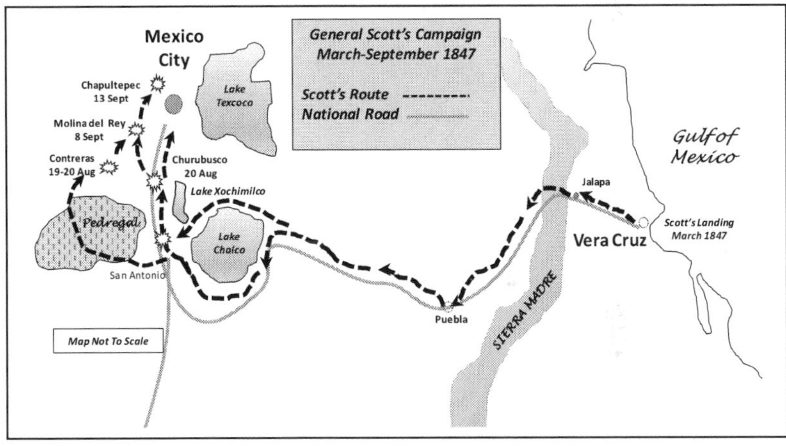

When Contreras fell, Santa Anna pulled his force back to occupy new fortifications, strengthen the defense, and cover the bridge spanning the Churubusco River at San Antonio. The Mexicans occupied a nearby Franciscan convent, named San Mateo. Its massive walls were twelve feet high and four feet thick. With part of his force in new positions, Santa Anna moved the more substantial portion of his force towards Mexico City. Worth would assault the Churubusco bridgehead, while the remainder of Scott's Army attacked San Mateo.

Hancock was under cover with his men away from

artillery fire, patiently waiting for orders and a return to the fight. While attacking the convent, Clarke ordered the Sixth Infantry to lead an attack on the bridgehead. The enemy guns quickly found their targets as the infantry began their assault. Hancock's men recoiled under the continuous fire. He spoke first, taking the commander by surprise in doing so.

"I'll lead the element in the assault."

"Well done, Winfield. When you are ready, move out and watch the fire from those guns."

Crouching as he went, with sword and pistol ready, he heard the bullets whiz past him as they moved along the bank. The results of the earlier assaults lay on the ground for the soldiers to see as they went forward.

"My God, they take the body apart," he thought, as he studied the dismembered infantrymen, here and there a dead Mexican soldier who was left to guard the crossing. Taking a deep breath, he suppressed the thought of carnage and moved along, soldiers at the quick step behind him. It was Hancock's baptism, and it came in the sheer volume of fire from all weapons that prevented movement on the causeway. The advance of divisions and brigades had devolved to a battlefield of company and platoon level maneuver, led by captains and lieutenants.

"The captain orders you to move around to the right and flank the position."

Hancock heard the words and their impact. Without hesitation, he gave the order.

"Follow me."

The order was given countless times on previous battlefields; however, this time, the words were Winfield's, and men moved at his command. The company swung right around the embankment and, in battle line, followed their lieutenant.

"Forward!" Hancock shouted as the line of infantrymen surged forward with him. Musket fire whipped past him as his soldiers took the volleys, some going down, some continuing despite being wounded.

They came in behind the bridgehead, crossing a water-filled ditch, and Hancock's infantrymen slammed into the strongpoint. The Mexican defenders, facing fire from the rear and fearing their line would be turned, fired quickly at the advancing Americans. They began to give way as Hancock's force weighed into them with bayonets. The close-quarters fighting would not allow the Mexicans to load and engage effectively. He turned to face the line and saw the Mexican officer turn towards him. Winfield held his pistol in his right hand, sword in the left. He quickly raised the weapon and fired, striking the man in his chest. The officer went down immediately, and the line began to break. The smoke and confusion interfered with his ability to control the infantrymen rushing in behind him.

There was a burning sensation in his leg, then sharp pain, as shrapnel passed through his leg below the knee. For a brief moment, his mind registered that he was hit, but the adrenaline and excitement within him forced him onward as the Mexican line withdrew, leaving the earthworks to Hancock's soldiers. Clarke's remaining units surged forward to the bridgehead, pushing their way over the parapet and into the Mexican line and hand-to-hand fighting. The bridgehead fell, and Hancock could see the Sixth's colors raised. The brutal fight was over, and Churubusco fell. Hancock was a brevetted First Lieutenant, promoted for "gallant and meritorious conduct" in the face of the enemy.

While the Americans resupplied, the Mexicans prepared and strengthened their defenses. The fight to the capital continued in early September. Captain Walker gathered the lieutenants around a map and read the orders.

"The division will move forward and attack Molino Del Rey, about a mile west of the castle of Chapultepec. The Sixth Regiment, with the rest of the brigade, will take Casa Mata. There is a defensive line connecting the two. We will strike the Mexicans there. I expect Santa Anna has placed more artillery in the castle, so move quickly once the firing starts. We move in the morning."

"Sir, how is Casa Mata constructed? Are we to maneuver around, as we did at the bridge?"

"It is stone buildings and earthworks, and the colonel plans on a frontal assault. We'll adjust as the fight progresses, but we'll take the earthworks first."

Walker ordered the company forward at dawn. To the east, the remainder of Worth's division began storming Molino Del Rey. Hancock and his men neared the position, and enemy artillery fired solid round-shot and 'grape,' cannon rounds with a dozen or more iron balls that spread when fired like a shotgun shell. Winfield was quickly becoming a believer in artillery supporting infantry.

"Charge!"

Walker bellowed the command, and the line of infantry went straight at the artillery battery, muskets down and bayonets ready. Up and over the works, they surged, and within seconds, multiple musket rounds hit Walker, who dropped immediately to the ground. The artillery had achieved its deadly effect. They held the battery position; however, most of the officers were down and large numbers of infantrymen. Hancock quickly determined the remnants of the company had to withdraw or face more losses. The Mexican infantry seized the opportunity and counterattacked, driving the Americans back. He quickly formed battle lines to meet the surging enemy and cover the withdrawal of the rest of the company, carrying as many wounded with them as possible.

"Volley fire!" Hancock ordered, searching for Walker in the chaos.

"Sir, the captain is down."

The sergeant couched next to him, continuing to fire, and taking Mexicans with each shot. Walker lay near the battery, severely wounded. The mini-balls ripped open his lower torso and broke the bones in his shoulder and right arm. Two of his withdrawing soldiers picked Walker up roughly and ran back, trying to stay out of the fire from the enemy who converged on the battery position.

"Winfield, you command," the weakened captain said as he slipped into unconsciousness.

The American artillery opened fire on Casa Mata, forcing the defenders back, while Hancock reformed the company and prepared to assault the works once again.

"Forward!"

The infantrymen moved at a slow run, and, as they reached the earthworks, Hancock raised his sword, pointing towards the enemy position.

"Charge!" Hancock's voice carried across the line.

The company of infantrymen crossed over the works and weighed into the Mexicans. Musket rounds whizzed past Winfield, and he could almost feel the heat as they passed his head, while others cut holes in his uniform. His sword raised and pistol at the ready, they braved the musket fire and swarmed over the position. The smoke from hundreds of muskets hung over the two forces as they fought brutally, hand-to-hand, bayonets and pistols, knives, and weapons as clubs until the Mexican line finally broke; slowly at first, then what remained of entire companies routed. Securing the position, Hancock stared at his blood-soaked trousers and, for the first time, realized his earlier wound had opened. In the excitement, he was unmindful of the pain, but no longer.

The assault on Molino Del Rey was underway to the east, and Worth's division took the position. Santa Anna's force withdrew under fire, then turned and counterattacked. The Sixth Infantry was ready and met the Mexican advance head-on. Artillery and musket fire combined to repulse the charging enemy once again. This time, as they withdrew from Molino Del Rey and moved towards Chapultepec, and the Sixth Infantry Regiment closely followed.

Winfield was devastated. Since Casa Mata and Molino Del Rey, he had been violently ill and in his tent suffering from fever and chills. Many men had fallen victim to illness during the campaign – some never to recover. The wound in his leg was insignificant compared to a disease. His misfortune was very difficult to swallow; however, his condition was under the care of the regimental surgeon, who had directed he hold back from the assault. It was inconceivable to him that he would miss the final fight. The sounds of the attack on Chapultepec were as close as if he'd been with Lieutenant Armistead's storming party, and it did not sit well with Winfield.

The success of the campaign, so far, had cleared nearly all defenses west of the capital except the formidable Chapultepec Castle. It stood on a hill 200 feet high, on the outskirts of Mexico City. The artillery began its bombardment on 12 September, and fired all day, resuming the next morning when Scott ordered the advance from the south and west. The defense was unwavering as the infantry fought their way up the slope. Once the soldiers reached the base of the walls storming ladders were used to get over the top. The Sixth Infantry circled to the north side of Chapultepec to cut off the escaping Mexicans. The castle fell, and the regimental colors of the Sixth Infantry flew from the ramparts.

Grabbing the blanket from his cot, he rushed past the medical personnel and, shuffling down the road, entered a stone building near the end of the town. Finding a stairway, he climbed the two flights and burst through a door to the roof terrace. The house could not have been better suited to his needs.

There was a panoramic view of the battlefield. Hancock could see the castle and the infantry holding steady at its base. The ladders were being brought forward and thrown up immediately against the wall, as blue lines climbed each one, pausing as they fought to get up and over. Some ladders tumbled or were pushed back by the defenders. Soldiers were exposed to fire from the wall as they climbed, falling when hit. Many who had reached the top were running along its heights firing. The defenders were fleeing or fighting and dying. Bayonets gleaming, terror struck the defenders. Winfield locked that piece of information away in the deep recesses of his mind.

"Bayonets strike immediate fear in the enemy."

Weak from his illness, Winfield still yelled encouragement as if he were leading the assault himself. Cheering, he willed them over the wall and watched their final surge as the firing died down. Barely able to make out the Sixth Infantry Regiment colors, Hancock could see them rising over the castle. Sinking to the roof exhausted, sweat-covered, Winfield felt satisfied.

"Glorious," he yelled.

Soldiers on the street below stared up at the lieutenant, who had finished yelling, slumping down to the roof, all his strength sapped from his excursion. They brought him back to the tent. As he lay there, Hancock was consumed with the thought he had not been part of the final assault. It overwhelmed and agonized the young officer.

The fortunate defenders who escaped retreated into the city. By late afternoon, Scott ordered his divisions to move forward, taking heavy losses from the Mexican defenders. The pressure forced the Mexicans to withdraw and counterattack with cavalry, which Scott repulsed. The Americans breached the defenses that evening, and General Antonio Lopez de Santa Anna, leader of the Army and Mexico, abandoned his capital.

The next day, Winfield wrote to Hilary about his disappointment at being left out of the assault.

"We have had to fight desperately to get here. It has been a deadly battle. It shakes one's soul to see the devastation war brings and what it does to soldiers. They are a unique group, able to overcome their fear and charge headlong into a determined enemy. I have never experienced anything like this before. It is terrifying and exciting all at once."

Winfield talked about life during the campaign and Mexico but failed to mention the fact that he seemed right at home in a fight. Hilary could easily read Winfield's desire to remain a soldier for some time to come. He was proud of his brother, as much as his parents were, but knew after this first exposure to battle and danger, he would never turn his back on soldiering.

"I am ordered to the hospital at the same time the final assault is going forward. I have missed the chance for greater things leading men in battle. Missing the fight will haunt me for the rest of my life."

He thought about his wound and added to the letter.

"I have been wounded, slightly. I tell you alone and ask that you not relay this to our parents. Mother will be upset. I will always feel that I should have been with my unit in the final battle."

The next morning, Scott's forces entered Mexico City. Winfield, nearly recovered, was back with the Sixth Infantry Regiment marching through the gates, as well. He could only imagine that there would be many more fights in his future, and he would not miss one.

Hilary read the latest letter with interest and the depth of his brother's disappointment. However, he knew his brother well. Winfield was heading for greater things in the military. The only issue would be breaking the news to their parents that soldiering had captured Winfield forever.

CHAPTER 6
OCCUPATION DUTY

After the capture of Mexico City, it would take politicians and diplomats nine months to work out the means of concluding the war. Hancock's new company commander, First Lieutenant Lewis A. Armistead had distinguished himself throughout the campaign and now replaced Walker, who was recovering from his wounds. Armistead liked Hancock from their first meeting, and the two formed a professional and personal friendship over their shared battlefield experience.

Replacements arrived, and among them was brevetted Second Lieutenant Henry "Harry" Heth, newly commissioned from West Point. Heth entered the room and set his bag down on the floor. Hancock tried to place the face and the circumstances; he had seen this man somewhere. His mind raced as he searched for recognition.

"I know you!" Winfield exclaimed as the new lieutenant stood inside the doorway. Somehow Heth was more than an acquaintance in Hancock's memory. Heth took less time to resurrect Hancock in his mind.

"The Military Academy. Of course, I remember Cadet Lieutenant Hancock and Benny's Tavern."

"My God, we are a long way from West Point. You were a plebe when I was a First Class. Your name, my good fellow?"

"Heth, Sir. Henry, but I go by Harry. I was a class of '47, and I am reporting to the Sixth Infantry. Sorry I missed the excitement earlier, and the fight is over."

"Welcome, Mr. Heth. Did I make your life miserable at the Academy? I hope so, and I'm sure you did the same to those who followed you. How is Benny?"

"He and his tavern are well. I ensured the tradition continued as you instructed." Heth smiled broadly, recalling the demerits he accumulated for being out of his room beyond the prescribed hours, but never caught for being at Benny's Tavern.

"Well then, occupation duty is vastly different from our previous excitement. No danger is lurking, but security and administrative duties are our daily tasks."

Heth liked Hancock immediately. The bachelors performed their duties and were continually seeking opportunities to experience the country and its beautiful women. Heth had found a willing accomplice in Winfield Hancock. From their initial assignment, the bonds of friendship would last a lifetime. Until their return to the United States, the young officers sampled the best Mexico had to offer the Americans.

Lewis Armistead and Heth sat inside a building commandeered as the company headquarters.

"It is something to behold. Winfield always says something smooth and inviting. The young ladies love it. Is it the uniform of an American officer, or the appearance of the man himself? I'm guessing it is both."

"You're always with him and seem to be enjoying occupation duty," Armistead observed.

"I enjoy Winfield's company and find it interesting he has had so many conquests."

"Be careful of her father, and of the governess who guards the young lady's virtue."

"I'm not as blessed as our handsome Pennsylvanian, but I'm doing well," Heth said, as two officers clicked their whiskey glasses and laughed.

Heth was good-looking and carried himself well, a product of Virginia society and West Point. Hancock was tall, strikingly handsome, and his demeanor captivated local young ladies. The young officers frequently attended socials given by the parents of lovely senoritas in Mexico City. The two officers were readying themselves for the latest social.

"I really must thank you. I believe I would not have an invitation to many of these socials, if not for you. The senoritas are enthralled with U.S. officers and you, in particular. I'm just happy to tag along. My hat is off to you, Sir," Heth said in his refined Virginian accent.

"Nonsense, my friend. We have yet another opportunity, and I have reason to believe you have done quite well yourself."

"Social?" Heth inquired, sure of the answer. "That makes three in the last couple of weeks. It seems the party will never end. At least it will last until we are finally back on U.S. soil. I also noted you had charmed at least as many young ladies during the same time."

"My God, Harry, are you keeping track?"

Hancock smiled with equal measures of surprise and pride.

"Just be careful, the fathers are ever-present."

Harry knew the appropriate customs and acceptable protocol for wealthy social events, coming from Virginia "blue-blooded" stock.

They arrived at the prescribed time to the home of a local dignitary, dressed in their best uniforms and presenting the appearance of professional military men. Wherever he went, regardless of the event, Winfield introduced himself in such a way that everyone knew he was in the room. Other officers had also been invited, including Colonel Clarke, still recovering from his wound at Churubusco. The colonel stood next to the host introducing his officers as they entered the well-adorned ballroom.

"Lieutenant Hancock, I wanted to tell you 'well done' for your actions during this fight," Clarke offered, as Winfield and Heth paid their respects to their commander.

"Thank you, Sir. I hope the Colonel's recovery has gone smoothly, and you are on the mend."

"Not much of a problem. I'll be back to complete health soon. Thank you for asking, Lieutenant. Who is this?" Clarke already knew who had joined his regiment, but studied Heth as a commander would when meeting a new officer.

"Sir, I am Lieutenant Henry Heth. I am fortunate to have been assigned to the Sixth and even more so while the unit is in Mexico."

Clarke recognized the slight Southern accent in Harry's response. "I gather from the sound of your voice you are southern-born, likely Carolina or Virginia. West Point, right?"

"Yes, Sir, Class of '47, and it is Virginia," Heth replied.

"Armistead is a Virginian, I believe. He is wandering about somewhere in this crowd. I have met a few other outstanding officers while we've been in Mexico. Robert Lee and Longstreet are also from Virginia. Well, enjoy yourself young lieutenant, but conduct yourself as the officer and gentleman West Point has made of you," Clarke offered, then turned to speak with one of the many dignitaries in attendance who wished a moment of his time.

They paid their respects to the host and hostess and were free to mingle, but the lieutenants somehow ignored most of the guests and focused, instead, on the unusually large number of young ladies who seemed just as interested in them.

"Winfield, we only have a few words of Spanish in our repertoire, they even less of English, but this lack of language hardly seems a barrier to you in your conquest of the young ladies of Mexico. I am always impressed."

"Tonight will be great for both of us. I assure you."

He scanned the room to find the loveliest young lady and make her his own, at least for the night. On this particular occasion, he focused his attention on the beautiful woman standing near the host. She moved into the garden outside, eyeing the lieutenants as she gracefully exited the room. Nodding to Heth, Hancock followed her through the doorway, taking a rose from the vase near the door. Heth could see through the open doorway as he watched Winfield bow and hand her the rose, introducing himself in broken Spanish. She was raven-haired with deep brown eyes, and her olive complexion added to her beauty.

"Lieutenant, I speak English. Perhaps that will be better for both of us."

"Perhaps it will. I am Winfield Hancock."

"And I am Isabella Castillo Garcia."

They spoke for a while, and she was fascinated with the handsome young officer. She spoke of growing up and of the beautiful country of Mexico. He offered the same about Pennsylvania and the United States. He longed to be home but had her convinced that without her, his heart would break.

Winfield spoke of her beauty, then professed his love for her in his best, yet rehearsed, Spanish. It was one of the few sentences he knew. She stared into Winfield's blue eyes and melted away, giving herself willingly to his embrace and tender kiss. He would visit again; this time, she would give herself to his desire.

Harry understood the signs and that his task was to intercept anyone, especially the "duenna," and provide Winfield time with the young woman. Hancock would naturally be dashing, handsome, self-confident, and profess his love once more, and win the affection of the young lady.

To Heth's surprise, a young lady approached, extending her hand. He took it gently in his and introduced himself. He was, after all, from a refined Virginia family. "This is going to be a good night for me, as well," Heth mused.

Hancock was on his own.

The diplomats completed their work, and the Sixth Infantry began its move to the coast and home. First Lieutenant Hancock served as the provisional quartermaster, performing so well that Clarke made the assignment permanent, to Winfield's dismay. It did, however, ensure he remained in Mexico to see the last unit depart the country. The Sixth moved to Vera Cruz, and

Hancock arranged for the movement of all personnel and wagons to the port for embarkation.

Dragoons and the Infantry shared a strong sense of camaraderie. Showing their appreciation for the foot soldiers, the Dragoons prepared large quantities of drink for the thirsty men passing along the route of march. The infantrymen wasted little time in consuming the liquor. Hancock was among them as the movement ground to a halt.

Lieutenant Colonel Gustavus Loomis, commanding the movement of troops, reached the bottleneck and its impromptu celebration. Angered, he began a long tirade, commenting on the poor performance of Hancock and his execution of the movement.

"I blame Hancock. If he had attended to his duty, this blockage would not have occurred; he has shamefully neglected his duty."

Hancock's record and performance of duty indicated otherwise. Harry relayed the commander's disparaging remarks about his performance. Temper rising, Winfield was outraged.

"This is insulting," he screamed at Heth. "Damn the chain of command."

It was in his nature to challenge authority, sometimes foolishly. Youth, arrogance, and liquor combined to bolster the lieutenant, and ignoring Harry's attempt to stop his friend from making a mistake, Hancock headed for Colonel Loomis' tent.

"By God, I have something to say to the fine colonel!"

"Winfield, you should reconsider," Heth implored.

The inebriated Hancock would have none of it and stormed off. Finding Loomis, Winfield challenged Loomis' statement on his failure to perform his duties. Replete with colorful language, he told the colonel no one is ever permitted to say he neglected his duties. Loomis could not believe the young lieutenant was speaking to him, the commanding officer, in this manner. Sitting rigidly in his chair, his anger building and with voice raised, the colonel fired back.

"Young man, you are an officer in the U.S. Army and must carry yourself accordingly. How dare you swear in my presence. This conversation is over. Go to your tent, sir."

"I will not let you or anyone else tarnish my good name." He started to rock back and forth from the drink. Loomis had heard enough.

"I am placing you under arrest."

He turned to Heth, who stood behind Hancock with a resigned expression. Harry quickly grabbed his friend by the arm and exited. Loomis smiled to himself at the sight of the two lieutenants. Back at his tent, still feeling the effects of imbibing the cavalry juleps, Winfield dropped onto his cot.

In the morning, Hancock listened as Heth relayed what had taken place.

"You swore at Loomis, you fool. You must apologize immediately. Do you even know that you are under arrest?"

"Arrest? Dear Lord, I have to make this right, Harry."

"Get cleaned up. We are going back to see Loomis."

Winfield, humbled by the experience, sheepishly asked for forgiveness. The colonel accepted the apology and said nothing more of the incident. Embarrassed by his actions, Winfield rightfully attended to his duties and the move to the port and journey home.

His performance of duty was of such high caliber that, upon his return home, he performed his quartermaster duties at Fort Crawford, near Prairie du Chien, Iowa, then on to Fort Snelling, Minnesota. Frontier duty was, once again, the order of the day. The excitement of Mexico would have to last for some time.

CHAPTER 7
LIEUTENANT HETH

Jefferson Barracks, Missouri

The bright morning sun rose as he stepped off the steamer in St. Louis, disembarking with other members of the regiment and ready for his next assignment. Hancock was an officer with battle experience gleaned from service in Mexico. The sight and smell of the battlefield had become a permanent part of him. He savored this new sensation of heightened adrenaline and danger that would not soon fade. Experience of this sort was a premium in the Army. Many of his West Point classmates also gained valuable experience on the Mexican battlefield and, more importantly, observed fellow officers and their ability in the most trying of circumstances. Some learned very early that the aggressive young Hancock was always at the forefront of his unit during a battle. The battlefields behind him, Hancock settled down to the more mundane garrison duty that stretched across the United States – and the Sixth Infantry was heading west.

He entered the headquarters, knocked loudly in crisp military fashion, and heard Brigadier General Clarke bark the customary "Come in!"

Winfield stepped through the door and came to attention in front of the general, seated behind the large oak desk. "Sir, Lieutenant Hancock reporting, as ordered."

"First, let me say we missed you these last few months," General Clarke began as Winfield entered his office. "Hancock, your efforts in moving this regiment from Mexico were exemplary. I need an aide-de-camp, and you are my first choice. I see no reason why you cannot perform the duties of the adjutant as well, so congratulations!"

Winfield quickly rolled the duties over in his mind.

"The adjutant is the military assistant to a senior officer, and an aide-de-camp handles the personal side. It makes sense to combine the two."

He focused on Clarke's words.

"However, it would behoove you to continue to keep your hand in the quartermaster's game. The lifeblood of an army flows through the quartermaster and his logistical expertise."

The general considered Hancock's recent success.

"You will serve as the new acting regimental quartermaster based on your exceptional performance. Alright, let's get started, Hancock. The adjutant's desk is just outside of this office."

The world of administration, of military orders published and received, of correspondence and record-keeping, was far removed from the line company lieutenant's position, but the awareness he gained enhanced Hancock's growing set of skills that he would leverage throughout his career. More importantly, he was always in General Clarke's company.

Armistead entered the headquarters to see Clarke with word concerning Harry Heth, now stationed at Fort Crawford. Winfield listened carefully as the captain informed the general.

"Harry Heth is gravely ill. Perhaps from his assignment in Mexico. I would guess dysentery from the description."

Hancock was surprised by the statement and listened as the captain read the dispatch.

"Harry had a touch of the illness in Mexico, but not too severe," Hancock offered.

"He is under medical care at Fort Crawford, but it hasn't helped. The doctor has recommended he be allowed to return home to Virginia and be with his family."

Leaving the general's office, Armistead paused at Winfield's desk. "Clarke must decide whether he remains in the regiment or released from further service."

"If he is released, I will request permission to accompany him back east to Richmond. With your endorsement, I believe Clarke will approve my request. My God, it is a thousand miles to Richmond. In his weakened state, I fear he may not survive the journey."

Clarke approved Winfield's request to take his friend home then take leave in Norristown. When Winfield arrived at Fort Crawford, he was shocked at Harry's appearance. His friend lost nearly one-third of his weight and was drawn and pale, almost ghostly. Hancock made arrangements, and they traveled by barge along the Mississippi River to St. Louis. Clarke, accompanied by his regimental surgeon, visited his two officers aboard the steamship. Clarke was startled by Heth's appearance and encouraged the lieutenant "to recover and return as soon as practicable."

"Doctor, I am less than optimistic about that young man's chances; however, these officers have surprised me before."

The doctor offered a grave prognosis. "We shall hear of his state within weeks. I'm sure, Sir."

With instructions from the surgeon, the lieutenants continued their journey to the Ohio River, resting for a few days in Cincinnati when Heth's condition worsened. Winfield ensured local doctors cared for Harry. With the forced delay in travel and better medical care, Heth's state began to improve. They bid farewell to river travel and departed for New York by rail. They experienced all the city offered and, to their delight, the abundance of young female companionship. It was a life far removed from the isolated forts of the Plains, and, once again, it was Hancock and Heth in Mexico.

The two friends headed for Washington by way of Philadelphia, where they called upon a Philadelphia doctor and close friend of the Heth family. Armed with "new" instructions and dietary changes, Harry was heading home to the care of his mother and sisters.

"I would be greatly pleased if you would call on my family in Richmond, but I understand your anxiousness to return home," Harry said as the two sat comfortably in the upper-class car of the train heading for Washington. "It is a short train ride to Richmond, and I am perfectly capable of making the journey on my own. I will always be grateful for your care and friendship. Perhaps towards the end of your leave, and before you return to the regiment, you may come to Virginia. The Southern belles would line up for a chance to meet Hancock."

Winfield laughed loudly, then thought about Harry's suggestion.

"Although I am under orders to escort you home, I see no reason why I shouldn't do as you say."

The sound of his voice still belied his hesitance to leave his charge before arriving in Richmond. They bid farewell to one another in Washington as they transferred to their respective trains.

Harry's condition improved through the remainder of 1849. Throughout his recovery, Heth continued his correspondence with others, none closer than Winfield. His health improved to a level sufficient to be recalled to special duty in Washington, and Harry rejoined the regiment by the summer of 1850, nearly 15 months after his health failed.

Norristown

It had been five years since Winfield had seen his family, and even longer since he set foot in Norristown. The mature and battle-hardened lieutenant needed to see his family once again. He left for West Point nine years ago and last saw his parents at his graduation. He returned far removed from the boy who went off to school and more experienced than the man who graduated from the Academy four years previous. Assignment to the frontier and battle experience in Mexico shaped the young man into the confident and courageous leader he had become.

"Win!" John exclaimed as he burst through the door and threw his arms around his older brother. "We've been getting ready for you since you told us you were coming home. Mother is beside herself, and Father can't stop talking to everyone in town that Lieutenant Hancock is returning for a spell."

Winfield watched his younger brother closely, the excitement in his voice at a high level, seemingly fully mature at 19-years-old. John was more than the boy he left behind years earlier. Hilary had completed his study of the law as their father wished and was practicing in the town. He'd catch up with him later.

Elizabeth heard John's voice as Winfield approached, her steps slowing as she neared the door. Lizzie did not want him to see her crying as tears welled up in her eyes. She could not tell if her tears flowed because she missed Winfield or a final release of the fear a mother feels when her child is in harm's way. Elizabeth stopped in the kitchen and stared for a moment at the unopened door.

"I hope I am not limping any longer from the leg wound in Mexico. Mother will be upset that it happened and equally upset I've kept it from her," Winfield thought briefly, then erased the thought from his mind. His wound had healed months ago.

"Mother, I am sorry it has taken this long to come home."

"Your father and I read and re-read your letters whenever you sent them — the things you have seen in such a short time. My stars, look at you, the handsome army officer brimming with confidence. We are so proud of you."

Winfield could not contain himself and moved forward, wrapping his arms around his mother. Lifting her off her feet, he held her tightly and kissed her gently on the cheek. They moved into the house and sat at the table, talking for what seemed like hours. The conversation drifted from topic to topic – the Army, Mexico, and Winfield's future. He tried to answer all queries and provide enough detail without needlessly worrying Elizabeth, ensuring that any mention of his wound would not find her ear. As they readied themselves for dinner, Benjamin walked through the door, and Winfield rose from his seat as his father entered the room.

"Father, I have missed you."

Benjamin considered his son in the way all fathers do when they have an overwhelming sense of pride.

"Well, Lieutenant, you appear very well, indeed." Extending his hand, he included, "Welcome home, my son."

Grasping his father's hand in both of his, Winfield thanked his father and expressed his joy at finally being home. The conversation, one of many he would have with his parents and brothers during his leave, continued well into the evening.

Finally exhausted, the family retired. It was as if no one wanted to move from the table for fear that they would not see one another the next morning. Benjamin stopped at the doorway, and turning to his son said, "Winfield, I'd like to talk to you about life after the Army." Winfield expected "the talk" with his Father about the continuing study of law at some point after the military. He had readied himself for a frank conversation of why he would remain in the Army.

After his experience in 1847 and 1848, the study of the law was far from his mind. Hancock believed he was thoroughly a soldier. The military discipline, the ability to exercise authority, and the rigors of field deployment were all elements that Hancock wanted to embrace. He was fast becoming an expert in the administration of a military unit through regulations and requisitions. After Mexico, he had a taste for harsher elements of war. The dangerous battlefield environment with two forces locked in deadly combat suited him. He sought distinction, understood it would come in time, and knew well the army was his calling.

"Father, you had planned for Hilary and me to study law. I respect you, but I've found that after the Military Academy, service on the frontier, and my experience in Mexico, I am well suited to lead men. The country needs professionals in the ranks. I have continued to study in this, my chosen profession."

Benjamin listened intently as his son articulated the reasons for his decision and the path he was following to achieve more responsibility and command his unit. He was, to his very core, a soldier – one who embraced the exercise of authority, the rules and regulations that drove the Army, and the experience and excitement of battle.

"I understand. Your brother has completed his studies and is in law practice. Somehow, I knew you would excel as a soldier. It suits you. I would ask you to reconsider, but that would be a vain attempt to have you stray from what you desire. You must connect in every way to your chosen vocation to succeed. The success you've achieved so far says everything." Benjamin paused, though he did not feel a sense of loss at his son's decision, and with a smile added, "You can always study law later."

Winfield smiled broadly and took his father's hand once more, then pulled him close, embracing Benjamin.

"Thank you, Father. I will make you and Mother proud."

"We are already beyond proud, my dear son!" Benjamin said, hugging Winfield even tighter.

The months passed quickly, and the townsfolk continued to welcome their favorite son throughout his stay. He connected with everyone: town leaders, both political and religious; shopkeepers; most of his father's clients; teachers; and friends who still resided in Norristown. There were excursions to Philadelphia, New York, Washington, and many points in between, but the soldier longed to return to the soldier's life.

CHAPTER 8
ALMIRA RUSSELL OF ST. LOUIS

Duties that supported the regimental commander continued to refine his military expertise and his penchant for preciseness in regulatory compliance. Winfield had become an exceptional staff officer, almost to the detriment of what might lay in his future as commander of infantry.

"I don't mind the position. It is a tremendous opportunity to learn about the Army at a higher level. Clarke is great to work for, but I should be in an infantry company," he confided to Don Carlos Buell, as the two sat outside the officer's quarters late one evening.

"I'm sure your time will come, Win. For the time being, you have St. Louis to explore, just like Mexico City. Do you appreciate how many ladies reside in this city?" Buell said, expecting Winfield to react and, in typical Hancock fashion, begin to devise some plan that would take them to the city. It didn't take long for the adjutant to see the opportunity.

"With the number of regiments consolidated at Jefferson Barracks, at least until they are split up and the companies dispersed across the Western Frontier, it is appropriate that the Sixth Regiment host a ball for its officers and the ladies of St. Louis," Winfield said.

"I serve as the acting regimental quartermaster, and, when we plan our social, I must make many trips to St. Louis to make arrangements."

"You are in!" Buell said excitedly.

"You're right!" Winfield said, satisfied with his solution.

First and Always: Rebellion

Winfield spent the next two months enjoying the city and its fairer population. St. Louis was the gateway to the West. The country's population was expanding and heading towards the frontier for new beginnings. They brought with them a mixture of cultures and customs that were visible throughout the vibrant Victorian city. It was this genteel world that Lieutenant Hancock had entered. His position as aide-de-camp allowed him to accompany Clarke as a guest of many of the city's most prominent people in their well-adorned homes. It was a significant departure from the spartan environment with which a soldier is intimately familiar.

"Sir, you've received another invitation to attend a social gathering in St. Louis. This time at the Mayor's residence. There is a second invite from Mr. Samuel Russell. He will host a gathering the following month at his Longwood Estate."

Hancock handed the invitation to Clarke.

The general read the invitation with a momentary pause before deciding.

"I'm inclined to send my regrets to the Mayor, but protocol dictates we shall attend. I recently met Russell, and he is a prominent business leader in the city. He seems to be a fine man, and it will give you a chance to get out from behind the desk. Accept his invitation also, and Winfield, you'll accompany me to both."

"Very well, Sir," Hancock said, smiling as he left the office.

It was the social custom in many St. Louis circles that the officers assigned to the area, particularly within the city itself, were often invited to attend private parties, galas, and public celebrations. Hancock enjoyed the assignment as Clarke's aide and adjutant, for which he would forever be grateful.

Standing just behind his commander as they entered the home, Hancock observed all the guests in their most elegant dress and lovely ladies moving around the room. The Russells stood steps from the door, greeting guests as each entered. It was Clarke's turn.

"Thank you for inviting me today. Let me introduce my aide, Lieutenant Hancock."

Clarke stood with Samuel Russell and his wife, Adaline. Mrs. Russell stared intently at Winfield, hesitating for a second or two, for there was something about him that caught her attention – perhaps a mother's intuition upon meeting the handsome young officer for the first time.

Hancock gently took her hand.

"I am pleased to make your acquaintance, Madam. Thank you for inviting me into your lovely home."

She merely smiled and shook the young man's hand.

Winfield dutifully stood next to the general, while he and Samuel spoke. Winfield surveyed the room quietly, seeking the most attractive young ladies. Unlike the past, it did not take him long to notice the beautiful young woman who was moving gracefully across the parlor, pausing to say something to each of the guests. It was Miss Almira Russell, the host's eighteen-year-old daughter. She was an extraordinarily beautiful young lady with blonde hair and deep blue eyes, a youthful exuberance, and a genuine interest in every guest whom she welcomed into the Russell home. "Allie," her friends called her, was a well-educated young woman, with an appreciation for the fine arts, and of music, in particular, which she would expertly play on the piano to entertain family and guests. People seemed to gravitate toward her and, even at the first meeting, one had a sense that she was well-loved and widely admired. She was the beautiful girl all young men sought when invited to a social gathering.

Allie scanned the room with her sister, Adaline, as they were warmly greeting guests, making their way into the parlor. They both noticed the tall military officer through the small crowd, and Allie turned to her sister.

"He is strikingly handsome."

"Who is?"

"That officer next to Father and the General," Allie said.

Almira was captivating, as Winfield watched with growing interest and a hint of admiration how she moved through the room, as a dancer might, not walking, but gliding from person to person.

"Sir, will you excuse me for a minute?" Winfield asked Clarke.

"I'll be quite fine, Lieutenant. Enjoy yourself, but we shall not overstay our welcome. So circle back every once in a while, and I'll tell you whether it is time to depart." Clarke enjoyed the sight of his aide, somewhat anxious and more than a bit focused on something or, better yet, someone.

He politely negotiated his move across the parlor, filled with increasing numbers of the Russell's guests. Momentarily losing sight of her in the crowd, and concerned that she had left the room, he finally arrived within an arm's reach of the attractive young lady.

Major Buell, whom Allie had met previously, stood talking to some guests as she approached.

"Major Buell, how nice it is to see you once more," Allie said, pausing long enough to allow the lieutenant time to close the distance between them. Although confident, as he always was in these situations, Winfield still hesitated when she turned in his direction. Their eyes met for the first time.

"Somehow, this beautiful woman is truly different. Not like all the others I've met," he thought to himself. Winfield's mind was racing. He could not tell whether he liked the feeling, for it was foreign to him.

Buell stood next to Almira. Turning, he nodded to Winfield with an approving smile, said, "If you please, Miss Russell, may I introduce our adjutant, Lieutenant Winfield Hancock. Winfield, this is Miss Almira Russell."

He was shaken by her and had not heard Buell.

"I am Lieutenant Winfield Hancock."

Buell held in a chuckle and only smiled, realizing that he had never once seen his friend in this unsettled condition before, given all of Winfield's earlier conquests.

"My God, he's captivated by this young woman," Buell said to himself. He accomplished his task – he had introduced the two. He then excused himself to mingle once more among the large group of guests.

"I understand who you are, Lieutenant. I am Almira Russell, and my father is your host today. Please call me Allie and welcome to our home."

Although the sound of guests in a myriad of conversations filled the Russell home, Winfield heard nothing but the sound of her voice.

Allie's smile almost gave her away as she tried her best to downplay the excitement in meeting this handsome young officer. She noticed the light hair and deep blue eyes, the confidence he exuded, and the military bearing that defined the man.

Hancock felt he must impress his new acquaintance, but somehow she seemed more, much more, than any of the many women in his past. Something from deep within swept over him with the realization that this beauty was meant to be in his life. All other conquests disappeared into the deep recesses of his mind.

"Almira," he rolled the name over and over again in his mind, then finally returned to consciousness and blurted out, "Thank you for the invitation, Miss Russell."

"I am presently the Regimental Adjutant."

"That's impressive, but perhaps you can explain what you do."

He was a bit confused as to why he needed to tell Almira more about himself. He hadn't done that with any other young lady in his past; however, he was taken by her beauty and poise.

"The adjutant is the military assistant to the Commanding General."

Allie tilted her head and nodded. It didn't matter what he said, only that he continued to talk to her. She felt the warmth build within her at the sound of his voice and the closeness standing next to this young man.

"I've never felt this way before," she thought.

First and Always: Rebellion

His life had changed forever. Samuel Russell glanced at the two and immediately noticed something different in his daughter. "I believe I'll see that lieutenant again," he said to Clarke, who nodded in agreement.

Samuel knew his daughter was captivated, and Adaline also watched the two young people who seemed to forget the social that swirled around them.

Clarke laughed to himself as he watched his adjutant, realizing the lieutenant's wandering days were coming to an end.

Every opportunity that placed Winfield in St. Louis was seized upon to be near to her. General Clarke was always supportive of his aide-de-camp. Within the limits of military protocol and the lieutenant's responsibilities, he allowed a bit more flexibility in traveling from the post to St. Louis. The general had already discussed as much with Mrs. Clarke, who was very fond of Winfield and Allie and enjoyed being a party to their courtship.

Winfield was aware of his military responsibilities. His trips to see Allie were tied, whenever possible, to the myriad of tasks Clarke assigned. Winfield did not know that Clarke, on many occasions, created situations allowing his adjutant to visit St. Louis. Other lieutenants would accompany Hancock from time to time, enjoying the company of the Russell's or Allie's friends. It was like the old days with Heth, only different.

The late summer warmth had gradually changed to fall. The winds were chilling as the two sat on the veranda of the Russell home.

"I'm quite cold," Allie said and rose to move inside to the parlor. Winfield reached for her hand, pulling her close to him. It seemed almost natural that the two quickly embraced. She fit so perfectly in his arms, and Winfield noticed a warmth holding her.

"I must talk to your father," Winfield whispered. She knew, and could hardly contain her feelings.

Samuel sat at his desk in the large office within the home. Surrounded by shelves of books and ornately decorated furniture, the large oak desk stood between

Allie's father and the young lieutenant. "I have heard you wish to speak with me," Russell began. "That sounds rather serious." Realizing this would be more a personal conversation, he rose from behind the desk and signaled Winfield to take a seat on the sofa. Russell sat across from him in his favorite comfortable chair.

"Sir, I am in love with Allie. I ask your permission to marry your daughter, but more than your permission, I ask your blessing."

"Winfield, I have watched you these past few months, and I am very impressed. You are a soldier and a fine officer. I have not met anyone that did not speak highly of Lieutenant Hancock. I must say there is some concern on my part. Almira was raised in these surroundings. Life in the Army has its challenges, and luxuries are rare."

"That is certainly true, Sir. However, I do not intend to be a lieutenant forever. I can offer Allie all the best that I have along the way. I can assure you she'll be taken care of, for I believe there is no one more important to me."

Samuel paused, then recalled Adeline's counsel that Allie loved her soldier. Winfield would undoubtedly take care of their daughter for the rest of his life.

"Winfield, Allie, and her mother will be happy when I say you have our blessing. If I haven't missed any signals, they have already discussed the wedding. My approval is a formality."

Winfield rose quickly and extended his hand, "I will love and care for her all of my days."

As his future father-in-law predicted, the wedding planning was entirely in motion. Winfield asked several officers to participate in the ceremony. Opening the letter from Harry, he read, with great disappointment, that his friend was unable to attend the wedding.

"I regret that my recuperation has taken more time than I expected. I am heartsick and without words to express my disappointment that I am unable to be a groomsman. I am anxious to meet the woman who brought Hancock to his knees."

Winfield laughed loudly. “We’ll host Harry when he finally returns to the regiment.”

Allie and Winfield married in January 1850 in her father’s house, filled with guests from throughout St. Louis and nearly all the officers of the regiment. General and Mrs. Clarke were there and satisfied that they had a hand in finally getting Winfield to settle down. General and Mrs. Harney were in the city, as well, and hosted the reception. It was, after all, winter in Missouri, and the weather failed to cooperate. It brought wind, thunder, lightning, and hail to the festivities. The lights in Longwood went out multiple times. Some thought this an ominous sign, but the young couple barely noticed. The ceremony continued in candlelight to the delight of the guests.

CHAPTER 9
NEW CHALLENGES AND NEW CONFLICTS

Their first year went by quickly as Allie settled into "army life," dramatically different than the one to which she was accustomed but found enjoyable. She was in love with her lieutenant and he with her. The proximity to her parents' home in St. Louis, and the city itself, which always extended to the army its most distinguished civilities, was considered a privilege and was truly appreciated.

"We're moving outside of the city. The headquarters is relocating to Jefferson Barracks, about twelve miles south of St. Louis," Winfield said to Allie.

"Will we find a place to call home?" Allie asked, concerned about the move. She had embraced life as a soldier's wife and prepared for the adventure, enduring assignments where quarters were less than adequate.

"I'm sure there are quarters on the military post that serve as the adjutant's quarters, but we'll see when we get there. I promise you that we'll have a roof over our heads."

"Yes, but will the roof leak? Winfield will take care of things, I'm sure," she said quietly to herself.

Upon arrival, Winfield received family quarters, which he deemed uninhabitable for the Hancocks. Allie's fear had become a reality. The house was keyless and, more importantly, the door was off the hinges. Winfield had requested the repairs be made for weeks after their arrival and finally sought the help of the post commander, the crotchety Colonel Braxton Bragg.

"There is nothing wrong with the quarters. This lieutenant should be glad we've accommodations for him," Bragg thought as he read Hancock's written request.

"The previous occupant was a major who found nothing wrong with the condition of the quarters. Who the hell is this Lieutenant Hancock to take issue with quarters being provided?" Bragg was growing angrier as he read.

Hancock was infuriated. One thing that defined Winfield was a sense that if ill-treated, he would not resign himself to the outcome. Regardless of the senior's rank, he challenged the offender. The harshness of the correspondence between the two officers reached its peak when Clarke interceded on Hancock's behalf, only serving to increase Bragg's disdain for Hancock.

"I command Jefferson Barracks, not Clarke," Bragg bellowed to his adjutant. The corrections to the Hancock's quarters followed, regardless.

When evening came, Allie and Winfield would always invite others to their dinner table. The officers loved being invited to the Hancock's for a meal and an evening of camaraderie in the otherwise austere environment, far away from their homes. It was a rare opportunity to depart from military tasks and participate in a somewhat refined social setting. The young couple enjoyed the company of the single officers, and Allie especially relished the rare opportunities when other wives were present.

The guests would arrive soon, but this was her time with Winfield, and she thoughtfully chose her words. Her excitement overshadowed what she wanted to say and to tease him with the news he hadn't expected. She couldn't help herself.

"We're expecting," Allie said softly, the evening light illuminating her golden hair, and, softly dancing upon her face, making her more radiant to Winfield.

Startled at the news, and never at a loss for words, Winfield stammered, "Expecting whom?" He knew full well what she was saying, but couldn't resist the impulse to play with her.

"We are expecting a baby!" She was uncertain whether he purposely toyed with her emotions, or this detail-oriented soldier was clueless in these matters. He took her in his arms and kissed her gently.

"I have only received wonderful news like this once before, and that was when you agreed to marry me," Winfield said quietly. His excitement was almost too much to contain, and she wrapped her arms tightly around him.

"Should we tell everyone or wait? I have no idea," Winfield said.

"There's no need to wait. We must tell everyone. We could send a telegram to our parents or possibly a letter, but that takes so long."

Their son, Russell, was born in October. The Russells were frequent visitors as new grandparents. Well-wishers stopped by the Jefferson Barracks quarters to offer their congratulations and, in many cases, leave some small gift for the newly-arrived Hancock.

Winfield continued to hone his staff skills over the next few years, reaching an exceptional level of proficiency.

He entered the office and removed his winter overcoat and scarf, protection against the Missouri November winds. Clarke came shortly after that as the sun began to rise.

"Come in here, Winfield, and I have something for you."

"Congratulations, Captain, you are promoted in the Quartermaster Department," Clarke said, as Hancock entered the office. Hancock was entirely taken by surprise at the announcement.

"Thank you, Sir! I don't suppose this was some hoax perpetrated by one of my friends? It would not be beyond their consideration," he replied. He smiled then said to himself, "I'd likely do the same thing, and perhaps I will."

"It is not a lark Captain. The Quartermaster Department needs your expertise, as do I."

Hancock nodded appreciatively at Clarke's statement. Clarke continued.

"We are also off to Florida, Fort Myers, to be specific. Your duties will continue to encompass the quartermaster's responsibilities."

"Very well, Sir. I'll tell Allie tonight about the promotion and the new posting." Little did he and Allie realize that she would be the only woman on the military post. Allie could tell it was difficult for Winfield to receive his promotion and not be selected to command a company, as he had hoped.

One common thread among all commanders was that their organizations required someone to effectively handle all the necessary actions that make a unit function properly. Soldiers must be armed, fed, clothed, sheltered, and moved when it is time. Skilled practitioners in quartermaster tasks were necessary, and real experts were rare. So commanders, from captain to general, always sought the right officer within their ranks. Hancock's commanders were no different. They knew he could handle the task with aplomb, and they, one after another, leveraged the young officer's skill to ensure their commands were successful.

"Allie is right," Hancock thought. "Clarke and Harney could see it, and they both assigned me quartermaster duties." In Mexico, moving the regiment back to the United States, and in Missouri, the name Hancock was at the top of everyone's list. When the time came for promotion, it was the Quartermaster Department, and not the Infantry, who offered a captaincy, and he accepted it. Winfield was heartbroken that the Infantry had allocated all promotions to Captain to other officers, his friend Heth included.

Fort Myers, Florida, was the base of operations for the force in its campaign against the Seminole Indians in 1856. Winfield studied background information as he sat at the makeshift desk in their quarters, reading aloud to Allie when he found something that would interest her.

"This is the latest installment of a long conflict with the Florida Indians. There were battles led by Andrew Jackson as far back as 1818 to curtail attacks on American settlers by the Seminole Indians. It was under Spanish control then, but they ceded the territory to the United States as part of a treaty in 1821."

"Where did the Indians go?" Allie asked, the displacement of natives a new topic for her.

"They were encouraged to move to the Indian Territory west of the Mississippi. Other Southeastern tribes refused to go, hence the second Seminole War. That was a fairly long-running affair – almost seven years. Some Seminoles did move west after that one. We had some discussions on this conflict at the Academy."

"That brings us to today's dust-up. Once we finish this action, I expect the remaining Seminoles will also be heading west."

"I do hope the baby will be alright here."

Hancock looked deeply into Allie's eyes, and the impact of what she said hit him forcefully. Ada Elizabeth Hancock was born in February 1857. Winfield couldn't help doting on the girl and continued to do so as she grew. The officers at Fort Myers enjoyed the opportunity to shower affection on the only baby on the post. Allie loved it.

As the situation in Florida began to settle, the regiment returned to the mid-west and was reassigned to Fort Leavenworth, Kansas. The country seemed to be in turmoil with abolitionists and anti-abolitionists at odds, and, in some instances, death and property damage resulted.

He served in the West during the partisan warfare of "Bleeding Kansas," and, crossing the Rockies to the Utah territory, where the Sixth Infantry arrived to quell a potential uprising when the Mormons tried to form their sovereign nation, and the Federal government balked. The "Utah War" was resolved without bloodshed, and the regiment received new orders for Benicia, California.

Hancock assembled groups of soldiers and teamsters while preparing to move a thousand men and all of their equipment westward over the Sierra Nevada range. As quartermaster, he was solely responsible for the logistics required to transit the country from Kansas to the Pacific Coast. California was another 800 miles away with the mountains between the Sixth Infantry and the San Francisco area. Hundreds of wagons and thousands of horses and mules trod westward, in a feat of unparalleled efficiency for a military organization, negotiating deserts and mountains. Along the way, Winfield sharpened his skills in staff and quartermaster tasks, which almost came naturally to the captain. He became an expert, valued and sought after by commanders at all levels. Winfield longed for his family and, once established in California, planned to bring Allie and the children to the Pacific Coast. It had been more than a year since he held his Allie.

Allie was content with her role as an army wife, one that was vastly different from the life she led in St. Louis. While Winfield moved with the regiment to western Kansas then to Utah and California, the Hancock family visited the Russell's at Longwood, then moved to the East Coast and Washington.

"My dear Allie," he could hardly contain himself. "I have been granted leave to return to you and move our family to California. I anticipate the journey to the East Coast will take some weeks, and expect we shall return by ship in the early Spring." Allie's tears began to fall as she read the words. They joined him, and, once again, established a new home in Los Angeles for the nomadic army family. This time, the living conditions were excellent, eliminating the necessity for Winfield to challenge authority.

CHAPTER 10
SECESSION

Across the country, the election of 1860 placed Abraham Lincoln of Illinois in the White House. Immediately, southern states began to increase their rhetoric for splitting from the Union. Secession and states' rights were the topic of the day. The heated discussions in Washington and state legislatures finally reached their peak, and the Confederate States of America was declared by February 1861. In quick succession, six states split from the Union. When word reached Hancock in California that Fort Sumter, in Charleston Harbor, had been fired upon and surrendered, four more states withdrew and joined the Confederacy.

In California, and throughout the Army, officers began to question whether their loyalty lay with the Union and preservation of the country as the forefathers envisioned, or with their respective states. Officers, among them many close friends, resigned their commissions and most agonized over their decision. A great civil war was upon them and the nation.

The Army was in turmoil. There were many occasions, once secession finally took root, that officers would visit the Hancocks to seek Winfield's advice or tacit support for their decision to resign from the Army and return to their home states. General Albert Johnson, a Kentucky-born Texan and the Division of the Pacific Commanding General, had become close to Winfield and Allie. It troubled Winfield that Johnson was sympathetic to the Southern cause. Close friends Armistead and Heth, both Virginians, felt an emotional connection to their home.

First and Always: Rebellion

Hancock and Heth, commanding a company in the Tenth Infantry on the Plains, maintained their correspondence. When rumors of secession began, Heth was a Union supporter and had even admonished fellow Southerners who resigned their commissions. When withdrawal from the Union became a reality, Harry's ties to Virginia weighed heavily upon him. Winfield could offer Harry little support, for Heth followed Johnson and Armistead and resigned.

"You must concur, Virginia has the right to withdraw if it feels compelled to do so, simply to preserve our way of life," Harry penned. Winfield read the words calmly, hearing Heth's voice as if they were sitting across from one another, sharing a whiskey. He could only imagine Heth wrestling with his decision then, finally, convincing himself he was right to join the Confederacy.

Heth continued, "I am sorry, but I feel compelled to do so. For God's sake, Winfield, even General Albert Johnson, has chosen resignation."

Hancock had the same conversation with so many others over the last few weeks. In his reply to Heth, Hancock wrote, "Harry, I offer you no advice on this matter. I will not argue the rights of states but for an undivided Union, not a country formed of principalities. I cannot sympathize with you, but your convictions must guide you. You are our dearest friend, and I hope you will make no mistake with your decision."

It was the last correspondence the two exchanged before the rebellion.

The Hancocks invited Johnson and a few resigning officers to their home before they departed California. He could see the pained expressions of some southern officers, torn between loyalty to their country and their state. Greeting Don Carlos Buell at the door, Allie remarked, "Winfield is distressed that some of his closest friends have chosen this path. If you would please talk to him, I'm sure Winfield would welcome your counsel. So many of our friends will find themselves in harm's way during the coming struggle."

General Johnson moved across the room toward his trusted subordinate.

"I am glad you are here in Los Angeles. Allie and the children will be safe."

"I damn well belong in a regiment, but this is my assigned duty!" Hancock replied. "It will not be long before I head east. You are departing, and I know Heth has resigned, as well."

Pausing briefly, he finally said with resignation and a slight tinge of sorrow, "I ask that you reconsider, Sir. We are both sworn to uphold the Constitution, and I cannot support allegiance to any state over the nation. Secession is wrong, simply wrong."

Johnson and others listened as Winfield continued very calmly.

"I care little about the slavery issue. That will resolve itself in time through the legislative process. It will meet its natural end in America. I loathe the idea that we should dissolve the Union as it is today. It is simply unacceptable, and those who pursue that end or support secession would, unfortunately, be considered traitors to the nation. My regret is that armed conflict may be necessary to resolve the issue. If civil war is the natural order of things, then I shall be obliged, for a time, to set my friendships aside and preserve the Union. May God protect us all."

Winfield's frustration that these officers were making a mistake was no longer hidden and evident to all. His charismatic personality allowed him to be honest without offending his friends and guests on this, their last night together.

Johnson thought for a moment, then slowly began, "I am a Texan, Winfield. It is my home and that of my family. If my Congressional representatives and the Texas population as a whole believe the state has a right, under that same Constitution you've mentioned, to forgo any direction from Washington in which they disagree, then that is their right. We'll not solve this here, so let us enjoy the evening. I pray that I am never in a position to meet you or any of my friends on hostile terms."

Winfield accepted the temporary truce in the name of camaraderie. The social continued with dinner and cordials, cigars, and good-natured ribbing and song. No talk that war may be upon them all.

The evening closed, and with it, raw emotion finally surrendered to tears as friends said their farewells. The Hancocks had grown very close to the officers. Allie was heartsick over the resignations, including General Johnson, to whom she had become quite close, not unlike a father and daughter. She prayed that she would not lose a dear friend either through differing opinions or, worse, armed conflict. Fate had other plans. Winfield understood brothers in arms today would be adversaries tomorrow, plying their deadly trade for which they had trained and honed their skills for years.

Allie let go of Winfield's arm, as the two bid good evening to their many guests, and with tears in her eyes, she embraced Johnson. "May the Lord keep you safe in his hands until this intolerable situation ends."

Johnson searched Winfield's face and eyes for understanding, saying, "Winfield, I say farewell. I hope you remain safe through this commotion."

He paused at the door, taking one final glance at the Hancocks, placing the picture firmly in his memory. Without a word, and confident he had made the right decision, Johnson smiled and taking his wife's arm, turned and walked into the warm California night. They would not see one another again.

"I have learned Harry Heth resigned. He is nearly as close to me as Hilary. I tried to correspond, but, like Armistead, he is a Virginian. God help them both."

No one imagined the carnage the North and South would impose on one another for years to come.

PART TWO. REBELLION

CHAPTER 11
FIRST AND ALWAYS

Washington, D.C.

"It's a disgrace, that's what it is. What was the name of the place, anyway? It seems to have slipped my mind."

Secretary Cameron spoke up. "Bull Run, Mr. President. It is Manassas or Bull Run, depending upon which side you are on. The Southern press is having a field day with this story."

"It is not a story, Mr. Secretary, but a real embarrassment for us. I find it unbelievable that the Union force lost its first battle. So, the Army wasn't as good as we expected, or the leadership was not adequate for the task. Either way, we begin yet again and hope there is time before Davis feels he can move on Washington. The country needs a larger army and a Commanding General capable of bringing it together. One who is ready for a fight."

Lincoln scanned the list of senior officers, each with a short resume and a list of essential qualifications.

"Who is George Brenton McClellan? Says here, he is a superb organizer and leader."

"A Major General, top of his class at West Point, decorated for gallantry in Mexico. It seems like everyone is a decorated soldier. He is one of General Scott's recommendations. He brought him here from Ohio to command the forces around Washington. Major General at 35 years old, not bad. Heard they call him 'Young Napoleon!' He'd be my choice, as well."

"You've mentioned Scott, and I'd like to speak with our Army chief about the action in Manassas. I believe he may provide additional insight that could inform our decision. A young Napoleon? Well, let's talk to the emperor before I decide."

"First and Always"

The Willard Hotel was a center of Washington activity. Its lobby continually filled with famous visitors. They sat on ornately covered sofas and chairs conducting a wide range of business or government meetings. The low hum of conversation heard as the Hancocks followed the bell captain and his porters to their room. They set the family's bags down in the center of the room, and, a gratuity in hand, returned to their station in the lobby. It was a lavish suite as one would expect in Washington, with paintings and colorful rugs accenting the walls and floors. There were separate bedrooms and a sitting area with sofa and chairs. The windows opened to a beautiful view of Pennsylvania Avenue, with the White House to the right and the Capitol building to the left.

The trip from California was exhausting, and although Winfield could have left his family in New York, they desired to accompany him to Washington. He dropped down on the sofa as ten-year-old Russell and his four-year-old sister, Ada, stretched out on the floor playing. Allie put her arms around her captain, kissing him lightly.

"How long will we be here, my dear?"

Winfield was unsure and shrugged, but he had two weeks before he needed to be in Louisville, his next posting. Allie laughed.

"After we unpack, why don't we stretch our legs a bit?"

The late summer evening was warm, and the sun was low in the sky. The city seemed alive and had much to offer. They had been traveling for days, and the thought of getting outside appealed to little Ada.

"Please, papa, let's go. I want to go right this minute." His lovely little girl was excited, eyes wide, jumping up and down, with her blond curls bouncing.

Winfield saw Allie in his little girl's face. They were both beautiful.

"What do you say, Master Russell, shall we explore the capitol?"

"Sounds like we should go immediately, and have something to eat. I'm starving!"

After dinner, they sat quietly on the park bench, across from the hotel, as the children chased one another. The sweet smell of summer, with everything still in bloom, hung on the evening breeze.

"What a beautiful evening. Washington is bursting with people. I have never seen so many soldiers in one place. I do not recall this many in Jefferson Barracks."

Allie slowly exhaled, but loud enough to get her husband's attention. He was quiet and deep in thought regarding the reason they were here – to change his posting. It was Winfield's last chance to influence the upcoming assignment.

"My previous service in the infantry, on the frontier, and in Mexico, must count for something."

He was focused, preoccupied, and Allie watched him for a few minutes before speaking.

"I know what you are thinking, Winfield. Who must I see tomorrow that could influence my assignment?"

Winfield looked quizzically at his wife. He believed, to his very core, that he could provide a valuable service as a commander, perhaps of a company of soldiers. He never shied away from a fight, and this one was for the preservation of the Union.

"Until recently, I belonged to an infantry regiment, and that should help. For God's sake, Allie, we lost the first battle two months ago in Virginia. If I go to a fighting unit, I could have an impact. I am just anxious to be included. I see that you're concerned."

"Concerned is too light a word, my dear. I am frightened about the prospect, but I love you and appreciate your desire to join the action."

"These repetitive support assignments take me further and further away from the infantry. The Army needs experienced infantry leaders more than ever."

They had always been honest and frank with each other. Allie smiled. It was not the joyous smile when a loved one does something that brightens your day, but one that says, "I appreciate your words," when, in your heart, you do not.

"I have watched you, Winfield, in all of our assignments, and you are an excellent and highly-regarded officer. However, I see your frustration at possibly being left out of this terrible action. That frightens me, but still, I must ask, why are you not satisfied when this next assignment would keep you safe and near?"

Winfield did not hesitate to respond. "Allie, I am a soldier, first and always."

He searched her eyes for empathy. Allie nodded, indicating he needed to continue.

"An army must have those things necessary for war. It is vital. I can find no fault with those who perform these tasks. I also agree that becoming a faculty member at the Academy, as you hoped I would, is just as safe. There are capable men to do such work, but that does not suit me."

"I know. I truly do, but my dear Winfield, you must admit that supply was second nature to you. Clarke and Harney knew it, and so did General Johnson. They all depended on your skill. If you feel that this is the wrong path, then you must do everything possible to help change your assignment from quartermaster back to the infantry." She paused for a moment, the emotion rising in her voice as she touched her husband's hand.

"I do hope that this rebellion is short-lived. I could not bear your loss, but I will support you."

A war to preserve the Union had started, and, as far as Hancock was concerned, the situation had dramatically changed. McClellan's Army needed experienced infantry officers. It had been so long since Mexico. It was the last time he felt the excitement of battle and leading men in a desperate fight against an equally determined enemy. He needed to do all that he could to make that a reality. To that end, he resolved to secure an appointment with any senior officer who would listen and was willing to help. He was also a professional, and if it were not possible to transfer, then he would move on to his assignment as a quartermaster in Kentucky. "Allie would love that," he thought, as he watched the children. Although she never expressed it, Winfield knew she feared for him if he were assigned. She was, in the end, a devoted army wife and would support him, regardless.

"This will work," he thought as he lifted Ada into his arms.

"It must work."

CHAPTER 12
McCLELLAN'S ARMY

The Army was rapidly expanding, with new regiments being formed and arriving from the various states daily, numbering in the thousands. Lincoln chose McClellan to command, and the general was actively recruiting officers with whom he was familiar. He promoted them as needed, and placed them in command positions as the Army of the Potomac, its new designation, organized for combat. McClellan had plans for a grand Army and needed experienced leaders. His recollection of fellow officers in Mexico and of his West Point classmates, both in and out of service, significantly contributed to his decision-making process regarding the potential he so desperately needed.

"Sir, I happened to be over at the Willard Hotel this afternoon and saw Captain Hancock and his family checking in. He is on your list."

General Randolph Marcy, McClellan's chief-of-staff, leaned on the empty chair in front of McClellan's desk. The general set his papers down, and recognition flashed in his eyes.

"That's excellent! Hancock, and many officers like him, are exactly the right officers we need. Marcy, I need you at the Willard."

Winfield's life was about to change. The decade since Mexico had provided him the opportunity for professional development. Skills he developed and under-utilized at the Academy were now fully leveraged. He read voraciously, digesting tactics and strategy from a history of battlefield engagements. He started to tell Allie about his readings when their conversation was interrupted by a knock at the door. Allie nodded at Winfield, then rose and crossed the room quickly to open the door. The officer kindly greeted Allie, then searching just past her, saw Winfield taking the few steps towards him.

"Please, come in."

Allie moved back as the officer stepped through the doorway.

"Captain Hancock, General McClellan sends his regards and welcomes you to Washington."

General Marcy stood at the door and extended his hand first to Allie, then to Hancock.

"Sir, please tell the General I am honored that he remembers me. I am equally honored to meet you once again. We were both with General Johnson in Utah a few years ago. It is a pleasure to see you again."

"Captain, the General is aware of your current orders as the quartermaster for General Anderson, in Kentucky. I am free to tell you he has other plans for you. Please remain here at the hotel. McClellan is extremely busy but wants to speak with you, likely tonight. May you both have a pleasant evening."

Marcy turned as Allie quietly closed the door. Hancock smiled broadly.

"I've served with Marcy but was unaware that George married Marcy's daughter. His father-in-law is his chief of staff. Interesting and unusual, don't you think?"

Allie shook her head. "Here's your opportunity, Win. I am confident that this will turn out well for you."

Marcy strode through the office door to McClellan's desk.

"Sir, I stopped by the Willard and greeted Captain and Mrs. Hancock, who is quite well. I have asked the captain to remain there. That was around 6:00 p.m. today. I am sure he is anxiously waiting for your message."

"Excellent! Winfield Hancock is a man of heroic courage and superb presence in action. I spoke with others who were with him in Mexico. Hancock and I were both brevetted first lieutenants for our service at Contreras and Churubusco. When General Harney was here, he mentioned Hancock and spoke highly of him. I need more like him in this army if we are to end this rebellion quickly, as Lincoln desires."

"What do you see for him? He hasn't commanded a company yet."

"He has a quick and correct eye for the ground. He'll be an outstanding brigade commander. He was the quartermaster for the Sixth Infantry's move from Kansas to California, a thousand miles over the mountains. That's an amazing feat."

"That's true. We were both with General Johnson in Utah. Hancock is an excellent officer, a bit headstrong, but someone I would want with me in a fight. You'll do well with officers like him."

"I'm not concerned about the jump from captain to brigadier general. He'll handle that with aplomb. Although I hear he is an excellent quartermaster, I knew the infantryman quite well. Winfield is more qualified to lead than many of the volunteer appointees."

McClellan went back to his papers as Marcy exited the room. They worked well into the evening, drafting messages and adjusting the organizational plans for the Army of the Potomac. McClellan stood, placing his hands behind his head and arching his back. The difficulties of command forced McClellan to spend nearly all of his day in the saddle, reviewing defenses and observing soldiers and their leaders. He and his staff were forced to accomplish administrative tasks late in the day. It was not surprising that McClellan summoned Winfield later that night. The relaxing conversation would be a welcomed relief.

"Get Winfield in here."

Marcy and Williams only smiled at each other. "We're on it, Sir."

Major Williams arrived at the Willard Hotel late in the evening, and Winfield opened the door.

"The general is ready for you, captain."

Hancock and Williams walked together the few blocks to McClellan's headquarters. General Marcy greeted Hancock once again, ushering him into a small sitting area. The officers departed the room for an adjacent office, so McClellan would not be disturbed. There was a table, strewn with reports, maps, and the myriad of papers that Hancock recognized and was well-acquainted with from his quartermaster duties. The youthful Army of the Potomac commander stood leaning over the table, apparently lost in thought, then turned to face Winfield dropping the papers in his hand. Hancock immediately came to attention, rendering a crisp salute.

"Sir, Captain Hancock reports, as ordered."

McClellan smiled and crossed the room from behind the table, returning the salute as he closed the short distance between them, extending his hand.

"It is a pleasure to see you once again, Winfield. I trust your family is settled here and comfortable."

"Allie and the children are quite well. Thank you for asking. How may I be of service?"

Hancock knew the opportunity to alter his assigned quartermaster path had come. Perhaps he could leverage the talent and influence of McClellan, who was already one step ahead.

"Lincoln has called for thousands of volunteers. States are providing them in a continuous stream. We need soldiers, but more importantly, I need capable officers to organize, train, and lead these regiments in combat. I see you, and many like you, filling that role as a brigade commander with appropriate rank."

The words momentarily stunned Hancock. An advancement from company level to brigade command was unheard of, but so was the Army's leap from the pre-war level of a few thousand to the massive force that would be the Army of the Potomac, with well over a hundred thousand soldiers. Winfield quickly calculated the possible number of regiments, brigades, and divisions as McClellan continued.

"I am well aware of your pending assignment, and can ill afford to have experienced infantry officers lost in support assignments. Don't misunderstand me. I believe those assignments are vital to the service. The responsibilities inherent in a quartermaster assignment directly affect the soldiers at the tip of the spear. You have demonstrated excellence in this capacity, and your previous commanders have succeeded based on your effort, as it should be. However, your service in Kentucky would not serve this Army well at this point. Your change of assignment is a task for my staff. I want you to get comfortable here with your family while my staff works the issue, but I need you to stay out of sight. For God's sake, Winfield, don't do anything on your own. By that, I mean, we'll handle it and no interaction with the Quartermaster Department, or anyone else on your part, is necessary."

Hancock was taken by surprise at McClellan's suggestion – more of an order. The general was already planning the reassignment, this time to infantry command. He could hardly contain himself at the thought of his good fortune. The years of professional study, demonstrating excellence in the most mundane tasks, honing his skills which had begun at West Point and developed over the last 17 years, had served him well.

"Sir, I am ready to assume whatever position you would assign to me. Brigade command and promotion, I am honored to be considered and ready to be assigned."

"Of course you will be brevetted to brigadier general, the appropriate rank for brigade commanders. I am sending you to 'Baldy' Smith. He commands a division in the Fourth Corps, under General Keyes."

They sat late into the night discussing West Point, their previous assignments, and their decorated service in Mexico. They recalled friends and classmates who resigned from the Army who they would likely face in this deadly conflict. It was dawn when they stood and, shaking Winfield's hand, McClellan welcomed him to the Army of the Potomac.

"Wait until Allie hears of this turn of events," Winfield said to himself as he departed for the Willard.

He was appointed Brigadier General of Volunteers on 23 September, and, after settling the family in the Washington area, departed for his new unit. Classmates at

James H. Kelly

West Point, the fates, and secession had destined many officers for stars in the conflict, on both sides. Armistead and Heth had already pinned on their general's stars.

CHAPTER 13
THE PENINSULA TO RICHMOND

"Hancock, I am damned glad you are here."

William "Baldy" Smith, was the division commander, his moniker bestowed on him while a cadet at West Point. He was standing, leaning against an upright tent pole, and taking a short break from the stack of administrative requests on his desk. Hancock saluted as he grasped Smith's outstretched hand.

"General Hancock, welcome to the division."

The title seemed foreign to him, almost out of place. A captain only days before, he was a McClellan-appointed brigade commander, and anxious to meet his regimental commanders. Baldy was a close friend and one year behind Winfield at West Point. He had been at Manassas when the Union force was defeated. He was now a division commander in McClellan's new Army of the Potomac. It would take months to equip and train.

Smith likely discussed officer assignments with the corps commander, General Keyes, and expressed his preference to have Hancock assigned to his command. He was delighted when the commander informed him that Hancock was indeed appointed.

Hancock was ready to take on the challenge, but first, he needed to hear what Baldy may have planned and what was in store for the division. The two sat down, and Smith spoke frankly to his friend.

"McClellan plans on taking Richmond, striking the heart of the Confederacy. He'll go through Manassas, then Centerville, where Johnson has his Confederates arrayed today. I gather they are about 100,000 strong, but George says that number is too low. The division needs training, and your time is best spent getting them ready."

"How much training have they had to so far? Any at all?"

"They have learned basic drills in their respective states. There are a few officers with military experience, but only a few."

Hancock knew this would have to be accomplished before the first units started moving south, but he was confident. Without saying, Baldy knew Winfield had this in hand and was well-equipped for the responsibilities and duties of command.

"We have three brigades in this division. The other two brigade commanders are Brooks and Davidson. Your brigade includes the 49th Pennsylvania, 43rd New York, 5th Wisconsin, and the 6th Maine regiments of infantry."

"How proficient are the commanders? Hopefully, some have prior service."

"No military service as officers. They are appointed regimental commanders by their respective states. I know you will ensure they are ready for command, regardless."

Smith and Hancock rode to the brigade together where Colonel Amasa Cobb, the 5th Wisconsin commander, was also serving as brigade commander. After Smith's introductions and a brief period of discussion with the remaining regimental commanders, Hancock thanked Smith and Cobb, then assumed command.

Brigadier General Hancock stood before his brigade for the first time. The regiments moved as though they had been in the Army for much longer than a few months. Thousands of soldiers, men of Maine, Pennsylvania, and New York, would soon learn what it is to be in service to the Union. Hancock was demanding in today's training and in tomorrow's execution, which he knew would come shortly after arriving in Virginia. His administrative expertise also made life difficult for his staff – at least until they reached the high level of proficiency he demanded.

While Hancock's demeanor was stern and business-like in military matters, he was amiable in less formal settings. He took pride in learning the names of every officer assigned to his command.

He naturally courted danger. When ordered to do anything on the battlefield, he ensured it was precisely done, to the credit of his unit, and without exception. Hancock cherished soldiers' lives but understood that command would mean sending soldiers to their death.

Hancock needed to select the rest of his staff and requested recommendations for aide-de-camp from the regimental commanders. The young officer stood outside the commander's tent and searched for something on which to knock that replicated a door. Opting for the wooden tent pole, he knocked and could see Hancock raise his head from the papers he held.

"Get in here, Lieutenant!"

"Mitchell, Sir. William Mitchell, 49th Pennsylvania. Reporting, as ordered."

The lieutenant stood rigidly at attention while Hancock sat forward in his chair, holding what appeared to Mitchell to be a personnel file. Hancock dropped the record and quickly found one with Mitchell's name.

"I am aware that you have an outstanding grasp for the tactical level, and you are an excellent horseman," Hancock began, then quickly said, "Stand at ease, Lieutenant. I am conducting an interview, not an ass chewing."

Mitchell immediately relaxed and remained standing in front of the brigade commander's desk. The "interview" went on for what seemed to Mitchell to be hours but lasted less than 30 minutes. The general laid out his requirements for staff officers and the necessity to be close at all times, especially in a fight. He was building his staff, and the young lieutenant was among few considered as an aide-de-camp.

"I have selected another lieutenant named Isaac Parker. Congratulations, William, you will join him."

Mitchell liked Hancock immediately. The general had a way to disarm subordinates and make them feel at ease in his presence, especially his aides. Each officer possessed the ability to anticipate his requirements, and he was creating a pool of young officers.

His brother, John, had joined the Army of the Potomac with the 49th Pennsylvania Infantry, like Mitchell, and Winfield made sure that Lieutenant Hancock was an assistant adjutant.

"That should calm Mother and Father," he thought and added the same news to Allie's letter.

Winfield was confident he could use John's talents in his headquarters and watch out for him at the same time.

Army of the Potomac

Smith's division established Camp Griffin on the surrounding farms. Winfield wasted no time in setting the regiments to training as infantry soldiers. To emphasize any direction, order, discipline, or clarification of his intent, in practice or battle, Winfield developed a penchant for "colorful language." It was an ability picked up in early assignments in the West and Mexico, but certainly from his mentor, General Harney, who used vulgarity as a second language. Soldiers understood Hancock's harsh and profane speech, some accepting it as soldier-talk, others were offended, but all would act immediately upon their commander's words. Hancock was well-educated from childhood and West Point, but perfected his manner of speaking, replete with its crudities, and was becoming widely-known throughout the Army as one of the most proficient general officers in its use – a tribute to his former commander.

Within months, the Army of the Potomac's numbers grew to more than 105,000. In Centerville, Virginia, about thirty miles from Washington, General Joseph E. Johnson's 45,000-man Confederate Army of Virginia waited. McClellan, always wary of the enemy's strength, notified the leadership in Washington that he believed Johnson's force outnumbered him.

McClellan believed that capturing Richmond was a matter of geography, with the two capitals only one hundred miles apart. The mountains bordered the region to the west and the Chesapeake Bay to the east. Several major rivers, running west to east, cut across McClellan's avenue of approach towards Richmond. The Rappahannock, Rapidan, Pamunkey, Chickahominy, James, and York rivers were all natural obstacles to be overcome. Fort Monroe was in Union hands and sat on the extreme southern end of the Virginia Peninsula, in Hampton Roads, ideally located to support the campaign. Although there were great rail lines for resupply, the waterways provided an interesting alternative. McClellan's staff began to work the details of a Peninsula Campaign from their Fairfax County Courthouse headquarters.

Smith, back from a council of generals, called Hancock and his fellow brigade commanders together to discuss the new plan and new organization. The Army of the Potomac would grow from four to six corps.

"We are the Second Division of Keyes IV Corps, and our objective is Richmond. Johnson has pulled back to Richmond. It would seem he expects our advance from the north; however, we will approach from the east and move up the peninsula."

The commanders stood quietly, assessing the impact of changing the route of a march that was underway — the logistics of shifting to a port for embarkation on all of their minds. Before Smith could continue, Brooks spoke.

"When do we leave? Where are we in the order of march?"

"Infantry, artillery, cavalry, and trains will depart from Alexandria. Support material and forage will leave from Annapolis. The III Corps is first in line on the 17th, and we'll follow."

Hancock, the former quartermaster, quickly calculated the number of railcars, wagons, and vessels to transport the large force down the Potomac to the Chesapeake and, finally, to Fort Monroe. Charters for steamers, schooners, canal boats, and barges would be needed.

"It may take a month to move this Army completely. There are 100,000 men, tens of thousands of animals, support wagons, and artillery caissons and limbers. Glad it's not me this time!"

Within three weeks, the quartermaster corps had delivered McClellan's Army to the peninsula. McClellan planned his advance up the peninsula, taking Yorktown, and leveraging the railroad for the move on Richmond. Confederate Major General John B. Magruder and General Joe Johnson had other plans.

Hancock was anxious to move his brigade forward and engage the enemy. He could not fathom why this Army was sitting, while it could go on the offensive. He was annoyed that Baldy Smith ordered another brigade, rather than his, to probe the line. Equally annoying, that unit broke through Johnson's line but had to withdraw for lack of reinforcements. It became clear that either Keyes or McClellan wanted no significant engagement.

"What the hell? This brigade was ready and available to reinforce." He started to show his frustration to the staff, then quickly corrected himself.

Army of Northern Virginia

Johnson was concerned with the growing Union Army and, to prevent being flanked by the Federals, pulled his Confederate Army back from the Rappahannock to Gordonsville, nearly 75 miles southwest of Centerville. The Federals initially pursued Johnson's Confederates; however, McClellan's new plan, moving the force by water to Fort Monroe, and threatening Richmond from the east, 74 miles away, forced Johnson to reconsider the defense. Across the line, Johnson worried that he would not be able to hold out against the Federals' superior numbers. He was also vulnerable to Federal naval gunfire and possible amphibious assault behind his lines. The Union controlled both the James and York Rivers and could move beyond his lines and attack the flanks, or cut off his route to Richmond.

Magruder's force dug in across the peninsula between the York and James Rivers. The Federals began shelling Yorktown, and Johnson ordered his divisions back from their positions to occupy a thin defensive line in front of Williamsburg. The line consisted of fourteen strongpoint or "redoubts," anchored by Fort Magruder in the center, sitting astride the major roads from Hampton and Yorktown. Johnson's apprehension increased, and he ordered the withdrawal from the line. Surprised by the retrograde, Hancock was, nonetheless, excited that McClellan would attack the line after more than a month on the peninsula. His brigade would finally get its chance.

Army of the Potomac

The Union Army pushed forward and eventually caught up with Johnson's rearguard near Fort Magruder. Major General James Longstreet's division was in position near Williamsburg, buying time for Johnson's trailing elements to move. He concentrated at Fort Magruder, placing regiments in the surrounding redoubts, but was unaware that Johnson's withdrawal removed soldiers from the fortifications on the extreme left of the defensive line.

Baldy Smith searched for an opening that would break the stalled offensive. With Keyes' approval, he planned to send a force forward and called Hancock.

"Winfield, take your 5th Wisconsin and 43rd New York, and Davidson's 49th Pennsylvania and move forward. I think there is an opportunity here, while another corps attacks the right of their line."

Hancock wasted little time in positioning the regiments forward of the Confederate defensive line, throwing skirmishers out. He could hear the sound of battle increasing to his left, near Fort Magruder. Along the road to Williamsburg, they found the bridge at Skiff Creek set ablaze by the Confederates. He turned to the cavalry officer accompanying his brigade.

"Get the hell up there and get those flames out before we lose the damn bridge."

The cavalry officer saluted briskly and galloped forward, taking most of the troopers with him, musket lead flying past them, and some hitting their targets as troopers fell. Before they could extinguish the fire, the captain ordered the soldiers to pull back. Hancock was mounted next to Colonel Stannard, the Vermont commander. His infantry regiment was in position beside him.

"Damn it all. Colonel, take four companies and get that fire out. Cover the far bank with fire, as it seems our friends across the way are determined to let it burn. Clear them out."

The Vermonters immediately ran forward at the double-quick. Stannard's companies sent volley fire across the creek, wading across to claim the far bank. Others quickly handled the fire, saving the bridge. The enemy withdrew, and the Federal infantrymen discovered muskets, tents, and wagons left behind. The Confederates were positioning themselves on the defensive line near Williamsburg.

By late afternoon, Hancock's brigade, with regiments from Davidson's and Brook's brigades, moved forward. His chance to meet the enemy head-on was here. The Confederate defensive positions were somewhere ahead.

"Line of battle."

The regiments positioned themselves on each side of the approach. Smith rode up and took charge of two regiments on one side of the road, while Hancock led the others. Anxious to press the enemy and retain momentum, they dressed their lines and advanced across an open field and into the wood line beyond. The woods were thick and tangled, making it challenging to maintain proper battle lines. Darkness added to the problem. Hancock's two regiments continued to shift to the right, unintentionally closing the gap between them and the two regiments under Smith's direction. Hancock halted to re-form his line, and Brooks, following with his brigade in a column, nearly intermingled with Hancock's.

"This is getting to be damned impossible. The trees, scrub vegetation, and darkness conspires against us."

Hancock and Brooks watched as the move bogged down. Smith briefly halted the regiments as Hancock's were within sight. He approached his brigade commanders and listened.

"I agree; this is difficult at best. It will be impossible once night sets in."

"We should hold the assault until daylight but will comply if you and Keyes want to press the attack. We must find the enemy's location. I've crossed roads that I had no idea existed."

The commanders quickly recognized the officer riding towards them was General Keyes.

"Place your regiments here for the night. Secure your area, and we will continue our assault at first light. I will remain here with you tonight, if you don't mind," Baldy said finally.

"Sir, we'd be pleased to have you with us. I can't promise the best meal, but it will do on this battle line," Smith offered.

Before daylight, instead of continuing the assault, Keyes wanted to probe the enemy's left flank.

"Winfield, pull back to the wood line behind us. I want to send your brigade to the right and see if we can gain an advantage. By the way, General, how is it you seem to be cleaned and pressed with that white shirt?"

Hancock smiled and, with a tilt of his head, said, "The valet, Corporal Mahan."

Army of Northern Virginia

Brigadier General Cadmus M. Wilcox was up, enjoying a cup of coffee that his aide had handed him. It was near dawn. The overcast sky was predicting that, later today, they would ride in the rain. Johnson planned on pulling back from Magruder's defensive line.

"Marcellus, are you ready to move?" Longstreet asked as he dismounted.

Wilcox saluted. "Where are we going?"

"I want you to move forward by 7:00 a.m. to Fort Magruder first, then forward and make contact with the Federals. Report to General Anderson. We want to hold them in place for a bit as we'll be pulling back later today."

"Perfect. Want some coffee?"

"No, thank you. I need to ride on to the right and see Hill and Early. Good luck, and I'll see you very soon."

Remounting, he turned his horse and moved past the sentries to the road leading north.

Army of the Potomac

Hancock departed for Smith's headquarters before the sun came up, finding Keyes and Smith together, with a map spread out on the table before them.

"Win, I want you to take five regiments, and a battery, to the extreme right of the line. Proceed up to the crossing at Cub Creek Dam, about two miles distant, and take possession of the enemy's works on the opposite side of the creek commanding the dam. I've received a report the enemy left that position." Baldy traced the route with his hand.

"Once you've secured the position, you are authorized to advance beyond, but only if you believe there is an advantage to be gained. If you need reinforcements, I will provide them when requested."

"I'd like to have a cavalry detachment screen ahead of me and between the dam and the York River."

"We'll see to that, but I need you moving soon. The road that crosses the Cub Creek continues towards Williamsburg. You may run into the rear guard of one of Johnson's divisions, as Hooker did. If that happens, get word to me so I can move Brooks and Davidson up quickly."

Smith turned to Keyes, who nodded in agreement. Hancock saluted and took the reins from Smith's enlisted aide who held his mount while the generals talked. Hancock called for his regimental commanders.

"Our force will include the 5th Wisconsin, 49th Pennsylvania, and the 6th Maine Volunteers. The 7th Maine and 33rd New York of Davidson's brigade, as well as Wheeler's artillery battery, will join us. All regiments will be ready to move early tomorrow morning."

Once the commanders departed, Lieutenant Cowen arrived and reported that his six-gun battery was to support the brigade. He was stationed to the rear and along the road heading to the east. The battery joined the line of march as the brigade moved along the Union right to the dam.

At first light, Hancock's force moved along the road. Reaching the intersection that would take them across the dam and to the redoubt, he positioned the 33rd New York volunteers. Turning left, he was soon within sight of the dam and could see the last redoubt, just beyond. Searching with field glasses, he could not see movement, and as Keyes pointed out, the area may indeed be absent of enemy soldiers. The water above and below the dam was too deep, ensuring any approach must come along the road.

Keyes arrived with a small element of cavalry to conduct a reconnaissance of the area bordering Cub Creek, from the dam to the York River.

"Winfield, are you ready?" The corps commander asked.

"Sir, I need the cavalry to screen my flanks when I move forward across the line."

"I agree, and will provide a regiment immediately."

Pressing forward, Hancock placed Cowen's artillery battery a short distance south of the creek, with a line of sight to fire directly on the redoubt to their front. Ordering the skirmishers forward, the 5th Wisconsin, followed by the 6th Maine, crossed the dam, and up over the redoubt walls. It was late morning, and the unguarded position was in Hancock's hands.

"Lieutenant, go back to the road intersection and inform Colonel Taylor that I wish him to move three companies of the 33rd New York to this position, immediately."

The lieutenant spurred his horse into a full gallop. The general brought his field glasses up once again to view

Redoubt 11, less than a mile to his left. It sat on elevated terrain that, if controlled by the Confederates, would put his newly-secured position in jeopardy. The plain between the posts was perfect for the assault, but the wood line bordering it would provide cover for the enemy to attack his rear once the assault began.

"William, get back to Generals Keyes and Smith that we hold the first position, and that we are assaulting the second. Tell them I need the reinforcements promised and request a brigade of infantry."

Mitchell rode off quickly.

Facing north, Hancock could see another unoccupied position between his soldiers and the York River.

"When the cavalry regiment arrives, they will screen right and survey the last redoubt."

He focused on the redoubt across the plain and how to take it.

Smith listened to the aide, Mitchell, and sent forward four infantry regiments with a battery of artillery. Directing the skirmishers into the open area between the two redoubts, Hancock reformed his infantry in line of battle. The artillery positioned itself in the center of the line, slightly behind the infantry. Ready for the assault and assured Smith's reinforcements were on their way, Hancock surged forward and took the second redoubt, unopposed.

"Why the hell are these positions abandoned? I can hear the fight farther down the line. If the reinforcements arrive, we can roll up the Rebel line from the left flank."

Longstreet's men were in position in the center of the line while the left of the line was "in the air" or undefended. Hancock quickly capitalized on the oversight and was working his way down the Rebel defensive positions. He finally reached two occupied redoubts that held Longstreet's infantrymen. Calling for the regimental commanders, the officers scanned the forward redoubts while Hancock talked through his plan.

"If we advance on these positions, we will provide the diversion that McClellan needs forward of the enemy strongpoint. He is trying to break the line with the other corps. Prepare once more for an assault. The last redoubt we've secured can adequately cover the right and left of the assault regiments."

The broad plain forward of their position extended southward, allowing the group to see Fort Magruder in the distance.

"Colonel Taylor, bring up three more New York companies and secure this redoubt."

Within minutes, the companies were moving and taking their positions. Satisfied with the New York infantry's placement, the general turned to his regiment commanders, Colonels Irwin and Burnham.

"Gentlemen, bring your regiments forward of this position and prepare to move when I call. Send skirmishers out about half a mile to the front. That should put them less than 50 rods from the enemy redoubt."

Irwin and Burnham moved immediately. Hancock spun his mount around to find Colonel Cobb and his 5th Wisconsin.

"We are in position, Sir. We should get this action started," Cobb said, anxious to begin their first engagement.

"Indeed, Sir. General Smith is providing reinforcements. We await their arrival." Through their field glasses, each could observe the Confederates at the top of Redoubts 9 and 10. Hancock then turned to Cobb.

"Cobb, they appear to be curious or confused as to who we are. Let's tell them."

With that, Cobb ordered the Wisconsin color bearer nearby to run to the top of the redoubt and place the National colors on the parapet, where the three 33rd New York companies were cheering. Hancock laughed at the New Yorkers' outburst and turned once again to Cobb.

"Colonel, move your regiment to the right of the guns once they are in place. The ground is good, and the buildings near the tree line will screen you."

Cobb saluted and headed back to the regiment. Confederate commanders reacted immediately, throwing their skirmishers forward. The Federal skirmishers did not take long to drive them off, and the fight on Hancock's end of the line began in earnest.

"Tell the skirmishers to lie down where they are."

The general's aide carried the order forward to the infantry line. Captain Wheeler, the artillery commander, halted his mount within feet of Hancock.

"Lieutenant Cowen is bringing up his guns, which he will place on the right and left of the redoubt. I want you to bring up your battery, but place your caissons in the rear of the redoubt." Wheeler wondered what the commander planned.

"Yes, Sir. We'll be up shortly. Where would you like the battery?"

"We are moving forward, young man. You are going with me."

Hancock was smiling, ready for action. Within minutes, Wheeler rounded the redoubt with his four guns. The general urged his horse forward, with Wheeler's battery in tow.

"Place your left gun here. Have you carried adequate canister?"

"Yes, sir. Our authorized load plus case, grapeshot, solid shot, and shell."

"Excellent! You'll need it very soon."

Riding back to the infantry regiments ready for battle, he moved down the line at a trot. The regiments stood firm while Wheeler's cannoneers began to fire. Still aware of the flanks, he sent skirmishers left and right into the woods to protect against a Rebel assault. He read the terrain better than most and knew that he could not adequately occupy the entire expanse with the units under his command. Reinforcements were needed, and he was still waiting.

The infantrymen could see the Rebels lining the parapets of the two redoubts to the front and the earthworks connecting the two, opening fire with muskets and artillery. Hancock's calm demeanor steadied the infantrymen who were facing their first real fight. They watched as Hancock rode along the line, ignoring the fire. The soldiers believed this was the general they wanted and deserved – a leader in the face of enemy fire.

The general rode to the center and watched from behind the battery, encouraging the cannoneers. They fired, reloaded, and fired again with a significant effect on the Confederate positions.

"Give it to them, boys. You are right on target."

They continued firing in preparation for the assault once the promised reinforcements arrived. It did not take long for Wheeler's artillery to drive the Rebels from the redoubts. The forward skirmishers fired at the Confederates as they emerged from the earthworks connecting the redoubts. Hancock's frustration increased realizing that surging forward and seizing the abandoned strongholds depended on the new forces Smith promised.

Army of Northern Virginia

"I am told that we have little coverage on the left. I can't explain why, but we may have one or more positions vacant as a result of the Union effort in front of Magruder. A Union force, probably brigade-size, has crossed Cub Creek Dam."

Jubal Early was concerned and sent the message to Longstreet. Early had become concerned about the Union's crossing when infantrymen who were pulling back from the extreme left passed the information to his headquarters. Longstreet sensed the danger even before Hancock was in position, but quickly read Early's message.

"Sir, I propose to move the brigade into those woods ahead and come upon the Union's right."

Early had given the order to prepare for movement and sent his aide to liaise with the cavalry detachment, already moving forward to screen towards the York River.

CHAPTER 14
GIVE THEM THE BAYONET

Army of the Potomac

Smith's aide handed Hancock a message. He opened it and read that he should fall back to his original position. Hancock obeyed orders from his superiors, but he failed to comprehend this order. He held two redoubts and could take an additional two, with the proper forces.

"Why in the hell do they not see the opportunity our position affords them? We can collapse Johnson's line."

Smith was sending him the regiments he requested and would likely move the rest of the division in this direction. Hancock anxiously sent a new message back, with a lieutenant from Smith's staff, telling the commander what ground he held and that he needed the support. It didn't take long for the reply to find its way back.

"You are instructed to fall back to your initial position. Our engagement forward of the center strongpoint and the left of the Army's line takes priority."

Hancock was irritated that neither Keyes nor Smith understood his position nor the advantages of attacking the Confederate left flank. A short window of opportunity presented itself.

"How can I pull back? Lieutenant Farquhar, come here. Take this down." Farquhar, a young engineer assigned to Hancock's brigade staff, dutifully pulled from his pouch the small pad and prepared to take direction.

"Ready, Sir."

"For General Keyes. Sir, I have been directed to fall back at a time when I hold enemy redoubts on their left flank. I have engaged the enemy, and the opportunity exists to turn his left if we reinforce here. I am told by

General Smith he can no longer reinforce this brigade due to action on our left."

Farquhar glanced up from his writing to signal Hancock he was ready to continue.

"We currently have the advantage. If we fall back, I believe we will fight for this ground again tomorrow, likely with more losses. It will inspire the enemy while adversely affecting my soldiers. Reinforcing this brigade and pressing our advantage may well relieve the pressure on our left."

Farquhar nodded. "Sir, is there anything further?"

Hancock nodded in the affirmative, "Just one more line. Tell General Keyes that I will obey the order to fall back if no answer arrives in a reasonable time. Signed, W.S. Hancock, Brigadier General."

"Get going! I need the answer as quickly as possible! Hopefully, the generals are together. Off with you, Lieutenant!"

Farquhar placed the dispatch in his leather pouch, pulled in the reins of his mount, and saluted. Sharply spurring his horse, he galloped away in seconds.

Army of Northern Virginia

General Hill rode up to the crest of the hill where Jubal Early sat, scanning the wood line.

"General Early, we've been given orders to move as you've suggested. I'm bringing up General Rains' brigade to take your place here."

"Very well, Sir. I'll move with the first element."

"I'll move with you," Hill said. "What marching order have you planned?"

"The 5th North Carolina will lead, moving on the right, followed by the 23rd North Carolina Infantry. The 38th and the 24th Virginia will move on the left."

General Hill rode with the right element and General Early with the left as the brigade negotiated the woods, determined to throw Hancock's brigade back. If they could move quickly, they would be in a position to capture Hancock's artillery, who were firing on Magruder.

James H. Kelly

Longstreet placed more infantry into Redoubts 9 and 10, while Confederate cavalry swept through the woods on Hancock's right ahead of Early's brigade. The Wisconsin skirmishers increased their firing to meet the increasing enemy presence.

Army of the Potomac

By late afternoon, and lacking any response, Hancock reiterated that he would wait for the corps commander's reply a "reasonable" time before pulling back, as ordered. Heavy rain started in the evening. Hancock planned to withdraw his force only a short distance in preparation for a continued assault. The poor weather would mask his movement. He still believed that Smith would see the opportunity before him and send reinforcements to retain the initiative.

Hancock went forward with the 49th Pennsylvania and saw that a Confederate regiment had entered the woods to his left in an attempt to flank the Union force. It was apparent Longstreet was attempting to envelop the Federal brigade. The Rebels broke through the woods to strike the Pennsylvanians, and Hancock ordered the regiment to pull back to the crest of a rise a short distance behind them. The 6th Maine regiment, closest to Wheeler's artillery in the center of the line, began firing at the advancing Rebels while the 49th Pennsylvania pulled back to reform. When the 49th had formed, the 6th followed suit, pulling back again and aligning with the Pennsylvanians. The battle line was ready for the Confederates.

On the right, the 5th Wisconsin engaged the enemy cavalry who were clearing the wood line, and with the artillery, checked the advancing Rebels. Hancock found Cobb and ordered him to withdraw to the crest with the other regiments.

Jubal Early's 5th North Carolina infantry emerged from the wooded area with the 24th Virginia, just behind the cavalry. Hancock's brigade was now under fire from both flanks. He moved with the retiring infantry regiments while assessing the situation and planning his counter-move. The artillery, having fired all canister rounds into the oncoming Rebel infantry, limbered up and pulled back themselves. They were just ahead of the onrushing Virginians, who were crossing a fence line and making a dash to capture the guns. Once clear of the woods, Early's regiments formed their line of battle and closed with the 5th Wisconsin. The battle raged across Hancock's front.

General McClellan was in Yorktown, overseeing the embarkation of troops and supplies that would move upriver around the Confederate force. Heavy rain fell, making movement difficult. Arriving at his headquarters close to 5:00 p.m., he found his force in a defensive posture, content with repulsing Longstreet's assaults. Adequate strength was available to breach the Confederate line and continue the pursuit up the Peninsula, but his offensive had stalled. The situation in the center of the line was vague, and the Confederate positions, except those forces in the wooded area forward of Fort Magruder, were uncertain. The only sure thing was that Hancock held two redoubts on the left of the Confederate line. The generals, who had gathered at the Whittaker House to meet McClellan, heard the heavy firing starting to the Union right, at Hancock's location, and he was miles from his nearest support.

McClellan instantly grasped that Hancock held the key to winning the battle. Abruptly he turned to General Smith and roared, "Damn it all! General Smith, get your two remaining brigades and Naglee's brigade on the road immediately. Head to Winfield. He seems to be the only damn one here who sees what to do, and he is, no doubt, in dire need of reinforcements."

Without a word, Smith moved quickly through the door, his remaining brigade commanders trailing him. Within minutes the regiments were on the road.

A corps commander spoke up.

"We are engaged in the center. Generals Hooker and Kearny are positioned east of the wood line near Longstreet's strong point, which he has likely reinforced."

McClellan angrily responded, "You are correct, general. Hancock is in position to roll up the flank, forcing Longstreet to fight both in the center and to the left of his line. He can only do so with sufficient force."

"Smith's column will move shortly. When he does, Hooker and Kearny will move forward into the woods, clearing them of Confederates, and assault the enemy works."

"Where the hell are the reinforcements? Smith is aware of my position, but not my current situation," Hancock said, as explosions interrupted the rearward movement of the skirmishers, rushing back to join their regiments. The sound of thousands of muskets reverberated across the open area. Smoke, barely rising above the soldiers, obscured Hancock's view. A musket ball ripped through Cobb's coat, taking with it a brass button. Hancock smiled at the colonel, who returned the glance with a "that was close" expression on his face.

"Well, Colonel," Hancock said to Cobb as the two officers moved with the infantry who were fighting their way back to Redoubt 11, "We'll take them on! Pour fire into them. I want to draw them in. There is no Confederate artillery on the field with the advancing infantry. I'll reposition our batteries to give you support."

The 5th slowly gave ground, pulling back, reforming their lines, and firing into the Confederates. Riding to the 7th Maine on his extreme right, Hancock ordered Colonel Mason to move, repositioning them to the right of Redoubt 11. The three New York infantry companies inside the redoubt were ordered out and positioned on the left of the Maine Regiment. Hancock was confident his right was secure.

Directing his artillery to take positions on each side of the redoubt, he watched as the heavy rains which soaked the ground were causing problems for the artillerymen's movement. Finding the battery commander, he redirected the artillery to post further back, behind Redoubt 11, in the open plain between it and the dam. Extending his line, Hancock sent two companies into the woods on the left, while Mason, with his regiment, did the same on the right. Hancock had envisioned the 5th Wisconsin retiring and occupying the redoubt, but as their withdrawal under fire was taking more time, he ordered four companies of Chandler's 6th Maine into the redoubt.

Hancock planned to feint. Once the infantry regiments were in the position, he began his attack. The Confederate regiments had been battling for some time and were at the bottom of the slope before Redoubt 11, only thirty paces from his line. They would not move back any further.

"Forward!" Hancock ordered.

Without hesitation, the entire line surged over the crest, stopping and firing two volleys at Early's surprised Carolina and Virginia Infantrymen.

"Charge, Gentlemen, Charge! We must give them the bayonet!" Hancock's voice echoed above the firing.

The line cheered as they charged down the slope and into the enemy, bayonets at the ready. The Rebels broke and fled back across the open area. Concerned about his flanks and rear, Hancock ordered a halt forward of the slope. The regiments, in the line of battle, poured their fire into the retreating enemy infantry. The companies in the redoubt and to the right or left of the position provided supporting fire for the charging infantry. Hancock's artillery sent rounds their way. The decimated 5th North Carolina and 24th Virginia left dead and wounded scattered across the open ground between the redoubts. The 23rd North Carolina, still in the woods, moved too far left and was engaged by Hancock's Maine regiment guarding the flank. The 38th Virginia finally emerged from the woods; however, before they could assist the two lead regiments, General Hill directed the units to retire from the field.

The regimental commanders followed Hancock's order and called "cease-fire." The effect on the enemy was so devastating that the second line of Confederate infantry promptly stopped their advance. Hancock, nonetheless, prepared for the counterattack to come on the right and in his rear.

"If I were them, I would try to dislodge this brigade and drive it back across the dam. It is the only crossing open if forced to withdraw," Hancock thought as he considered the Rebel assault. "Where the hell are the reinforcements?" he said to himself.

When the assault began on the center of the Army's line, McClellan initially rode forward. Hearing the battle raging on the Confederate left, he headed for Hancock's area. Although Longstreet's Confederates put up a determined defense, the Union III Corps, with Kearny's and Hooker's divisions, was reinforced throughout the day, driving the Confederates before them. Longstreet finally withdrew – continuing the march westward towards Richmond.

Without the requested reinforcements, Hancock would not pursue the retreating enemy, and held his position, securing both of the Confederate's left-most redoubts. He sat upright in the saddle as the Confederate officer approached under a white flag, requesting that they are allowed to retrieve their dead and wounded, to which Winfield readily agreed.

General Smith arrived at Hancock's location as the remaining regiments of Brooks and Davidson were closing on the dam behind Hancock's position.

"Well done, Winfield. The division is closing on this end of the line, but it would appear the engagement is over. Longstreet had to react to your presence on his left. I don't expect he'll counter-attack any time soon."

"Sir, the regiments were magnificent. It was their first, and they disputed the ground inch-by-inch. When the Confederates were within thirty paces, we surged forward and weighed into them. I understood the order to pull back to the first redoubt, but we were engaged when the opportunity presented itself."

Hancock felt that he owed the division commander a brief explanation of his brigade's action. Smith understood, then rode forward to see the regimental commanders. The rain continued, and Hancock's troops bivouacked in the pouring rain on the field they had won only hours before. Hancock could hear the sentries challenge the riders coming from the dam. Even he was surprised to see General McClellan, with his adjutant, Seth Williams, still mounted and being escorted to Hancock's makeshift headquarters in the redoubt.

"Winfield, I hear you had quite a day. Longstreet hit you pretty hard, did he?"

"Sir, I wish I could offer you a drink. Perhaps later. I appear to be without my usual comfort items. It appeared to be a brigade or more attacked from the wood line. They were from Hill's division and Jubal Early's brigade, including the 5th North Carolina and 24th Virginia. I gave them safe conduct to pick up their dead and wounded scattered everywhere in front of the redoubt. Our 5th Wisconsin was magnificent, and Colonel Cobb was truly outstanding. Taylor, Mason, Irwin, all excellent and held their ground in this their first action."

"I knew I was on solid ground when I promoted you back in September. You were superb today, truly superb. Have the reinforcements come up?"

"The 3rd Vermont has arrived from General Brooks' brigade. The rest you've passed on the road in."

"The rest of the division will be here shortly. Well done, Winfield. Please convey my thanks to all the regiments. We'll carry this fight forward in the morning."

The two generals spoke for a short while and, when Smith arrived with the remainder of the division, McClellan departed once again for the headquarters. Hancock entered Smith's headquarters tent and found the general with a glass of whiskey and water, which he offered to Winfield. The two men welcomed the brief respite from battle, but both were anxious to pursue Johnson's Army.

"There's the white shirt again. I am astounded you have someone who ensures you have one every day, battle, or not. I must tell you that your plan was brilliant, waiting for the proper instant to change from defense to offense and the coolness you displayed and that of your soldiers, so steady. That was the key to victory. I wish to commend you for such an outstanding display of generalship." Smith knocked his glass against Hancock's.

Winfield could only thank Smith for such praise, and asked: "What's next?"

When time allowed, Winfield was in his headquarters tent, writing to his dearest Allie about Williamsburg.

"Today, my men behaved brilliantly, capturing the first colors in this campaign. They fought extremely hard and were determined to succeed. Unfortunately, we have lost over 100 men."

When Allie read the letter, she could not help thinking about the danger her soldier was now facing. "Lord, protect Winfield and the men in his charge," she whispered.

McClellan also corresponded with his wife, but his words carried a different message. "Hancock was superb today!" The title was picked up by the press shortly after that and followed Hancock for the rest of the war.

General Johnson continued his movement off the Williamsburg line and towards Richmond. By month's end, the two armies would clash once again when Johnson struck Keyes' IV Corps at Fair Oaks along the Chickahominy River. Franklin's Corps was further north, and General Hancock's brigade could only listen to the sounds of battle.

Army of Northern Virginia

The momentum changed with a single shot! Lieutenant General Johnson was wounded, and the command of the Army of Northern Virginia was in the hands of General Robert Edward Lee. One of his first actions was to move Jackson's force from the Shenandoah to Richmond. The Union was quickly learning that General Lee favored the offense. He employed Generals Longstreet and Jackson with a combined strength of 60,000 men. McClellan would be cautious to the extreme, leaving the Federal force open to an aggressive Confederate attack.

First and Always: Rebellion

Numbers didn't matter to Lee. The Army of Northern Virginia would carry the fight to the blue-clad soldiers. Lee would pursue the Federals with Longstreet and Jackson's corps and move north while McClellan withdrew to Fort Monroe.

CHAPTER 15
NORTHERN INVASION

Army of the Potomac

The regiments headed downriver, first to Newport News, then on to Aquia Creek on the Potomac, arriving in late August. Hancock stood on the landing, watching the long line of infantry soldiers disembark from the barges. The scene was chaotic. Two corps had already landed, and Franklin's VI Corps was compounding the problem. Thousands of soldiers and hundreds of wagons, all were trying to distance themselves from Aquia.

"They have done well these past few months. Unfortunately, we did not press our advantage when Johnson was outside Richmond." John could always tell the level of frustration in his brother Win's expression, although the general always hid it well from his subordinates. He was just quietly venting.

"Longstreet and Jackson, under Lee's direction – we may have to closely review at our strategy, as I'm sure McClellan is already working on the next move. Pope is moving in Northern Virginia and has already engaged Jackson somewhere around Culpeper, unsuccessfully, I might add. I hope he doesn't find Lee before he is ready."

In one quick movement, Hancock was in the saddle moving to the division headquarters. General Smith had sent for the commanders just minutes before. Walking into the house his staff had secured as his headquarters, Smith found Hancock, Davidson, and Brooks discussing the trip to Newport News and the congestion at Aquia.

"Did the Quartermaster Department execute their task too well? It seems elements of three corps moved quickly and are gathering near the landing," Davidson said, with a hint of sarcasm in his voice.

"I question the ability to move away from the docks, but that is our problem, not the quartermaster's." Hancock's previous experience with the quartermaster's role deflected Davidson's criticism and, to some degree, defended the transporters, placing the problem in the hands of infantry commanders.

"Indeed, we've done extremely well in getting the division inland from the river," Smith said as he approached his three commanders.

"We're moving north to Washington. Our assignment is the defense of the capital. The division is ordered to move from here to Alexandria. We should handle the 35 miles without a problem, even in this August heat. Prepare to move, gentlemen. Hancock's brigade will lead, then Brooks and Davidson. Remember, we are in Virginia. General Stuart is out there somewhere with his cavalry and could probe our move, so security is needed."

Baldy Smith suspected that Lee's Army was moving farther north and that the division would see action soon.

"Franklin has just informed me that Jackson is closing on Manassas and that he has already attacked and destroyed Pope's supply depot. Washington may be in his sights before long." First glancing at Brooks and Irwin, Hancock turned back to Smith and wondered aloud what he believed everyone was thinking.

"Are we in support of Pope? Lee will not waste time bringing Jackson and Longstreet together. If McClellan and Pope's forces join, Lee will have more than he can handle."

"I don't think we have received that order yet. There's always a chance, so keep that thought in mind as an alternate mission. We could be called upon to move south quickly. Currently, it's Alexandria and defending the capital," Smith replied.

James H. Kelly

Army of Northern Virginia

The failure of McClellan's Peninsula Campaign dismayed Lincoln. His new Army of Virginia was moving south, so Lee directed Jackson to move and intercept Pope. General Lee was confident the combined strength of Longstreet and Jackson, with tactical daring and maneuver, would defeat the Union force present near Manassas. General Longstreet, with half of Lee's Army of Northern Virginia, was still north of Richmond.

Lee moved quickly to engage Pope's Army. Splitting his force, Lee planned to flank the Union Army first, then strike. Sending Jackson's force north, then East, the Confederates found themselves behind Pope's forces and attacked the supply depot. The lines of communication now threatened, Pope withdrew to Manassas and engaged Jackson's corps.

The Second Battle of Manassas had begun, and, for two days, Pope sent his force crashing against Jackson's line. Longstreet's Corps was on the move and closing quickly on Manassas. With Pope focused on Jackson, Lee saw his next opening against the Union's left flank, which was "in the air." Longstreet's 25,000 men attacked on 30 August. The fight lasting several hours, Lee and Longstreet were both on the field directing the movement of brigades and artillery, and personally braving the Union fire. They swept Pope's Army, and the demoralized Federals headed back from Manassas for the second time.

Lee surveilled the Maryland line; it was free of any Union forces, but he remained wary of the Army of the Potomac.

Army of the Potomac

President Lincoln received the news of General Pope's defeat with frustration. Pope was out, and reluctantly, George McClellan once again commanded the "new" Army of the Potomac, over the objections of Edwin Stanton. Incorporating what remained of Pope's Army, McClellan was without equal in organizing and equipping an Army – and he rebuilt the Army of the Potomac in days.

Hancock was a McClellan supporter; however, there were those times when he saw things differently than his commander. In Williamsburg, when ordered to withdraw, he delayed his movement realizing, that he held an advantage and could turn the Confederate line. Hancock was a soldier, and obeying orders from his superiors was fundamental to army order. He believed in assisting his fellow commanders, if he were able to do so, but expected the same in return. On the battlefield, he instinctively knew what to do without hesitation – a trait that ensured his continued battlefield success at the most critical of times.

Army of Northern Virginia

The conference room was unusually quiet, considering a large number of people were seated around the table. Nearest the President's chair was Secretary of War George Randolph and Vice President Alexander Stephens, with other cabinet secretaries either seated or standing, making casual conversation. General Lee arrived with his adjutant, Captain Taylor. Davis' secretary greeted them and ushered the general to his seat. As Lee stood, pulling his chair back from the table, President Davis entered the room, eyes immediately locking on Lee.

"General Lee, it is so good to see you. What news do you bring regarding the Federals and the whipping your Army has given them? I apologize, my anxiousness to hear your report has overcome my manners – please be seated."

"Thank you, Mr. President. We have done our job well these past few months. The Federals have suffered a series of setbacks. Although we suffered at Malvern Hill, not far from here, General McClellan continued to pull back and has withdrawn from the peninsula; General Pope and his Army of Virginia were beaten soundly in Manassas."

"Here, here," the assembled secretaries chimed in and slapped the table, as Lee continued.

"I believe Lincoln intended to bring these two armies together into one force. Generals Longstreet and

Jackson interfered with that plan over the past few days. We threaten Washington, as McClellan did to us here in Richmond. However, I would caution that we cannot win this contest by defending our cities alone. Lincoln has succeeded in merging the armies, as he intended earlier, and the Army of the Potomac defends Washington, with General McClellan commanding once more."

Lee continued, "We have been fortunate that McClellan shows his hand in his excellent strategic planning, but suffers from timidity in its execution."

Secretary of War Randolph spoke up, "What then, General Lee, do you propose?"

Lee scanned the room then looked directly at President Davis, "It is time the Army strikes north. I intend to take Harrisburg, then Baltimore."

Davis believed the action would likely cause the Union to sue for peace when Lee threatened Washington. Lee departed with approval from Davis, and the Army of Northern Virginia was on the move.

Generals Hill, Rodes, and Anderson surveyed the crossing site from the heights above Point of Rocks on the Potomac, 12 miles north of Leesburg. "The crossing is perfect, and we can move the division quickly. I want to be across the Potomac and in Frederick by late morning."

"It's short of 15 miles," Rodes offered. "The soldiers marched hard these last two weeks. Thankfully resting in Leesburg was an excellent decision. The Federals are still around Washington."

"We could be near Harrisburg before they even start to move," replied Anderson, "and then, perhaps, we could discuss terms. I wonder if General Lee is leaning towards Pennsylvania?"

"Well, I believe General Jackson would rather draw the Yankees out from around Washington, then destroy the Army of the Potomac. He knows McClellan well – even graduated with him from West Point. That may be General Lee's intent. First, gentlemen, let us address one state at a time. Let's get to Frederick before General Jackson gets there," Hill cautioned as the three officers rode off towards the crossing.

Jackson crossed the Potomac River at Whites Ford, northeast of Leesburg the next day. By 7 September, Lee's force was in Frederick, Maryland. The Confederates cut rail lines and communication between Washington and the garrison at Harpers Ferry, Virginia, 20 miles west, located at the confluence of the Shenandoah and Potomac Rivers. Harpers Ferry held an armaments factory and 12,000 Union soldiers. A second garrison was to the west in Martinsburg, Virginia. Lee expected both to withdraw once the Army crossed the river. Neither Union garrison moved.

Army of the Potomac

Lincoln, Stanton, and Halleck were aware that the Confederate Army was moving north of the Potomac. Washington was secure, and it was time to pursue Robert E. Lee.

"General Marcy, did you read these orders from Halleck?" McClellan asked.

"I reviewed the orders before bringing them to you. It is time we destroy the Army of Northern Virginia. Lee is in Frederick already; probably has designs on something farther north, or possibly Baltimore."

"He could turn this way and threaten the capital, but he'd run headlong into this Army. I want the order to move written immediately. Contact Franklin, Sumner, and Burnside. Tell them the Commanding General requests their presence with their division commanders. We'll move on multiple routes towards Frederick before dawn tomorrow, the 7th."

Army of Northern Virginia

Longstreet dismounted and entered the building Lee's staff had borrowed as the headquarters.

"Sir, we are consolidated here in Frederick. Everything went smoothly and without incident. It is as if the Federals are unaware that we are in Maryland."

"General Longstreet," Lee rose to greet his right-wing commander. "I do appreciate the report, but make no mistake, they will come."

"I believe we must shift west to Hagerstown and open a line to Winchester and the Shenandoah. If we are successful, I propose we move into Pennsylvania. There are two garrisons, Martinsburg and Harpers Ferry; I had hoped they would withdraw upon our approach. They have not, and we cannot leave them in our rear area if we are to proceed."

Longstreet studied the map. The Army would have to be divided to accomplish the various missions.

"Sir, the complexity of multiple objectives with this Army may well be too difficult to achieve."

General Lee agreed, "General Longstreet, the Union Army is not currently a threat. Stuart will find them and screen our movement."

Jackson spoke up, "I believe we can quickly defeat the garrisons in order; the only difficulty is the distances traveled and time." Jackson and Lee were generally of the same mind during a battle, and he understood Lee's intent.

"General Jackson, you will cross back over the Potomac, south of Hagerstown, with three divisions and approach Martinsburg from the north. Their garrison appears to be less than 2,000. Then continue along the Potomac to secure Harpers Ferry. I estimate the garrison strength is nearly 10,000 men." Jackson nodded thoughtfully, and Lee continued, "General Longstreet's divisions under McLaws and Anderson will move south and occupy the heights north of the Potomac, east of Harpers Ferry. General Walker's division will recross the Potomac, as well, and take the heights south." Lee could see Longstreet was uneasy with the split in forces.

"General Longstreet, Hill's division will move over South Mountain, two miles from Harpers Ferry, to block any Union retreat from Harpers Ferry. If practicable, take Hood and Jones' divisions and continue to Hagerstown, where we will consolidate. I shall defer my decision on Pennsylvania until then. Gentlemen, what are your thoughts?" It was Lee's style to solicit comments and suggestions from his generals when discussing plans.

Longstreet could already see the Army split three ways, and was skeptical. He would comply with his commander's orders, once issued.

"Sir, McClellan will come eventually, and if the Federals arrive while we are divided, he will take the opportunity to strike each element independently. I am concerned that we may not be able to concentrate in time to meet his threat."

"The distances are not too great, and the movement would be rapid should that need arise."

"We are forcing the capitulation of two garrisons. I would have preferred the Yankees withdrew once we crossed the Potomac, but they haven't, and we must eliminate that threat. I would recommend we survey the crossing sites at Shepherdstown, once we settle Martinsburg."

"General, I believe McClellan will be slow to move," Lee countered, "and we will be concentrated in Hagerstown, perhaps even before his lead corps reaches South Mountain. However, I agree with you regarding Shepherdstown and would ask that in your move on Harpers Ferry, you send a small force there. We may need it."

They discussed some additional points of the plan until Lee was satisfied, and he issued the order the following day. On 10 September, Lee's Army left Frederick, and within 48 hours, McClellan's Army arrived in the city.

Army of the Potomac

The Union XII Corps had just arrived in Frederick. Its three divisions and scores of regiments were settling down after a long day's march. Typical of infantry soldiers, they dropped their haversacks and started small fires for coffee and cooking. The infantrymen carried or picked up along the route of march, items that Marylanders handed them – eggs, beef or pork, and vegetables.

Corporal Barton Mitchum and Sergeant John Bliss, of the 27th Indiana Infantry, had just arrived and were seeking a place to drop down and rest. Mitchum leaned his musket against a split rail fence bordering the road and saw the white paper, standing oddly against the post.

"What's this?" Mitchum said as he bent to retrieve the paper. "Neat little package for some officer, I suppose."

He unwrapped the small package, and a series of hand-written papers fell away from a few cigars.

"This is something official, and says here it is for Brigadier General Hill."

"What have you got there, Barton?" Bliss asked as the corporal handed him the documents.

"I believe it is some directive or orders, from a Rebel headquarters, with some adjutant's signature."

Pausing, Bliss read aloud. "Headquarters, Army of Northern Virginia, Special Order 191." Pausing briefly, he added, "We should bring this to the captain."

Bliss headed in the direction of the company commander, with Mitchum trailing, cigars in hand.

"Sir, Corporal Mitchum saw these papers near the fence line as the regiment was settling in," Bliss continued, "and they appear to be official. Thought I should get them to you immediately."

"Thank you, Sergeant Bliss," Captain Knop said as he took the papers.

"One more thing, Sir. The paper held a couple of cigars. I don't smoke, and if you do, they are yours. If not, they'll make for a good trade."

Knop laughed, "They are yours, sergeant."

Bliss saluted and headed back to the fence line where, just hours before, the Confederates sat. Knop read with amazement Order 191 from the Headquarters, Army of Northern Virginia. He held a copy of Lee's order intended for Hill. Before this fight was over, Bliss would be a First Lieutenant in Company F, and Captain Peter Knop would be dead.

Later that evening, McClellan held Lee's order. He understood the disposition of the Confederate forces and

Lee's plan to attack Harpers Ferry. Longstreet was heading for Hagerstown, Hill was near Turner Gap on South Mountain, and Jackson, with Walker and McClaws, was going to Harpers Ferry. McClellan turned to Marcy and held the papers up.

"Here is the paper with which if I cannot whip Bobbie Lee, I will be willing to go home." The Army needed to move over South Mountain quickly, and be in a position to strike and defeat Lee's elements one at a time.

"Seth, send this wire to Washington," the general directed. "I have Lee's plans and will trap them if my men are equal to the emergency. Will send you trophies." Williams transcribed the general's message and handed it to the orderly.

"This goes immediately," Williams directed. The orderly headed for the door. The confident tone of his message to Lincoln informed by McClellan's persistent belief that Lee outnumbered him.

CHAPTER 16
SHARPSBURG

Army of Northern Virginia

General Stuart entered the headquarters, and Lee cordially greeted his cavalry commander.

"General Stuart, it is always good to see you."

"We see McClellan is moving towards South Mountain. His pace is much faster than our previous meetings, and I am concerned he grasps our intentions. How that came to be, I cannot fathom, but I trust the intelligence. I have personally observed the Union column."

Lee thought for a moment.

"That is disturbing news, and we will adjust accordingly. I expect the Federals will be cautious in deploying, and we have time. Thank you, General. Major Taylor, send a message to General Longstreet to join us here. I need him in planning our move."

The Army would cover the three gaps over the mountain. Uncharacteristically, Lee began to question the probability of success in Maryland and started to formulate a plan to move back into Virginia.

Army of the Potomac

Hancock read the orders just handed to him from Baldy Smith's headquarters.

"Our orders are to move with the division through Crampton's Gap, seize Rohrersville in the Pleasant Valley and engage and destroy the Confederate division located there. We move early tomorrow morning."

The division was already moving towards Crampton's Gap, six miles south, and the southernmost passage over South Mountain.

"The division will establish positions on the eastern side of South Mountain, as the corps' reserve. General Slocum's First Division will lead the corps through the gap."

Colonels Cobb and Burnham were with Hancock along Burkittsville Road, east of Buckeystown.

"Gentlemen, if the Rebels are defending, then ready your regiments for we may see action as soon as tomorrow morning."

The Corps fought its way through the gap to the sounds of battle in the distance at Harpers Ferry. Jackson's assault was underway. McLaws' infantry and some cavalry defended Crampton's Gap, and Franklin's force swept them from the field. The VI Corps was ordered to go to the aid of the Harpers Ferry garrison but stopped their advance once in the valley east of the mountain. General Franklin showed he could move just as slow as his commander and friend, General McClellan.

Hancock's brigade headed down the west side of the mountain with the remainder of the Second Division and started their movement towards Harpers Ferry and Jackson's force. The distant sounds of battle at Harpers Ferry slowed, and General Franklin, believing the garrison had already surrendered, stopped his advance and remained in position on the west side of South Mountain. Hancock was unconvinced the battle was over to his south. He rode to Smith's headquarters.

"We haven't heard if the garrison has fallen, have we? Should we not at least send the cavalry forward to assess the situation?"

Smith looked at his anxious brigade commander.

"Winfield, I want in this fight as much as you. But Franklin believes it is over."

"The force at South Mountain was only part of the Army, probably Longstreet, and, by the sound of it, Burnside's force has beaten them badly. A second force at

Harpers Ferry means Lee has split the Army. We are in between those two forces. Why the hell are we not moving on them? We have the strength to defeat each of Lee's elements, one at a time!"

Hancock's instincts were correct, and his eagerness for battle was rising. Smith wanted to apply that eagerness at the right time. He knew Winfield would bristle at his response.

"Seems McClellan has other plans and wants to catch the bulk of Lee's Army somewhere near here. So we'll hold and await our orders."

West Woods and The Cornfield

South Mountain was behind them, and the Army began deploying along the high ground outside of Sharpsburg, Maryland – along Antietam Creek on 16 September. Hooker's I Corps was in the north, near the Upper Bridge, and held the right flank; Sumner's II Corps was to the left, with the Middle Bridge; and Burnside's IX Corps anchored the left at the Lower Bridge. McClellan ordered Hooker across Antietam Creek to assault Lee's left flank the next day. He intended to cut off Lee's approach to Hagerstown. Before the day was over, Hooker's skirmishers engaged elements of Major General John Bell Hood's Confederate division in the East Woods. The sky opened up as darkness fell and combined to end the fight, both sides withdrawing.

McClellan held a two-to-one advantage over Lee, while Hooker yelled for reinforcements. McClellan ordered Mansfield's corps to move behind Hooker's, then ordered Franklin's VI Corps up from their reserve position. Hancock was once more moving to the sound of battle. Smith's division was placed in reserve, a task that did not sit well with the aggressive Hancock. The regiments anxiously awaited the start of the fight.

Hooker's divisions moved forward before dawn the next morning to seize the plateau near the Dunker Church, over a mile away. Converging on Miller's cornfield, they could see Confederate bayonets as the regiments positioned themselves to counter the Union thrust. The artillery opened with canister, firing over the heads of the blue-clad lines and into the Rebels, blasting sections of the corn and people aside. The effect was devastating as the line of soldiers closed on one another, screams of courage and pain mixed over the sound of weapons.

Initially sweeping the Confederates from the field, Hooker threatened Lee and Jackson's left. Jackson called on John Bell Hood's division, who attacked out of the West woods and across the Hagerstown Pike into the Union brigades. Pushing the Federals back, they restored the Confederate line, but at 80 percent casualties. They forced their way into the Union reserve, located at the edge of the cornfield. The fighting raged throughout the morning in the West Woods, and finally, both the I and XI Corps pulled back north. Mansfield's corps was on the move to join the fight, as Hooker's corps withdrew.

The Sunken Road

General Sumner led his II Corps forward to support Hooker sending two divisions, under Generals Sedgwick and French, across the battlefield to clear the West Woods. They found units scattered across their front from Hooker's fight against Jackson, the majority in between the two divisions. Sedgwick continued towards the Hagerstown Pike and the West Woods. French shifted to the center of Lee's line.

Sedgwick's infantry met the Confederates on the far side of the woods. Lee ordered Walker and McLaws, who had just returned from Harpers Ferry, into the fight. They joined elements of Richard Anderson's and Ambrose Hill's divisions and slammed into Sedgwick's left flank and rear. The Union soldiers were rolled back and withdrew northward, towards Hooker's corps artillery. Within thirty minutes, the ferocity of the attack took 40 percent of Sedgwick's division.

French's Third Division shifted south against Lee's center. The low farm road connecting the Hagerstown and Boonsboro Pike provided a natural earthwork behind which Longstreet's infantrymen readied themselves. Brigadier General Daniel Hill, of Jackson's Corps, took full advantage and positioned George Anderson's and Robert Rodes' brigades, and other smaller elements, along the "Sunken Road."

French moved forward with Weber's brigade leading. His first line reached a low ridge where the infantrymen could see the Sunken Road, and the Rebel forces sixty yards to their front.

"Forward," Weber ordered, with each of his three regimental commanders repeating the order. The 1st Delaware on the left, 5th Maryland in the center, and 4th New York on the right stepped off together.

Army of Northern Virginia

Rodes watched as the blue line started their descent from the small ridge and readied his brigade, each man watching the oncoming infantry and searching for his target.

"Steady men, they will present themselves shortly."

Five Alabama regiments were crouched down below the edge of the road, just enough to protect them, while allowing clear sight of the oncoming Yankee line. Anderson's North Carolina regiments were right of Rodes, along the road as it turned slightly to the right. Weber's three Union regiments spread across the front of all nine Confederate regiments.

"It is time," Rodes thought, as the Union line reached the bottom of the hill near the Sunken Road.

"Rise, Alabama! Dress the line! Dress the line!"

Anderson's men followed suit. The infantry rose immediately and readied themselves, weapons charged and primed.

"Shoulder, arms." The Union rank drew closer.

"Fire by rank! Front Rank – Ready! Aim!"

The veteran infantrymen lowered their weapons and picked out their targets. Within a second or two, Rodes commanded, "Fire!"

First and Always: Rebellion

The volley was deafening; smoke immediately obscured the view of attacking and defending forces. The Union line staggered, then halted.

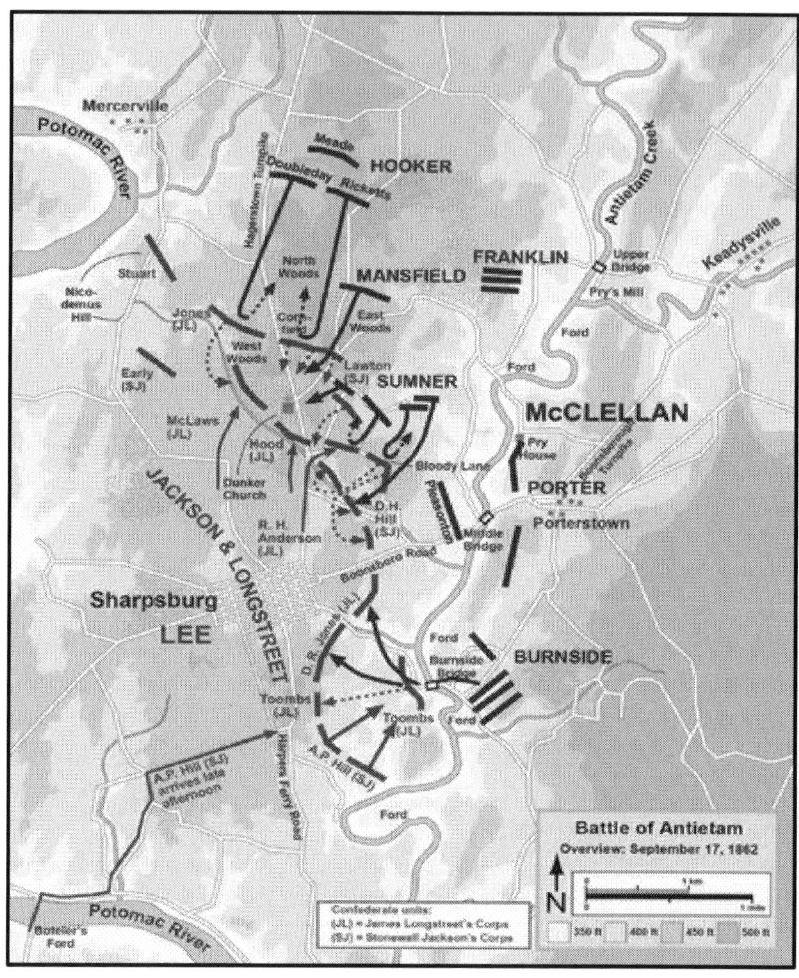

"Second Rank – Ready! Aim! Fire!"

The Union line reeled as the second blast of fire hit them, and downed more than a quarter of the battle line. Weber's men started to slowly withdraw and move up the ridge from where it had just come. Confederates were firing at will. Near the top of the ridgeline, the 1st Delaware Infantry turned and fired one volley, then disappeared over the top of the ridge. In minutes, French pulled his entire force back over the rise.

Army of the Potomac

Brigadier General Israel Richardson's division moved forward in support of French's assault. They crossed Antietam Creek with Thomas Meagher's Irish Brigade leading. The Irishmen took their position on the right, and Caldwell's brigade, following behind, took their place on the left. When the Irish crested the ridge, the Rebels opened with a volley creating significant gaps in the oncoming line. The undulating Maryland farmland first exposed and then hid the oncoming Irish as they closed on the Sunken Road. Meagher's regiments topped the second rise only twenty paces from the enemy, and, on command, leveled a volley. Screams of dying and wounded men and animals, explosions, and thick smoke from thousands of rounds all combined to create a field of terror as the two opposing lines delivered their fire.

Caldwell sat calmly watching Meagher's men trading fire with their adversaries and could see a rider heading his way. Richardson's aide-de-camp reined in his horse near Caldwell.

"Sir, General Richardson directs you to relieve the line held by General Meagher's brigade," the young lieutenant yelled over the firing. "The Irish Brigade is in front of the Rebel line and blasting away. They have taken a beating, and loss is heavy, but they have accounted well of themselves. Unbelievable to watch."

The bullet passed through the young officer just above the right eye, and death was instantaneous. Caldwell watched as he fell from the saddle. Turning to his aide, who had reached for and missed the falling adjutant, the general yelled, "Get back to Richardson, behind Meagher's brigade, and tell him we are moving. Also, send my regrets that his adjutant is down. Go and damn quick!"

The officer stayed low in the saddle to stave off an equally gruesome fate and galloped back to the division commander. Caldwell moved quickly down the line, directing each regiment, by "right flank," to move behind Meagher's brigade. He then faced left, aligned his regiments, and passed through the retiring Irish Brigade. The battle was his.

In the low road, Hill frantically called for reinforcements, and Lee sent Richard Anderson's division with Wright, Posey, Pryor, and Cummings' brigades. The continuous fire from French, and then Richardson's division, had taken its toll. The Confederate center was outnumbered two to one, but Anderson's division was arriving to reinforce Hill's line, bringing Wright, Pryor, Posey, and Cummings' brigades. The new regiments positioned themselves in the road, among Anderson and Rodes' men. Caldwell's brigade surged over the small crest, taking with it some of Meagher's brigade, and the Confederate line wavered.

To the left of the Union line stood Colonel Francis Barlow's combined 61st and 64th New York regiments. Barlow maneuvered his regiments forward and positioned his infantry to envelop the enemy.

"Left oblique!" Barlow commanded, and the regiments turned slightly left.

"Right turn," and the regiments swung right, staring down the length of the Sunken Road.

"Regiment, Halt! Fire by Rank! Ready! Aim!"

The infantrymen could not believe they were looking down the long enemy lines who were facing forward to meet the rest of Caldwell's brigade. They selected their targets in seconds.

"Fire!"

The explosive sound of the volley, sending hundreds of deadly rounds into the "bloody lane," caught Wright's startled Alabamians by surprise. The destructive enfilading first broke Wright's line, forcing their surrender. The effect down the line was immediate. Units started to give way as the center of Lee's line collapsed. Barlow's soldiers entered the lane and poured fire into the Rebels, who fell in heaps.

Rodes, on the left of Hill's line, learned the 6th Alabama Regiment, on the end of his battle line, was taking enfilading fire. He ordered the Alabamians to refuse the line. Mistaking the directions from Rodes, the Alabama commander, instead of meeting Barlow's threat, ordered face about and retire. The regiments to their left followed suit, and Rodes' brigade vanished from the Sunken Road – the units pulling back to the Piper farm.

Richardson ordered Brooke's brigade forward to break the line. Caldwell's men moved into the road, stepping over the bodies of hundreds of Confederates, the carnage shaking seasoned veterans. Barlow moved down the road near the intersection of the Sunken Road and the Roulette farm road, facing Rodes' right flank. Caldwell then moved his regiments up and out of the way to the south and the Piper farm. The sporadic musket fire and continuous artillery signaled a lull in the fight. Caldwell rode forward and stopped briefly on the southern side of the Sunken Road, in the Piper cornfield. Barlow rode with him as they moved behind the regiments heading south. Turning back to the road, Barlow said, "They lay two and three deep in spots."

Caldwell nodded and added, "It is just as bad behind us. Hundreds of blue uniforms littered the fields leading up to this road. The Rebels found their targets today. I have heard it isn't much different on the northern end of our line."

Through his field glasses, Caldwell could see movement, as Rebels were maneuvering through the farm and around the flank. Longstreet sent four regiments to the left of the Union line in an attempt to retake the road or stem Richardson's advance. The Federals shifted to meet the threat. Barlow's New Yorkers moved across the field with the rest of the brigade, taking fire from the remaining Confederates near the Piper farm. The Confederate artillery continued to pour case-shot and grape at the maneuvering Union infantry. A case-shot exploded near Barlow, taking the colonel down with shrapnel to his lower body.

The division commander approached the rear of Caldwell's and Brooke's brigades when his horse was struck in the neck and went down hard, Richardson jumping as the mount fell.

"We've got them on the run! Pour it into them, boys!"

Richardson ran into the lane and up to the south side. His men pressed forward, pouring volley fire and hurling back the Confederate line trying to retake the road. Richardson secured another mount to ride to an artillery battery in the rear of the division, intending to reposition the guns. The exploding Rebel artillery shell took the general off his feet and back against the rail fence that bordered the farm lane. The sergeant accompanying the general was killed instantly when the exploding round tore the upper part of his body away and killing soldiers on either side. Struggling to breathe, Richardson could see that the hole in his chest was pouring out blood and life. He closed his eyes and surrendered to unconsciousness.

Caldwell arrived, dismounted, and knelt beside the fallen commander. Two artillerymen tried in vain to stem the flow of blood from the jagged wound. The commander was taken from the field and died shortly after. Taking temporary command of the division, Caldwell repositioned the brigades from the Sunken Road and awaited the Confederates.

CHAPTER 17
DIVISION COMMAND

Word reached McClellan's headquarters quickly. Accompanied by his aides and a small cavalry detail, he rode into Hancock's brigade headquarters around 1:30 p.m. along the Hagerstown Pike.

Hancock had received orders to protect II Corps artillery positioned behind Sedgewick, whose attack was smashed by McClaws earlier in the morning.

"Winfield, where are you?"

The Army commander returned the salutes of the small staff as he dismounted and headed for Hancock, who was talking with his regimental commanders nearby.

"Here, Sir. If you are here, then something is up for this brigade."

"Not so much for the brigade as for you, my trusted lieutenant. Colonel Cobb, I'm glad you are well and present, it makes this easier. How is the 5th Wisconsin?"

McClellan extended his hand to Winfield then to Amasa Cobb.

"Very well, sir. We are ready for action at your command."

"Winfield, Israel Richardson is down, mortally wounded. Do you know him? He commands the First Division under Sumner. They are located here in the center, near the small farm road that is worn low. I've not received a new report, but I hear the fighting was fierce, and casualties are high."

McClellan indicated the position on the map Hancock had spread out earlier.

"Over the last two hours, French and Richardson's assault pushed the Confederates back from the road. Longstreet could be observed, on the high ground beyond, directing an artillery battery. Winfield, I am here to tell you that you are the new First Division Commander. Sumner is located just behind the line. Find him first. I've already sent Marcy to notify him and Franklin of my decision. Baldy Smith is also aware. I believe General Caldwell has assumed temporary command."

"Sir, shouldn't General Sumner elevate one of his brigade commanders?"

"I am promoting you to division commander, Winfield. I'm sure Sumner agrees with that decision."

Turning to Colonel Cobb, he said, "Amasa, congratulations! You are in command of this brigade."

"I'll depart immediately. There is lead everywhere in the air. Be careful, Sir."

McClellan knew his decision to move Hancock was correct – as it had been in Williamsburg when he turned the Confederate line.

Hancock headed towards his new division along the Sunken Road, accompanied by Mitchell, Parker, and the orderlies. The battlefield, littered with the dead and wounded soldiers and hundreds of horses from both sides, displayed the carnage resulting from the last eight hours of combat. He had never seen anything like this before. Neither Mexico nor Williamsburg provided such a spectacle, and, as he galloped across the killing field, he saw the immensity of the fight and the devastation it would bring unless it ended quickly. Hancock was ready for battle.

"They need to see their new commander on the field," Hancock thought, one of a thousand things rushing through his mind. As he galloped towards the fight, his adrenaline and battle senses were reaching their peak. Courage, fear, anticipation, and uncertainty were all coming together inside him, and Hancock loved the feeling. Approaching the division, he pulled back on the reins, his horse letting out a rush of air, and turned suddenly towards the Sunken Road. He would ride around the left of French's division and into the "bloody lane."

The soldiers knew the name – Hancock. His reputation from Williamsburg spread. The loss of Richardson, at once, saddened the soldiers; however, his replacement inspired them. Partially protected by the low road, they began to stand and cheer as they watched their new commander ride the length of the battle line and waving his hat, in that small, dangerous space that separated the two armies.

"Well done, my boys. Ready yourselves for their return," Hancock called out.

The occasional shot from a North Carolinian's rifle zipped past him, as the Rebels tried to end his command before it had begun. He ignored the threat and would continue to do so in the future.

Brooke's brigade held the right of the division line, and Meagher the left. Caldwell had reached the road and held his position slightly to the rear to counter any attack on the division's left flank. They were still trading shots with the Confederates. In the chaos not two hours ago, Richardson had been in the road bringing order, leading his troops and positioning regiments as they drove the Confederates from the position. He was on foot after his mount was killed under him. The division performed its assault with deadly effect.

Hancock galloped fast enough to negotiate the road and announce his presence to the battle-weary brigades, yet carefully to avoid trampling the hundreds of Hill's and Anderson's infantry lying dead and wounded the length of the road. He rounded the left of the division and headed behind the line, where Caldwell awaited his arrival with the few staff members who had accompanied Hancock. The soldiers knew their new commander was with them, and they prepared to continue the attack on his command.

Stopping on the backside of the hill that provided cover from the Confederate firing, he dismounted. They could hear the line still cheering their new commander's arrival.

"Welcome to the First Division, Sir. I wish it could be under better circumstances. I received a message earlier that you would be arriving to assume command."

Hancock noted and appreciated the lack of animosity in Caldwell's voice, sometimes an issue in changes of command. They could hear the continuous whiz of bullets passing overhead as they stood on the rearward slope of the hill, short of the Sunken Road.

"Thank you, General. What is the condition of our division?"

"We hold the road, but the Rebels have been able to reinforce beyond the house on the far hill. The brigades have paid a heavy price to get here. After General French attacked our right flank, General Richardson attacked. Meagher's Irish Brigade led, followed by Brooke to the right and my brigade to the left. Meagher lost over 70 percent."

"It seems the battle in our center has slowed, once the Sunken Road was ours, and General Richardson went down," Hancock said.

"We have new orders. We will hold our position and defend it. I see that the soldiers and their officers are anxious to surge ahead, especially after the drubbing they gave Longstreet's infantry. But, we are to repel any attacks to our front. Let's get that to Brooke and Meagher, and have them meet me on the road."

His aides moved immediately to disseminate his orders. Hancock could not comprehend the rationale behind McClellan's directive given Richardson's advance on the Sunken Road and Hill's retreat. It was time to press the attack.

"Men, stay there until you are directed to move. We must hold this place at all hazards." The Confederates opened with artillery, falling among the line of infantrymen.

Hancock found a significant gap existed between Caldwell and the Irish Brigade, which he filled with two regiments from the division reserve. Artillery was crucial to fill the void, and the First Division had none in support.

"This is unacceptable, not to mention complete bullshit!" Hancock exclaimed to Parker and Mitchell, his ever-present aides. "Alright! Here's how we'll handle this. The VI Corps is to our right rear. Get this to General Slocum and tell him I need the assistance of a single battery to secure my line. If he is unable to help, then go to General Smith."

The brigades continued to take the Rebel bombardment, believing it was a prelude to a Confederate push in the center. Mitchell returned in minutes and handed Hancock a message which read, "Congratulations on the assignment. A battery is heading your way. Regards, Slocum."

Hancock held up the paper. "Better timing is not possible. I hope you conveyed my thanks to General Slocum?"

"Sir. I led the battery here myself, and they are moving to the left, near General Caldwell's force."

Captain Emory Upton moved his New Jersey Light Battery behind Caldwell's brigade. Hancock was waiting in the road near the Roulette Farm when Upton came to an abrupt halt.

"Captain, are you ready to wreak havoc on the hapless bastards?"

Upton smiled. "Where shall we unlimber, and who shall we kill first, General?"

The Stone Bridge

Across Antietam Creek Brigadier General Robert Toombs positioned his brigade of Georgians – nearly 500 infantrymen. The Federals assaulted with one or two regiments at a time, trying to cross the bridge and seize the heights. Tombs easily repulsed them.

"Move around. Goddamn it! We'll lose the division on this bridge. Find another way across," Rodman yelled at the regimental commander.

The mini-balls sounded like a buzz saw, ripping into the columns, four men abreast, as they tried to storm across the bridge. The 11th Connecticut Infantry began the attack, and withdrew, leaving a carpet of blue strewn across the bridge. Toombs' sharpshooters had found their targets time and again.

Brigadier General Williams pulled hard on the reins leaning well back in the saddle as the horse came to a quick stop.

"Sir, General McClellan must know the status of your attack. It appears to him that you've made little progress. I'm directed to tell you to attack the bridge at once, against all hazards. He must have your corps sweep the right of the Confederate line."

"Inform the general we will attack by 11:00," Burnside replied. Saluting, Williams quickly disappeared, heading back to McClellan.

"Send two regiments forward," Burnside ordered.

A second aide was sent and reported that, by noon, Burnside had not yet crossed. McClellan was livid at the half-hearted attempt to seize the bridge and called for his Inspector General, Sackett.

"Colonel, go to Burnside and tell him, at the point of a bayonet if you must, to seize the bridge immediately. Stay there until that happens, then report back to me."

The infantry, supported by artillery, surged across the bridge in the early afternoon and reached Toombs on the far side. With lines of battle formed, Burnsides' men sprang forward. The defense crumbled at the weight of the overwhelming Union infantry force and began to pull back to Sharpsburg.

Army of Northern Virginia

"A messenger from General Lee informs me that they are being pressed hard by the Federals. The situation in Sharpsburg is dire." Ambrose Hill searched the faces of his brigade commanders, each man anxious as they listened to the battle raging miles away from Harpers Ferry.

"Your men are tired, I know. We have more than 15 miles to cover and little time. We will move at the double-quick whenever we can."

Hill's infantrymen sensed the urgency and closed the distance within hours. In the early afternoon, the head of Hill's column reached the area south of Sharpsburg. On order, they slammed into Burnside's advancing force.

Major Taylor rode back from the line to find Lee behind Longstreet's line.

"Sir, General Hill is attacking the Federal left flank and has stopped their advance on the town."

"I suspect that the forced march and immediately going into the fight has depleted Powell Hill's force," Lee replied. "When this line is stable, we shall ride to General Hill's location."

Burnside ordered the corps to withdraw to the bridge believing Hill had an advantage in numbers. The Confederates controlled the heights once again. The bloodiest day of the war was coming to a close.

The sun rose on the 18th over two battered and bloodied forces, sorely hurt and still in lines facing each other over a field filled with thousands of dead. Lee stood with his back to the Potomac; his regiments fought out from the previous day's battle.

Army of the Potomac

Late that evening, Hancock sat at the field desk his staff set out for him. They knew the general would take time to complete his correspondence once the lines were somewhat quiet.

"Dearest Allie," he began, "It is late evening after, and a tough day has ended. We lost Israel Richardson today, and I am in command of the division. Baldy Smith was very supportive of the move, and he has confidence in Amasa Cobb, who assumed command of the brigade. General McClellan directed the move personally. He had ordered that, in the morrow, we do not participate in hostilities, as he expected some reinforcements to arrive before he desires to recommence any movements to the front. I expect you shall read of this engagement, and I will confirm the losses are staggering."

Hancock's soldiers readied for an attack that never came. That night, Lee withdrew unmolested into Virginia. Nearly 23,000 men were down, with 5,000 dead, and the Battle of Antietam was over.

Weeks passed, and McClellan held the Army in position.

The October evening breeze brought an uncomfortable chill to the officers gathered in Hancock's headquarters. Greetings and small talk complete, the general began.

"We are to move tomorrow and cross into Virginia through Harpers Ferry. The corps will survey Charles Town, eight miles from Harpers Ferry. We must determine if the Confederates are in that area. I expect Lee may have some of Stuart's cavalry there. We will move to Bunker Hill and Winchester, 12 miles west, and see if Lee has anyone lingering there as well. The I Corps searched north of us from Shepherdstown to Kearneysville. The Rebels have likely moved farther south, hence our mission. General McClellan is planning to move the entire Army."

"When do we leave, Sir?"

The distinct accent rose above the group of senior officers. General Meagher was never at a loss for words and asked what everyone was thinking.

"Will we be able to pursue the enemy if we find him there?"

Hancock shared their frustration. His commanders had sacrificed much of their brigades at Antietam. They also understood the price Lee had paid for the recent battle – the army casualties so high that the campaign ended, and Lee withdrew across the river. They all wondered, as did Hancock, why the Army did not follow through and crush the Confederates when it had the chance.

"Lee is bleeding, and our chance to crush him was not lost in Maryland," Caldwell added.

"We are moving by the morrow with an additional one or two regiments. It is our task to identify whether Lee still occupies ground further West in the valley before he moves his Army. We shall engage the Rebels if we find them."

The war had, once more, returned to Virginia.

Lee continued to move the Army of Northern Virginia south through the Shenandoah Valley, out of the Union forces' reach.

CHAPTER 18
ACROSS THE RAPPAHANNOCK

Washington D.C.

It was well into Autumn. Lincoln sat pensively, staring out of the window at the people passing by. He often did when contemplating the complex issues of the troubled nation. It had such a relaxing effect on him, watching life outside the White House, and a part of him wishing a return to life as a small-town lawyer once more. He wondered about Davis' Army, achieving several victories over the last year. He was encouraged to invade Maryland and Kentucky. The First Lady walked up quietly behind him. Placing her hands on his shoulders, she leaned forward, pressed her head to his and held him for a moment.

"Mary, it will not be long before people tire of this conflict. I am confident that the Union will prevail; however, I spend much of my time convincing people of that, and that the war is going as planned. With the terrible showing so far, people will eventually question my ability to manage this war."

"My dear, the Lord plans that you are here, in this house, and at this time. You must lead this nation out of the darkness. I trust you will find the way. You always have in the past."

"I argue with my cabinet every day regarding the road ahead. You should not be troubled by the demands of this office. Your kind words do warm my heart, and I thank you for that. Let us join our guests."

Lost in thought, he walked out of the room with his arm around the First Lady.

"The country needs a victory before this year ends. That would silence the detractors and restore the nation's confidence. And, if we could end this conflict and preserve the Union, all the better."

Mary squeezed her husband's arm and returned to the family quarters.

The great Army, bloodied from battle in the Maryland countryside, replenished and sitting idle across the Potomac plagued him. He quietly considered McClellan's future. Stanton appeared in the hallway and nodded to the President.

"Perhaps it is finally time," he said to himself.

Seeing Stanton, Lincoln began, "My general refuses to move, and I have tried to prompt him, even visited his headquarters. If the Commander-in-Chief must motivate one of his generals, then I would submit we have the wrong man in command. I have given him all that he has asked; however, the situation is beyond caution and planning on his part. The people will not wait much longer for a victory. It must be today!"

Lincoln's voice rose to meet his growing frustration.

"Is it pure laziness on McClellan's part, or is something akin to a blatant disregard for my orders? What will the critics say – that Lincoln once again is unable to lead as Commander-in-Chief?"

He strode down the hallway, Stanton, breathing hard as he tried to keep up with the President.

"McClellan has allowed Lee to pull back to the south, lick his wounds, and heal. We recognize the nature of the Confederate soldier, and their steel when it comes to a fight. How can I wait any longer? I will not! We must find a new commander who will act."

Lincoln stopped and turned to Stanton, who handed him a list of possible candidates for command. He and Halleck already anticipated Lincoln's decision and prepared the listing. The President stopped at a window and watched a company of soldiers march past the White House.

"Halleck's recommendations are included here as well?"

"Yes, Mr. President. We anticipated that a change was needed, and this list represents the major candidates."

The evening sun had set, and Stanton and Halleck sat in the Secretary's office when the officer arrived.

"Mr. Secretary, General Halleck, you wished to see me?"

"General Buckingham, please take a seat. Secretary Stanton and I have a task for you, directly from the President."

Buckingham sat up a bit straighter, hearing this was from Lincoln himself.

"You are to report to the Army of the Potomac in Virginia, and there you will personally deliver these orders." He handed the general two envelopes.

"You must see the sensitive nature of these orders, and I do ask that you read them both before you depart. I need not remind you that you carry the full weight of the President's authority with you."

Buckingham thought the last statement was rather ominous. He stared at the envelopes, and the names ascribed to each.

"I will depart for General Burnside's headquarters as soon as I pack. I believe this will take one or two days, but I will report after I deliver each envelope."

"Very well, General. I am uncertain whether this task may take you to more than two locations currently planned. Time will tell. I expect to hear from you tomorrow evening," Halleck said. "Have you any questions?"

"None that I can think presently. The task is pretty straight forward, Sir." Buckingham saluted and left the Secretary's office.

"What do you think he'll say once he finds out, for the second time, he is no longer in command?" Stanton thought aloud.

"It is the right thing to do. I'm more interested in what Burnside's reaction will be," Halleck responded. "Twenty-four hours, and we'll see."

They set out into the snowy night for the ride to the headquarters in Rectortown. McClellan was aware that a special train had arrived from Washington carrying General Buckingham. The train stopped near the headquarters, and, instead of reporting to McClellan, Buckingham left the railway and proceeded, in a driving snow-storm, to make his first visit to the IX Corps and Major General Ambrose Burnside, in Orleans, Virginia.

Army of the Potomac

The Army spread out across Northern Virginia.

"General, I would ask what brings you from Washington in this foul weather?" Burnside asked, a concern already rising within him.

"Sir, it is a pleasure to see you. General Halleck and Secretary Stanton sent me, and as you can imagine, the sensitive nature of my call forces me to arrive at an inconvenient time."

"Well, perhaps we can get right down to business. At least have some coffee. It is excellent even for an army in the field."

Buckingham thanked him, removed the envelope addressed to Burnside, and handed it to the General, who read the General Order first. "War Department, November 5, 1862. By order of the President of the United States, Major General McClellan is relieved from the command of the Army of the Potomac and that Major-General Burnside takes command of that Army."

It was signed for Stanton by the Assistant Adjutant General. General Burnside briefly stared at Buckingham with disbelief and trepidation in his expression. Raising his eyes from the letter, he asked, "What is next, General?"

"Please accompany me to General McClellan's headquarters. I was to see you first then continue to McClellan. Once he reads the order, I am confident he would want to meet with you immediately. If we are together, that will aid in this process substantially."

The two generals prepared for the ride to McClellan's headquarters, and Burnside, turning to his chief-of-staff, ordered, "Get the disposition of each corps and division in this Army. If we have Lee's location, get that as well."

McClellan knew at once he had been relieved. He sat alone in his tent, writing to his wife when Buckingham knocked on the tent pole at 11:30 p.m. and requested to see the general.

"Of course, come in out of the cold. General, it is good to see you again."

"I think we had better tell General McClellan the subject of our arrival."

"I am anxious to hear why you've come, as well. It is late, and the weather is deplorable. That portends serious business."

McClellan tried to lighten the atmosphere for a brief moment and took the envelope Buckingham offered. McClellan read Order 182 first, from Stanton: "By direction of the President of the United States . . . relieved of command of the Army of the Potomac and that Major General Burnside take command."

"Well, Ambrose, I turn the command over to you! General Buckingham, if you will excuse us for a few minutes, I would like to talk with General Burnside privately."

Buckingham thanked McClellan, excused himself, and stepped outside where Marcy and Williams were waiting. Although neither officer expected McClellan to over-react to the orders, they were relieved when he had taken the news calmly.

"I shall go with you to Warrenton, perhaps for the next couple of days. I want to provide you with all the information I have currently regarding this Army and Robert Lee's."

"Thank you, General. It is greatly appreciated." Burnside shook McClellan's hand. He'd always been loyal to McClellan.

"Buckingham, I thank you, sir. Your task is complete. My staff will see that your accommodations are ready. I will see you in the morning."

Winfield Hancock was loyal to McClellan, but he understood the need to move the Army forward and pursue the enemy. Refitted and readied for action, he questioned the long period of inactivity. It was not in his nature to sit, even though the time was used to train and prepare. The delay only served Lee's purpose. When word spread of McClellan's relief, he became aware of a move within the officers' corps to resist the change. Soldiers loved McClellan, but that did not warrant blind loyalty at the expense of order and discipline. Hancock gathered his officers together for a council and to address the discord within the officer ranks.

"This is the United States Army, and it must have discipline." Hancock searched the faces of each officer to determine how each man was taking the abrupt change in command.

"I hear the Army isn't satisfied with the change in command. Many considered Lincoln's treatment of McClellan ungracious and coming at an inopportune time. We are still at war, gentlemen. I do not sympathize with any movement that would seek to resist an order from the Commander-in-Chief. How can that serve our purpose? It is, therefore, a useless exercise bordering on treason."

He could feel his temper rising, but was quick to control it and calmly alleviate the concerns of his officers.

"I want each of you to keep in mind that we serve the nation, not a man."

Army of Northern Virginia

Major Taylor walked through the headquarters with the latest dispatches for the general.

"General Lee, we have read that the Federal Army has named Major General Ambrose Burnside as its new commander. I have heard he is a capable officer, with some success on our North Carolina coast earlier this year. It was his corps at the lower bridge in Sharpsburg."

"This is unfortunate. George McClellan is a brilliant officer. Were you aware that we served together as engineers? I had come to rely on his cautious nature when maneuvering against this Army."

Major Marshall, Lee's aide-de-camp, entered the room and quietly took a chair, while Lee continued.

"Good evening, Major. We were discussing the recent relief of General McClellan."

"Yes, Sir. I've heard. If I read the Northern press correctly, there is growing criticism for Lincoln's management of this conflict. Perhaps McClellan's delay in moving after Sharpsburg prompted this decision?"

"I anticipated that the longer he commanded, the more difficult it would have been for us to counter his moves. So it is to be Ambrose Burnside of whom I know very little. Our Army is finding its way back from a low point in morale. When ordered, they will do what is required. General Burnside may yet provide us the opportunity for the battlefield success we seek."

"Sir, he was slow in front of Richmond, as well. I assume they have reconstituted, since Sharpsburg."

"I suspect Lincoln, and the North for that matter, are quite anxious for a victory. The Sharpsburg engagement was not a clear victory, although we were forced to withdraw across the Potomac."

Army of the Potomac

Stanton demanded Burnside's new plan. After all, it was the delay that had gotten McClellan relieved. Richmond's capitulation was, once again, the objective. This time the Army would strike from Fredericksburg. Burnside's first order of business was a reorganized force, creating a new command level between his command and the corps commanders. There were three "Grand Divisions," each with two corps, supporting artillery and cavalry. Burnside selected Hooker, Sumner, and Franklin as the Commanding Generals. The reconstituted Army strength was 130,000 soldiers.

In their planning, the staff identified the Richmond, Frederick & Potomac Railroad playing prominently with an ability to support the large Army of the Potomac in a winter campaign. General Herman Haupt, the Union expert on rail transportation, agreed on the use of the RF&P railroad as the only rail that could meet the Army's requirements, and, therefore, it was a necessity.

"I intend to deceive Lee into thinking our objective is Culpeper or Gordonsville. We will concentrate the force in the vicinity of Warrenton. That will hold Lee's Army near the upper Rappahannock." Burnside was confident.

Hooker, Sumner, and Franklin listened, each wondering who would dash for Fredericksburg.

"We shall move quickly to Fredericksburg and clear the town of the small Confederate force there, seize the high ground south of the town and drive south to Richmond. I will carry this plan to Washington tomorrow. Are there any questions or, more importantly, any objections?"

"Who will stay in Warrenton to fix Lee's forces?"

Franklin was more to the point as his fellow Commanding Generals pondered the same question. "Who stays behind?"

"Whoever stays must be prepared to meet Lee's force head-to-head if he crosses the Rappahannock." Hooker was already thinking through the engagement and what additional forces he would need if Burnside selected his Grand Division.

"I am requesting thirty days of supplies positioned at Aquia on the Potomac. Crossing the Rappahannock will require pontoon bridges at Fredericksburg."

Washington D.C.

Lincoln was uncertain about the plan, given the degree of risk it entailed. A river crossing to assault Fredericksburg, dependence on pontoons and multiple bridging sites, and winter all created doubt in the President's mind. He bent down to stoke the fire in his office.

"Send this to General Burnside. I approve of your plan to move on Fredericksburg, then Richmond, and you have my complete confidence that you will be victorious.

Whatever you need in this campaign, make me aware, and we will accommodate. I would caution, however, that the demands of a winter campaign plan require its rapid execution. Signed, A. Lincoln."

With the President's approval, the Army began its march in mid-November. Orders to move boats and supplies to Aquia Harbor and Belle Plain, each less than a day's journey from Fredericksburg, were issued. He needed to secure the town before Lee could mount a defense. The Confederates were spread out to the west as far as the Shenandoah Valley.

Army of the Potomac

Burnside arrived at Stafford Heights, across the river from Fredericksburg, and read the latest message from the engineers that his aide handed him.

"The engineers assigned to build the pontoon bridges are in Washington with thirty-six pontoons; forty more boats are arriving by 15 November. The Quartermaster is busy bringing together the necessary horses and wagons to make the overland trip to Fredericksburg, and, if all goes well, we will send them forward by the 16th or 17th. It will take several more days to reach you. Signed, Woodbury; Army Chief of Engineers."

General Woodbury knew from the start that a delay was inevitable, but failed to make the point to Burnside. Rapidly crossing the Rappahannock River and seizing Fredericksburg before Lee knew he was there was key. Burnside's plan could unravel with a delay, and Lee would not waste time moving to counter the Federals.

Hancock, with his aides Mitchell and Parker, watched the division march into Falmouth. They were the first element of Sumner's Center Grand Division. Spurring his horse, he rode forward to observe the city from the heights above the river and saw that they had, indeed, beaten Lee to the prize. The city was lightly defended by a small contingent of Confederates sent by Lee earlier, around 1,500 soldiers. He searched intently through his field glasses and could see the streets of the town rise sharply above the riverbank, then continuing to climb to the southwest, like arrows pointing to the high ground called Marye's Heights. Turning to the left, Hancock could see the Rappahannock River continuing its path to the southeast. A rail line came from behind his position, crossed the river on the southern edge of the city, then continued along the river passing in front of a far ridgeline. The Richmond, Fredericksburg, and Potomac rail lines were destroyed and the bridges burned. Prospect Hill was farther back from the river, almost a mile, and an open plain lay between it and the river.

"What I do not see are the pontoons. They were to be pre-positioned in the Washington area. The engineers should have started moving here at the same time as the Army. I think we have a problem."

The small group of riders approached. Hancock saluted as Sumner arrived, accompanied by the new II Corps commander, Darius Couch.

"How does it appear, Winfield? The river is wide, but the engineers will throw the bridges up quickly, I expect."

"Sir, I don't think the boats and bridging equipment have arrived yet. But the city appears clear of Lee's men, except for a few Rebel mounted troops I observed from here."

"Damn it all! We should be surveying adequate fords and grab this city immediately. Burnside isn't far off. I'll get a message to him and ask where the hell are the engineers?"

The Army could ill afford to have a delay in the boats' arrival or, worse, a surge in the river, making it too high for wagons and artillery to ford. Any advantage of beating Lee to Fredericksburg would be lost. The light was fading, creating shadows on buildings, and obscuring their view of the city's residents going about their evening business. Hancock and Couch scanned the high ground beyond the town and knew the Army must be on the heights before Lee arrived.

The courier from Burnside's staff arrived. "Message from General Burnside, Sir."

Sumner quickly read the message. He became visibly upset and thrust the paper into his coat.

"Establish your bivouac sites and post pickets," Sumner directed.

It would take two more days for the rest of the Army of the Potomac to arrive – much longer for the pontoon bridging equipment.

Army of Northern Virginia

Longstreet's I Corps was on the march east from Culpeper Courthouse, while Thomas "Stonewall" Jackson's II Corps was moving from the Shenandoah Valley. Lee understood where Burnside was heading and ordered his Army to concentrate around Fredericksburg.

"Jackson's corps must travel 150 miles to reach Fredericksburg, and the Federals are on the march ahead of him."

Lee stood with Taylor and read the latest report from Longstreet, who was quickly closing on the city.

"Concentrating the Army here has become a race. I believe General Longstreet will be able to hold in Fredericksburg if the Federal Army moves across the Rappahannock. We must be prepared to reduce the pressure on his corps, for he would not be able to stand against the entire Army of the Potomac." The adaptable Lee thought for a moment.

"Send a message to General Jackson, if his movement is such that he closes on the rear of the Federals, he is to attack the rear or flanks, if practicable. Burnside would have to hold part of his force to meet Jackson, therefore splitting his force."

The long columns of Longstreet's Confederates arrived on the evening of 20 November. Generals McLaws, R. H. Anderson, and Pickett's divisions were weary from the rapid pace of the 35-mile march and, at the same time, exhilarated, as the soldiers and their officers steeled themselves for another chance to whip the Union. It had been months since Maryland and Sharpsburg, and the replacements and recruits were ready for the fight. The hardened veterans in each Confederate division were taking their positions in Fredericksburg and preparing to meet Burnside's Army.

Army of the Potomac

Sumner thought about the planned crossing of the Rappahannock into Fredericksburg and had sent his concerns to Burnside earlier. In his message, Sumner highlighted the danger from both Confederate artillery, likely to concentrate fire on the bridges, and from infantry musket fire from the city buildings overlooking the river. Instead, Sumner recommended fording sites below the city and, once across, turning his force into Lee's flank. General Burnside balked at Sumner's fording idea, thinking that should the weather cause the river to rise, Sumner would be caught on the other side without adequate support and cut off from the Army.

Nearly two weeks had passed while the Union Army sat in camp. The situation in Fredericksburg was briefed to the President every day, and his uneasiness prompted a meeting with his Army commander at Aquia, on 27 November.

Lincoln listened while Burnside talked of crossing at Fredericksburg and of the problem he was experiencing in obtaining the necessary bridging. He also admitted there was risk involved in any crossing. Once across, he would drive Lee from the city as the army moved beyond Fredericksburg.

"I would prefer that Burnside's case was more favorable," Lincoln later said to Stanton.

He desired an almost "risk-free" crossing, ensuring the Confederates could not fall back from Fredericksburg, gather their strength, and defend Richmond. It was apparent Burnside had no plan to cut off Lee's Army if it moved.

The engineers arrived in late November. Convinced that he could move forward before Lee concentrated all his combat power, Burnside directed a survey of crossing sites above and below the city. The next day they found one south at Skinker's Neck, 15 miles away. Burnside was anxious to move.

The Commanding General convened a council of war with his Grand Division commanders upon his return.

"We shall have the advantage and attack Lee's right flank and rear. Begin moving to the fording site on 6 December."

The weather conspired against the Army when a winter storm brought the movement to an abrupt end and forced the corps back to their camps. The crossing downriver from Fredericksburg was no longer undefended. Jackson's men had arrived days earlier and were in position along the heights near Skinker's Neck. Within a week, the commanders gathered once more to hear the final plan. The force would cross the river in Fredericksburg without regard to Lee's concentration and positioning for defense. The surprise was lost.

Franklin's Grand Division, the main effort, would initiate the attack against Jackson's corps on Prospect Hill. Sumner's Grand Division would assault Marye's Heights as a supporting attack. The combined assaults would prevent the Confederate command from reinforcing one or the other. The Grand Division commanders agreed.

Burnside was confident.

"If well-executed, we can split Lee's force and seize the high ground beyond Fredericksburg."

His subordinate commanders were less confident, but they would carry out the Commanding General's orders. Hancock felt that alternatives needed to be considered to save thousands of soldiers from slaughter at the base of Marye's Heights and Prospect Hill.

CHAPTER 19
BURNSIDE'S WRATH

Army of the Potomac

Hancock dismounted, handing the reins to Parker. Looking south to Marye's Heights, he could see the Rebel artillery emplacements near the crest. Scanning the panoramic view of Fredericksburg from the river to the heights, he pictured what would happen when the brigades assaulted. Zook and Caldwell remained mounted a few feet away and watched their commander.

"The Confederates are moving along a road below the hill, and only their heads and shoulders are visible. Can you see them? It is a low road, much like Sharpsburg. They will fire on us from behind significant cover."

The officers let that ominous fact sink in and began their planning to overcome the Rebel advantage. Hancock noted the vast expanse that ran from the heights to the outskirts of the city. Fences divided the land with the occasional house or other buildings visible. Once the assaulting force emerged from buildings, it would be under constant artillery and musket fire.

Unquestioned obedience to orders always had its place, and he, as much as any officer, understood that cardinal rule. In the heat of a fight, it was imperative. Winfield closed his eyes and thought of the potential slaughter. Seeking a redeeming element in Burnside's battle plan, he found none as time had conspired against them. He believed the generals must bring the situation to Burnside's attention and, hopefully, result in a viable change to his plan. Hancock's frustration was rising, knowing the price to be exacted from his soldiers once the Confederates had solidified their position.

Couch walked his horse forward and joined Hancock. Zook and Caldwell excused themselves and returned to their brigades. When the two generals were alone, Couch could see the determination on Winfield's face.

"I see your concern. You are asking: How do we maneuver against the heights?"

"The plan desperately needs change, Darius. It presents too many disadvantages that I fear are nearly impossible to overcome. Rather than simply voicing opposition to the plan, it requires the presentation of alternatives."

"Well, let me start by saying the pontoons have arrived."

"We've waited 22 days for the bridging equipment. While we sat along this river, the enemy has not been idle," Winfield said in a low voice, as the two discussed Burnside's plan of attack.

"I will ask French and Howard, but it sounds like we all have reservations."

"It's not a matter of meeting the enemy here. It is an opportunity to consider a different avenue of attack."

Burnside distributed his plan to each corps. Couch and his generals stood in Sumner's headquarters to receive the commander's guidance. After listening to his description of the battle plan, the Grand Division Commander was surprised by his officers' criticism, Hancock first among them. Both Couch and Hancock believed the current plan was excellent had it been executed before Longstreet and Jackson prepared defenses. That time had long since passed.

"There has to be a better way for us to seize the high ground," Hancock said to Couch, only steps from their commander.

Sumner overheard Hancock's remark and quickly asked, "Why is it so? Burnside surely is delayed in crossing, but we are here. When Franklin carries the Confederate right, we shall move on the heights."

At the Army headquarters, the Commanding General surveyed the entire room. He learned of Sumner's meeting and summoned all general officers. Searching their eyes one at a time, he paused for a moment when his eyes met Darius Couch. His gaze was more than an acknowledgment of an officer's presence. It was a little sharper, almost piercing, as he shifted slightly right to Hancock, standing next to his corps commander.

"Your duty is not to throw cold water on my plan, but to aid me loyally with advice and hearty service."

He conveyed to the generals present in his headquarters that they had no right to express their opinion regarding the Army's movements.

"You have personally taken issue with my plan, General Hancock."

Hancock noticeably straightened, not yet at a full position of attention, but preparing to take the verbal onslaught Burnside seemed intent on directing at him.

"Sir, if I may explain, and I meant no disrespect nor disloyalty. The delay we have experienced in crossing the Rappahannock has enabled the enemy to enhance his position on the heights greatly. There has been ample time for their forces to assemble. Should we not consider this and perhaps adjust our plans accordingly?"

Burnside was outraged that a subordinate general would first question and then propose a change to his plan – a plan he had developed and played out in his mind over and over, seeing his force carry the left and then the heights. It would give the President his much needed victory.

"General, you are mistaken."

His voice rose loud enough that the entire room could hear. Some turned to listen to the exchange; others shifted and tried to ignore the criticism of Hancock. All registered the tone and nature of what Burnside was saying.

"I am appalled at your lack of respect and devotion to me personally and to this Army."

Hancock was struck by the accusation, feeling the anger building within him, but continued to hold his temper. He was a soldier to his core and understood his commander's wrath would likely pass soon.

"I apologize if I have caused the General concern. I only wished to convey that the situation has changed due to the delay in crossing the river, and we should consider alternatives."

"General Hancock, I have formed my plan and expect its complete execution by officers and soldiers alike. I demand loyalty, respect, and devotion. I will not stand for disloyalty among my officers. If you feel you are unable to carry out my orders, perhaps it is time for you to withdraw from division command."

Hancock's demeanor changed, preparing for a confrontation. Anger built within him as he struggled to maintain his temper. The tension rose within the room, each officer expecting Winfield to respond in kind.

Sumner was appalled by the statement and quickly turned to face Burnside with an expression conveying that this was neither the time nor the right circumstance to make such a statement. Sumner trusted the abilities of both Couch and Hancock implicitly and could ill afford the loss of either commander.

Sensing that this discussion had risen to a higher emotional level, Couch immediately interjected, placing a hand on Winfield's shoulder – an unspoken attempt to convey he would handle the situation.

"Sir, I'm sure General Hancock meant no offense. We both recognize his service and must have him in the coming engagement. If I had ever done anything in any battle, in this upcoming fight, I would do twice as much."

Burnside was unmoved and angered, but he also understood the need for leaders like Hancock and Couch. As in any battle, a loss would come soon enough for many division, brigade, and regimental commanders. Longstreet's soldiers would ensure it. Burnside could ill afford to lose leaders who could carry the day. The humbled staff and commanders set about the business of battle.

Hancock was outraged when he and Couch walked out of the headquarters, while Sumner stayed behind to speak with Burnside. Hancock's nature would not allow injustice of this kind, indeed, and not upon his name nor his service to the nation.

"In front of all the Corps' senior officers? Is Burnside that Goddamned insecure that he calls our loyalty and service into question? Blind obedience is one thing, but we have an obligation, based on our positions and experience, to render useful advice to our commanders."

Couch understood the frustration, and his quiet demeanor stood in contrast to the fiery Hancock, as he tried to calm his division commander.

"Perhaps, the column of brigades will reach the works quickly. French's division will lead. You can bring the second wave against the Confederate line. You must be on French's heels when he goes for the enemy works."

"This will be difficult, at best. If I were up there on the heights, I'd have the open area and the town targeted within my artillery's range. However, I am a soldier and will do what is ordered by my commander. I only sought to highlight the concerns that Lee is prepared to take us on."

They walked quickly to their horses and, retrieving the reins from his orderly, Hancock saluted.

"Good evening, Sir. We will be ready when you call."

Couch returned the salute. Hancock rode back to his division, and Couch continued forward to Chatham Manor, overlooking the river. It was yet one more opportunity to search beyond Fredericksburg and the hill, silhouetted in the evening light. He wondered if Winfield might be correct.

Army of Northern Virginia

McLaws and Barksdale stood just on the river's edge.

"They'll come along this stretch of the river bank."

"The city itself is an obstacle to them. We can reinforce that by placing additional muskets throughout these buildings. I can spread my soldiers out along this street and in the houses."

"That's a certainty. I'll send you more regiments to enhance the defense." McLaws looked back and saw Hanover Street extending to the heights.

"We can cause him to bleed right here at the river's edge, but we likely will not defeat him here. Half the Army of the Potomac is across from us and, it appears, the rest of that force is facing Jackson. They still have to get across the river. General Longstreet has ensured the open area beyond the city is nothing but a killing field of artillery crossfire."

Barksdale brought his field glasses up and could see some movement.

"The engineers are scouting the banks. There are not many places available upriver, so this is likely the place to cross. I've positioned my Mississippians already. Dusk is coming on, but we'll prepare. Your orders, Sir?"

"Hold here in place, and I'll send regiments forward. I want them to focus on the southern approaches in case the Federals cross farther south then turn north into the city. I have Kershaw, Cobb, and Semmes' brigades on the heights behind works. Anderson and Ransom's divisions are in position, as well. When I tell you to withdraw, don't delay. Pull back through the city and join the division on the heights."

"I will, Sir."

"God help them if they plan to assault here."

Army of the Potomac

The engineer captain searched the river bank for miles, above and below the city, and found three adequate sites to build Burnside's bridges across the Rappahannock: two in Fredericksburg for Sumner, and one farther south, for General Franklin's force. Working very early in the morning, and under cover of darkness, to help conceal their efforts, the captain and his fellow commanders estimated that they could complete their tasks just after sunrise. The commanders needed a plan beforehand to quickly move thousands of men, artillery, and support equipment across into Fredericksburg.

Hancock looked at the 400-foot wide river and the planned crossing sites.

"How long would it truly take to cross this river when the Rebels begin firing? Remember what happened on the southern bridge at Antietam? We lost hundreds of men and valuable time because of a few hundred well-positioned Georgians."

The staff listened quietly as their Commanding General spoke. "Antietam may pale in comparison to the crossings here."

He had heard enough "estimates" and wanted to be personally ready when the time came. It was not that he completely doubted the engineers' ability, but there were other considerations. After all, he reasoned, these were the same people directed to have pontoons here two weeks ago. That was a prerequisite for a successful advance into Fredericksburg, and that did not happen as originally planned. A plan, he knew, that he was wed to, regardless.

Captain Hancock had observed his older brother many times before, having served as his assistant adjutant general these past twelve months. There was something different this time, not that many would be able to discern the change in the general's demeanor. That would take a brother, and John could read the concern behind Winfield's eyes. The general always seemed to carry the weight of his command position with ease, as if he were born to it. This battle would be no different in that respect. The general would lead his division into the tumult at the base of the heights as coolly as if on parade. His troops would see their commander amidst the firing and drive forward with him.

John knew this time Winfield would have preferred another course of action than that which Burnside had committed the Army and in the face of what was a hardened defense. He watched his brother and the process he went through before each engagement, seeing the battle progress in his mind, working out the details of firing and movement on the heights, and finally achieving success as they swept up and over the heights. It was a marvel to observe.

Months before, in Sharpsburg, there had been no time for planning as he raced to assume command from the wounded Richardson amid a fight. These soldiers and officers were his charges, and, as Winfield expressed to John earlier, he would lead them with all the skill and experience that he possessed. Marye's Heights was going to be a straight-on bloody fight as brigade after brigade slammed themselves against the wall, like waves crashing against a rocky shoreline.

"What are you thinking, Sir?" John asked. He always ensured the proper military courtesy was extended to the general even though they were brothers.

"I'm thinking about contingencies. Simply those things that could go wrong or alternative ways of doing things in the heat of this upcoming battle. Something always goes wrong and quickly. We'll adapt, as needed. I want you to stay at the rear of the division as it moves forward. I'll need Miller, Rorty, and Parker on the field."

"I can ride with you on the field."

"That you can, but I feel that initially, you should hang back with Rorty at the guns. I'll send for you."

"Yes, Sir. I understand, but the soldiers will quickly grasp that you are, somehow, protecting me. I prefer to ride at your side," John shot back, this time the brother, not the lieutenant.

"You're right, John. I do you a disservice as an officer. Alright, ride with the staff, and keep your damn head down!" Winfield relented.

"Don't forget your letter to Allie today," John replied.

Most officers were busy writing home to family.

Hancock already ordered a few regiments to cover the engineers and secure the sites, but the city must also be cleared of Confederates so that Sumner and Couch could ready the force for the assault. Completing his vision of the battle, he saw the many units lined up on the cross streets in battle order. Although difficult in the extreme, the brigades would be ready to conduct their advance on the heights.

"And what of Lee's artillery?" he pondered. "I think they have, more than likely, targeted the streets and various buildings."

Burnside thought about his artillery. So did General Henry Hunt, the Chief of Artillery, who would cover the crossings. It was getting late, and Hunt gathered his commanders just before midnight at the Lacy Manor, in Chatham.

"I want to protect the engineer teams on the river, and that effort will begin within the next few hours. We are also to check any Confederate movements on the plains in front of Franklin, who is moving into position."

Hunt could see the artillerists were anxious to ply their trade after being idle for so long.

"Ensure that we provide counter-battery fire, but have shot and canister ready." Nearly 150 artillery pieces of various types lined Stafford Heights as if one large battery occupied the position. Hunt placed additional artillery farther to the rear near the Phillips House and Burnside's headquarters. All were ready by 2:00 a.m., long before the engineers began their work.

Hancock's three infantry brigades were on the move once more. They took their positions behind the Lacy House, on the heights above the river. Riding slowly with Zook late in the evening, they discussed the dash into Fredericksburg when the bridges were ready. He especially liked Colonel Zook, who was also from the Montgomery County area, his home. They talked of nearby Valley Forge, and of the county where they both grew up. They spoke of the Schuylkill River and visiting there after this fight. The rest of the Right Grand Division set their bivouac sites nearer the Phillips House, where both Burnside's and Sumner's headquarters sat.

"We need to move fast," Hancock cautioned. "I expect to be under enemy fire the whole time."

Zook agreed and asked, "When will we move?"

"I believe by daylight, but we'll see how the engineers fare. We'll have half the damn Army behind us as we enter the city."

They dismounted and entered the Lacy House, greeting Hunt and his officers. It was time to bring his commanders together and discuss the pending fight. He found an empty parlor and removed his hat and overcoat, then took a seat with Zook, Meagher, and Caldwell. The warmth of the fireplace provided a brief respite from the bone-chilling cold. They could hear the engineers outside, making their way to the river.

"The engineers should start the bridging within the next couple of hours. Are the 57th and 60th with them?"

Zook turned from the fireplace.

"Yes, Sir. The regimental commanders have already moved forward with the engineers. They'll do well, and I expect they will fall in with the brigade when we cross."

"Once we head for the bridge, move quickly. The Rebel artillery will attempt to strike the bridges, and lines of blue make attractive targets."

"I'm more interested in how we clear the city, as I fully expect those bastards across the river have infantry throughout the buildings."

"When you get your brigade over the bridge, move left down the first street you reach, so we don't bunch up at the far riverbank. There will be enough confusion, but the corps must be across and begin the assault as soon as we are ready."

"Thomas, how are the Irish?"

"Right as rain, Sir. We will waste no time getting over the water and into the town. Sir, if I may? General Burnside has taken issue with you, as we were all witnesses. Is there . . ."

Hancock interrupted the Irish commander.

"There is no issue. We will carry out the orders. I am prepared to adjust as the assault progresses because once we are on that field, it is how agile we become and how we can adapt that will carry the day."

All three commanders witnessed Burnside's tirade and knew of Hancock's temper. They were impressed that he held it while being reprimanded by the Army commander. For the next hour, they talked of the march, the next move, and of the war in general. No one mentioned the heights outside of Fredericksburg. Each officer was confident and courageous enough to assault the waiting Confederates, but believed he would not come off the hill unscathed – no talk of mortality.

The long lines of equipment, containing scores of pontoons and support wagons, made their way in the early morning darkness from the Stafford Heights to the river. Engineers immediately began pulling boats from their wagons and sliding, or carrying, the pontoons down the embankments to the water's edge. Efficiency was the key. Working in eight-man teams – each with a specific function and sequenced to facilitate bridge-building – the engineers set about their work on all three sites. Stealth was impossible as engineers hammered planks into place. The freezing temperature would climb to mid-day warmth, but before dawn, the chill went right to a soldier's core.

"Sergeant, I can't feel my damned fingers," the private said to his section sergeant quietly.

"If they start shooting, you'll forget about the cold, right quick," the sergeant answered, then added, "and try not to get wet, you'll freeze before the sun rises."

The soldier picked up his end of the 27-foot plank, headed for the end of the bridge, and the next pontoon. The sergeant now began to wonder about the Rebels. He had seen the pickets earlier; they were missing from the shoreline. It was near dawn, and the engineers, who had worked on the middle crossing since 3:00 a.m., were near to the middle of the river. The upper and lower bridges had just begun construction. Across the river, the Mississippians readied themselves.

CHAPTER 20
BRIDGEHEAD

Army of Northern Virginia

Barksdale was in position with four of his regiments and one additional that McLaws provided in support, all along Sophia Street. It was just before dawn when new light overtakes darkness, and there is movement, as stillness gives way to life waking up for the new day. On the Rappahannock, the Confederates could see vague outlines of the partially-completed bridges nearing their side of the river but waited until the bridge builders were closer and the targets assured. Breathing steady, hearts pounding, the fight about to begin, each man swallowing the excitement that was building up inside as they carefully took aim and waited for their officer's command. Seconds before the volley, even the morning chill could not prevent the sweat from running down their faces. As the day started to break, the engineers were aware that they were observed but unaware that they were in the sights of hundreds of muskets. The Rebels positioned themselves behind fences and walls, in and under houses, and any place that afforded cover. The mist was lifting a bit more.

"Fire!"

The soldiers on the bridge turned, almost as one, hearing the deadly command. The volley shattered the early morning calm and sent men running for their lives off the bridge. An engineer private stood motionless, frozen in fear, holding the plank he was preparing to lay on the bridge up in front of himself in a vain attempt at protection. He never felt the bullets hit as they passed through wood and his upper body. The soldier dropped to his knees, hesitating for a moment, and, still clutching the plank, rolled off the end of the unfinished bridge into the

Rappahannock. Thousands of mini-balls surrounded the scattering engineers as they dropped down on the deck, others peppering the planks and pontoons, the canvas shredding, churning up the water.

A second volley sounded, reaching the far bank of the river. Lieutenant Parker, mounted and sitting slightly behind Hancock, saw two of Zook's soldiers collapse. The rounds passed through each man's body at the same instant, the two falling against one another without a sound, as if settling down for a rest after a long march. After the volley, the stillness returned, punctuated by the occasional sound of a wounded engineer, caught in the open on the bridge, or the scream of a draft horse hit multiple times and in its final gasps for life.

Zook sat firmly in the saddle, and his horse shuttered at the sound of the volley. Steadying his mount, he watched as the newly-arrived soldiers began to buckle. Moving behind them, and forcing them back into line, "Steady men. It is time for our response."

The sight and sound of their brigade commander, fortifying their resolve as they prepared to fire, the infantrymen firmly stood their ground as workers sought cover behind the stacks of bridging lumber and boats. The 57th and 66th New York Regiments waited for the smoke to clear, hanging low from the second volley, and just enough that they could see the flash from the muskets hiding in the structures across the river.

"Ready! Fire!"

Returning a volley fire of their own into the smoke, they were unaware that their fire had little effect, with most rounds hitting the river's embankment at the far side. Reloading, they fired again. The well-covered Confederates along the river were encouraged that they could throw back any attempt to cross by the Federals. Barksdale had positioned five regiments along the river to stall the Federals. They would give Lee more time to prepare the defensive line from Prospect Hill to Marye's Heights.

"In a short time, Burnside's Army will surge, then it will be a difficult fight in between all of these houses."

Barksdale read McLaws' note to himself.

"If pressed, remember we are delaying the force. The real fight is on the heights behind you." The brusque Mississippian filed that away.

"I pull back when I damn well please," he said to himself.

Lee, Jackson, and A.P. Hill surveyed the ground that sloped away towards the vast plains and the river. It was the extreme right of the Confederate line. Although the mist had not yet cleared, the sound of the bridge construction near Deep Run, about two miles north, found its way up the hill to their position.

"They will come across that open farmland once they have enough infantry across the river. We can slow the Federals with artillery at the bridging sites, but I want you to hold your defensive positions along this high ground."

Since Antietam, Jackson almost instinctively knew Lee's intent as he planned for a fight.

He smiled. "They have always been cautious in their execution, and I expect the same from Ambrose Burnside. When he comes across that open area, we can destroy him with artillery. That is a vast area for enfilading fire."

Lee continued, "It appears they will have three sites across the river: two at the upper end and one lower, in Fredericksburg itself. Longstreet has moved men forward in the city to delay the Federals there. I am surprised Burnside has chosen to cross in the city, but we will meet that portion of his Army when they assault the heights, which I do expect. Our position is strong there, and I believe Burnside is fully aware of this, and any assault there will be a supporting one. His main effort must be here."

Jackson reviewed the placement of his corps with Lee, both satisfied that the defense would effectively check Franklin's advance. The sun just began to show itself when the explosive sound of many regiments sending their deadly volley at the Federal engineers turned the heads of the generals towards Fredericksburg. The sound echoed down the river and rolled up Prospect Hill.

"It begins," Lee said, as newly-promoted Major Taylor handed the general the reins.

"Indeed!" Jackson responded as he and Hill saluted. The Commanding General returned the salute and rode away – his most trusted subordinate had everything well in hand.

Army of the Potomac

At the southern end of the city, the engineers scrambled to complete their bridges. The firing at the middle and upper bridges masked the construction at the lower site. As the mist rose from the water, the Confederates could completely see the bridges. Sharpshooters continued to harass the engineers; however, by late morning, the bridges were ready for Franklin's Grand Division to cross. McLaws anticipated Franklin turning north. He reinforced the southern end of the city with new regiments to prevent Franklin from moving forward, although the Confederates could not restrain his crossing.

Franklin read the message from headquarters, "You are not to advance until the Fredericksburg crossings are complete and Sumner's force is across and occupying the city. Signed, Burnside." He could hear the fight building in the upper part of Fredericksburg. The middle crossing, just below the burned-out railroad trestle, was covered by Hooker's IX Corps regiments, the 89th, and 46th New York. The fog was a blessing and a curse. It concealed the bridging operation the 50th Engineers were conducting, but also hid the Fredericksburg wharves where Barksdale had the 8th Florida.

"Stay low, and keep moving," the captain cautioned as his company moved back to the river bank. The sound of the musket seemed to echo off the river bank a second before the round snapped the captain's head back, taking with it a large portion of his skull.

"How the hell are we supposed to get this done," Sergeant Drewey yelled to the Captain, "with that infernal firing by those sons-of-bitches in the houses?"

He didn't see the round had just ended his commander's life. And so it was throughout the early morning hours; firing, killing and wounding infantrymen and engineers, slow progress, and returning fire.

Hunt listened as Burnside's aide conveyed the Commanding General 's direction.

"Concentrate fire on the town. Silence those infantry troops along the river's edge and clear the way for Sumner's division to cross."

The order passed to his waiting artillerymen, and the guns along Stafford Heights roared, striking the houses and other structures along the banks of the Rappahannock. The concentrated cannon fire brought down walls, roofs, and fences with an exploding shot. It wasn't long before Fredericksburg was war-torn, almost rubble.

With the mist dissipating, the Confederates had a clearer picture of the sites and engineers. The Federals bravely tried to continue the construction, only to be thwarted by the murderous Rebel fire, as Barksdale's sharpshooters continued to take careful aim, then fire. The dedicated engineers tried to ignore the deadly missiles as they worked – and they tumbled into the cold water of the Rappahannock one after another.

"We need to clear that damn river bank," Hancock started to say, but Lieutenant Miller was a step ahead.

"Sir, shall I get back to General Hunt with a request?"

"Absolutely. You are wasting time here, so get moving," the General snapped.

Hunt saw Hancock's aide riding towards him and, with a hand wave, said, "Lieutenant, General Burnside has already ordered that we commence firing. Tell General Hancock we will continue to concentrate fire on the river bank opposite the bridge sites, but Burnside has ordered a general bombardment. We'll either drive them out or bury them where they are hiding."

Miller saluted and returned to Hancock, who maintained a guarded optimism about the artillery's ability to drive the Rebels away. Hunt's guns pounded the city for hours, some solid shot passing through buildings without effect, others collapsing wood and masonry onto the Confederates using the lower floors or basements for cover. The Rebels dug in deeper.

"They need to dislodge those men from their positions in what will remain of the buildings in Fredericksburg," Hancock said to Couch.

"I trust Henry's ability to bombard the place, but it must be cleared or bypassed, and that isn't possible unless Franklin is successful on the left."

Fredericksburg and the Rappahannock required a new tactic, without precedence – a river crossing of infantry, using boats. Once landed, they would secure the site then expand the area outward, clearing the Confederates before them. When Burnside read the proposed plan, he readily agreed. Hunt sought volunteers to make the assault and turned to Couch.

"Hunt has suggested a river crossing of infantry," Couch offered.

"We'll go." Hancock said quickly, "Zook and the Irish are ready."

"I need you ready to move your division in force. I'll have Oliver provide the force."

Colonel Norman Hall and his 7th Michigan Infantry readied themselves as they held their position near the northern-most bridge site. Four officers and one hundred men, in four boats, would establish a bridgehead.

Hunt directed his artillery to increase their fire on the section of the city adjacent to the river, and the intensity unnerved many of the Confederate infantrymen. By mid-afternoon, the 30-minute bombardment ended, and the infantry detachments moved quickly down the slopes and into the waiting boats, a signal for the enemy musket fire to begin. The firing raked the boats, initially taking a toll until, to the surprise of the soldiers paddling for their lives, the shooting slowed, then stopped.

"Sir," the Mississippian said in a low tone to his Lieutenant only feet away, "I can't see them. The damn boats are all hidden."

The officer saw for the first time that the river bank was slightly higher and blocked the view of his marksmen. The Yankee soldiers would reach the bank.

"Get ready! They will come over the bank in force."

The fortunate Michigan infantrymen, 70-strong, landed and climbed the embankment. Soldiers, used to lines of battle 100-men wide, were forced by the buildings and streets into smaller groups of five or ten. They encircled houses loaded with Rebel marksmen, and killed or captured many, as they drove the bulk of McLaws' regiments back from Sophia Street, running along the river. Hall reinforced the 7th with the 19th Massachusetts, who moved to the right upon landing. Sumner had a foothold, a bridgehead, and the Federals surged.

The engineers returned to the two upper bridge sites, swiftly finishing the construction without the suppressive enemy fire. While the engineers worked, the 20th Massachusetts also crossed in boats as 300 more infantrymen came ashore all in support of the 7th Michigan, the tip of the spear.

The soldiers at the middle crossing saw their opportunity, and the 89th New York ran to the boats and began their crossing. Opposite them, on lower Sophia Street, Barksdale's men opened fire. The 46th New York, along the far bank providing protection, fired over the heads of the assault force with devastating effect on the enemy shooters. The New Yorkers landed their boats with ease, rushed over the city wharves, and across Sophia Street, driving the enemy before them. The engineers immediately went about their work finishing the bridge, and the 46th New York rushed up and across the bridge.

The battle for the city was still raging as Howard's brigades, under Hall and Owens, were all across and fighting house-to-house to dislodge the Confederates.

Soldiers encircling a house took fire from the surrounding buildings. The enemy was everywhere. It was battle, unlike anything they had ever experienced before. Infantrymen pursued infantrymen street-to-street, through alleys, over fences and walls, around houses, churches and businesses, and behind rubble created by Hunt's earlier bombardment. The light was fading, and the Confederates found that delivering accurate fire was becoming difficult. McLaws knew, as more Federals surged across the bridges, that the city was untenable, and he ordered Barksdale's Mississippians to withdraw at dark. Colonel Hall and Colonel Owen's men settled in for the night along Princess Caroline and Sophia Streets.

It was evening, and the Army of the Potomac finally had their foothold in Fredericksburg. Miles south, Franklin sent Baldy Smith's VI Corps forward, over the bridge and into the open area along Richmond Road, then rescinded the order. Burnside feared the night crossing would create too much confusion, so he ordered the Army back to camp.

Fredericksburg

The division prepared to move that evening with the knowledge that once the bridgehead was secure, the infantry would rush over the bridges. Before Longstreet could finalize his defense, Hancock and the rest of the II Corps would have the chance to move on the heights.

"Perhaps the morning will bring the assault on the Rebel heights." Hancock took another draw from the cigar as he and Zook watched the infantry clearing the houses.

The delay in orders was not exclusive to Franklin's headquarters. Sumner rose early in anticipation of the Grand Division's river crossing. The sun was up, and there was a coolness in the air at the river's edge. Hancock rode down the ravine from the Chatham Manor, ordering his division across the bridge. He could see the last part of French's division crossing on the upper bridge to his right, while his division moved quickly across the lower of the two, Meagher's Irish Brigade leading, and on to Sophia Street.

Hancock returned the salutes and salutations of the soldiers marching past who were ready for battle. The soldiers marveled at their general, his very presence inspiring and appearance every bit the confident commander who would lead them to victory. Winfield was aware of his effect on his soldiers, but it came naturally, without effort to cultivate a persona. He crossed the bridge and rode along the front of his division, marshaled along the street nearest the river. Pausing at the intersection of Sophia and Hanover Streets, he could see the ground sloping from the river's edge to Marye's Heights. It would be an uphill climb under fire to the low wall. For some reason unknown to Hancock, the Army had come to a halt. Rather than maintain their momentum after clearing the city, the Army of the Potomac held in place, once again giving General Lee the advantage.

Where Lee was an adaptable and agile commander, Burnside was cautious, somewhat inflexible, and unwilling to change. Lee and Longstreet took the extra day to strengthen their defense further, and the heights were unassailable. The delay in town also had a damaging effect on Sumner's Grand Division, including Hancock's men. Order and discipline were in decline. Soldiers and officers replaced anger and frustration from the hard-fought urban battle with lawlessness and larceny. Once the Confederates soldiers and the majority of the civilian population withdrew from the city, individual homes and businesses were left unprotected and at the mercy of Union soldiers.

Hancock rode up Princess Anne Street with his brother, John, and Isaac Parker. Everywhere he looked, soldiers were liberating homes and businesses of property, food, and, of course, liquor. They came upon one soldier exiting a house with what appeared to be glass urn and an arm full of kitchen utensils, while accompanied by another soldier carrying clothing. Hancock was livid observing the criminal acts and drew his pistol demanding, "You are vile sonsofbitches! Who are you, and what do you mean by committing such thievery? To which regiment are you assigned? I will shoot you myself, right here."

The soldier was startled to see the general pointing a pistol at him and dropped the glass urn, shattering it on the cobblestone walkway. His comrade released the clothes he held and raised his hands in the air.

"Please, General, I am sorry for this offense. I meant to send these things home."

"It is thievery, plain, and simple; you are a lowly sonofabitch. Goddamn you if you are First Division soldiers."

Hancock was aware that Howard's two brigades crossed, but it did not matter; the Union soldiers were part of this Army, and, by default, subject to his wrath. Past the soldiers, Hancock could see chaos as Union soldiers pushed furniture and personal property out windows. Books, papers, and paintings littered the street, fires were ablaze, and bottles and glassware smashed.

Infuriated, Hancock turned to Parker. "Lieutenant, I want you to go back to General Couch, and if you can't find him, then go to Sumner. Tell them what we have seen here and that I respectfully request the Provost be sent with a detachment. You might add that I am on the verge of shooting these scoundrels whenever I find them."

Turning then to John, he said, "I'll be damned to hell before a soldier in my command stoops to this low level of behavior. Get word to every brigade and regimental commander. Behavior like this unacceptable. I will court-martial the commanders if they do not get control."

The more regiments that crossed over the river and were in the city, the larger the problem became. Wholesale looting and destruction of personal property were underway.

Hancock continued to the river crossing where French and Howard waited to discuss the movement on the heights. Along the way, he continued rebuking officers with a string of vulgarities to restore order. Within an hour, the Army Provost was posted on the bridges, taking property soldiers were trying to carry away and sending them back to their regiments, or arresting them.

On the heights, the Confederate artillery helped restore order when they fired into the city, on buildings and intersections already targeted, as soldiers dropped their booty and reassembled as units. It would take the remainder of the day to bring an end to the wholesale destruction and vandalism.

Hancock faced Mitchell, riding at his side. "I will not let this stand. Who are these miscreants? If they survive this battle, I will see them again." Mitchell took the note but needed to let the general refocus on the assault. Turning to John, he said, "His anger will pass when the bullets begin again." John Hancock knew this was indeed true of his older brother.

Couch's adjutant, Major Walker, rode up to Hancock at sunset.

"Sir, General Couch sends his compliments. He has been ordered by General Burnside to move the corps to the left, march along the Rappahannock, and connect with General Franklin's Grand Division. You are to prepare the division for movement."

Hancock looked at the young major and said, "Tell General Couch that when directed to move, we shall be ready."

Before he had a chance to discuss the order of movement with the brigade commanders, Couch met him near the river's edge.

"The Commanding General has rescinded the order to move left along the Rappahannock. Remain in place and establish bivouac along the streets you hold, no fires."

Hancock was confused, and he wondered aloud, "Does the Commanding General have an actual plan for this assault?"

He didn't expect an answer. Couch wondered the same thing but kept it to himself. Another day was lost, and Longstreet put it to good use. In Hancock's mind, every day, every hour he delayed would translate into hundreds of casualties.

Army of Northern Virginia

General Lee stood atop the heights and was satisfied with his line. It connected two salient that formed naturally by Marye's Heights on the left and Prospect Hill on the right. The Confederates were well entrenched. Longstreet's I Corps was in a firm position, his line extending from the Rappahannock River, across Marye's Heights, southwest of Fredericksburg, to Jackson's II Corps. His divisions deployed left to right with Anderson, then Ransom and McLaws on Marye's Heights, Pickett, then Hood's division straddling the road that ran between the salient.

Jackson continued the line across Prospect Hill to Hamilton's Crossing. Where Longstreet used the low road and wall at the base of Marye's Heights as part of his "works," Jackson had both wooded and open terrain, marsh, and rail line cutting across his front. The Confederates created earthworks and prepared. Jackson deployed three defensive belts, with A.P. Hill's division in the first line, Taliaferro and Early in the second, and D.H. Hill on the right behind Early, as the Corps reserve.

Army of the Potomac

General Franklin was furious over the lack of direction as the time clicked by. He still had not received orders, and the tension continued to rise.

"What in God's name is taking Burnside so long? I am at a loss regarding our direction, gentlemen. We must be ready. I believed we should have moved on Lee yesterday, and he has gained one more day to ready himself."

"Sir, General Burnside felt that you should have a penciled copy of the order. We anticipate the final version being transmitted by wire shortly."

The irascible Franklin was a detail-focused leader, as were most West Pointers, and as cautious as his close friend and classmate McClellan. He carefully read the order and was struck by its vagueness.

"It says, we are to keep the command in position for a rapid movement down the old Richmond Road. I'm to send at least a division to seize, if possible, the heights near Hamilton Cross Roads. What in Christ's name does 'at least a division' and 'if possible' mean?"

Franklin read it over again.

"Sir," Reynolds replied, "we are the main effort in this fight. A division assault is something less. Don't you agree?"

"I would have thought so before this order, but I will not deviate from these instructions. John, you will send a division. Make sure he is supported and emplace your artillery accordingly."

"We'll comply, as written. I have little idea what Burnside intended to do here, but we'll follow the letter of the order. That said, General Meade will lead his Pennsylvania Reserves."

Meade stared briefly at his two senior commanders.

"My division can take the hill, but I must have reinforcements to hold it."

He saluted and excused himself to ready his 4,500-man division.

Army of Northern Virginia

Near dawn, Longstreet mounted up and rode along his defensive line, starting with Major General John Bell Hood's division on his right and connecting to Jackson's left flank. Sitting quietly on their mounts, Longstreet and Hood could hear the voices of Union officers carried on the dense fog that covered the field. The Federals were not far from Anderson's brigade.

"They'll be coming soon, Pete," Hood said. "It sounds like they are forming in the plain this side of the river, but in front of Jackson. Marye's Heights and Prospect Hill are slightly forward on your flanks. If the Federals figure it out, they may come directly at you. I'll make sure Colonel Alexander's artillery is covering your front. You'll need the extra firepower. I'd be surprised if Burnside comes straight up the hill."

The crossing sites were about a mile to the east from Hood's position overlooking Deep Run. One could not see fifty yards in the mist. The Union voices, giving commands, gave the impression that the Federals were much closer, and Hood thought Longstreet might be correct, and the initial attack may well come against his section of the line. They were ready. Longstreet moved on and rode the line past General Pickett's division in the wooded area between Hood and the heights, then past Lafayette McLaws' and Robert Ransom's position, whose regiments were nearly shoulder-to-shoulder along the stone wall on Marye's Heights, in ranks that filled the sunken farm road. General Anderson's division spread a bit more to secure the left flank of the corps.

"Thank God," Longstreet mused, "the Yankees were slow, once again."

Prospect Hill

The mist lifted with the morning sun. The soldiers on the high ground south of the city glimpsed the faint line of smoke coming from Meade's Third Division soldiers moving across the plain between the river and Prospect Hill. Marye's Heights provided Longstreet's Confederates an opportunity to focus on the right of the Union line. His soldiers watched while Sumner's Right Grand Division positioned themselves in the streets of Fredericksburg, readying themselves for their part in the action.

Meade formed his lines of battle in the open as Hill's brigades, positioned along the RF&P railroad, watched and waited. The rail line ran across the plain in front of Jackson's line and, for Hill's brigades, provided additional cover for the infantrymen as they prepared to take the assault. General Reynolds ordered Doubleday's division to Meade's left securing the Corps, and the Army's left flank. Reynolds then placed General John Gibbon's division to the right rear of Meade.

Confederate artillery on Prospect Hill had initially remained quiet so as not to give away their position and delay the counter-battery fire of Hunt's massed artillery north of the Rappahannock. Meade's division was visible by every artilleryman on the right of the line. Fifty batteries opened in a murderous crossfire. The artillery rounds tore infantry companies apart, creating holes in the advancing lines. Meade rode between the two leading units, Sinclair's and Magilton's brigades. To his left, he saw a single artillery round dismember four infantrymen in a fraction of a second, then pass in front of him. Lines wavered in the fire, then moved forward, at the rail line. On command, the Confederates fired a volley at the Pennsylvanians, and many in the front rank went down; some, including the regimental commander, tumbled back into the ranks behind. Confusion reigned for a brief time as the Union lines hit the rail line one after another, some regiments mixing with others. Meade and his commanders restored the order, and the brigades moved forward, up and over the tracks into Hill's Confederates.

Meade could see Sinclair yelling "Forward" as he stood atop the rail line, his brigade screaming as they went over the top, turning into the left flank of Archer's Rebel brigade. In seconds, he saw Sinclair go down, shot from his horse. At the same time, Magilton's men went over the rail line and turned right into the flank of another brigade. Conrad Jackson's force followed Sinclair and attacked head-on into Archer's front. The melee lasted only minutes, and the Confederate line buckled quickly as Sinclair's regiments slammed into Archer. The 19th Georgia broke and began to move off the line and to the rear. The regiments to their right, in turn, began to pull back as the Union soldiers worked their way down the line.

"They are on the run; after them, boys! Charge!"

The fire was all around Meade, who seemed oblivious to it. Atop his horse and on the highest point of the rail line, the general made a prime target. One of the aides went down hard on the rails, and his horse was hit by an artillery round, taking the hindquarter away. The startled lieutenant moved to the backside of the rail line, cleared his head, and searched for another mount. Dead and wounded men and animals were everywhere in the plain. He couldn't leave the general, so he grabbed a wandering, panic-stricken horse. The lieutenant remounted and quickly rejoined his general, who gave him an approving nod.

Mini-balls filled the air. Meade could almost feel one ball as it passed through the crown of his hat, a second tore his coat sleeve as he held his saber high. The soldiers crouching behind the rail line looked up to see their general, and, glaring at the men, Meade let loose a verbal assault.

"Are you damned cowards? Get up, get back with your regiment, and roll these bastards back over the hill!"

Meade brought the flat edge of the saber down on the closest man, a lieutenant, and the men surged up and over the rail line. They would rather brave the Confederates than the mean-tempered Meade.

The tenacious Union division had broken through the Confederate line and, moving left and right, had created a breach that was several hundred yards wide. Meade had conveyed his concern to both Reynolds and Franklin that, after securing the hill, he would not be able to hold the ground without adequate reinforcements. He desperately needed support to reinforce success. Meade twice sent his aide to the rear requesting assistance from David Birney, who refused to move until ordered by Reynolds.

Meade fought to control his temper amid the battle. He rode back nearly a mile across the plain and found Birney and his staff.

"General, you will move your Goddamned division. I do not care that you demand orders from Reynolds. The fight is to your front, and your soldiers are needed as I waste time discussing orders with you. I am the senior officer on this battlefield. You will immediately move forward in my support, or you will suffer the consequences when this engagement ends. We will not lose this battle because of your insistence on the correct protocol. How damned ridiculous is that? Do you hear me?"

Meade could barely control his temper.

Birney was taken entirely by surprise at the harsh tone and manner of Meade's verbal attack, but he knew enough to answer in the affirmative, saluting.

CHAPTER 21
CARRY THE ENEMY WORKS

Hancock rode back down Hanover Street to meet with his commanders. He wanted them to hear the battle plan directly from him before French moved out of the town and up the heights.

"Gentlemen, I have received the order, and we will carry it out against all hazards. I am fully confident that you will do your duty."

The officers knew, by merely looking past the town at Marye's Heights, the difficulty anyone of them would have in an assault.

"The brigades will be in a column."

Samuel Zook's thoughts had drifted, concerned that fog covered the city, making it difficult to see the heights.

"We would likely follow the lead division, under French. Hopefully, the wave of blue would increase with each successive division to overwhelm the defenders. The ground doesn't appear to be too bad."

He remembered the Mill Race and fences, thinking that perhaps French's men would handle the obstacles first. Zook heard the general's tone changing, yet still very calm about the entire assault as if it were a quick exercise in overpowering your enemy.

"Samuel's brigade will lead the assault for this division. If the brigade falters, Thomas will pass through and take the lead with the Irish Brigade. Thomas, you will likely pick up soldiers from French's division earlier, then Zook's brigade. Unless they are wounded and making for the rear, bring them into your force."

Meagher was never at a loss for words, but in this instance, all he could think of was carrying the enemy works.

"We will not falter, Sir."

"That is commendable, Sir. If you do hesitate, through no fault of your courageous Irishmen, John Caldwell's brigade will advance and pass through your lines. I know we can prevail. The corps' success rests on constant pressure. When a line waivers, the next element should pass through, over, and so on until we carry the enemy's works." Hancock smiled as he always did before a fight.

"I will be on the field with you," he said.

Each officer knew where their commander would be, without saying so. Officers shook hands and wished each other luck in the fight – war's terrible reality a part of each man. Some made light of their situation as soldiers often do to choke down fear and trepidation. Many thought this a futile act that would end in the slaughter of countless men, but they were soldiers and would commit everything within themselves to succeed in this effort.

The division stood on Sophia Street, commanders taking the opportunity to pass final instructions and encouragement to the soldiers. The sound of French's attack reverberated against the building walls, hardening some, unsettling others as they stood. Smoke from the battlefield drifted through the streets. Longstreet's artillery had, indeed, done their job well. They could easily target moving Union columns, exacting their payment before the soldiers had a chance to move against the heights.

Thomas Meagher was a leader, fighter, and a hero to most Irish Americans for his previous actions against the crown. This time, he would eloquently appeal to the soldiers' Irish national pride and the love for their newly adopted country. Bloodied at Antietam's Sunken Road, the Heights were to be the next trial for these Irishmen. Hancock would depend upon their example and bravery as they moved on the stone wall. Meagher took a group of orderlies and headed down Sophia Street, reappearing with bundles of green boxwood.

"My gallant lads, here is a symbol of our land, both old and new, of our families, and our heritage. We shall wear the green proudly on our caps and show the enemy who they fight today. If we fall, we will not fall as nameless soldiers among the sea of blue. We shall die as Irishmen."

Each of the 1,200 officers and men filed past and picked up the green, and, following their general's example, placed it in the brim of their hats. Accompanied by Hancock, Meagher walked the line of regiments, addressing each in turn. The sight of the two generals an inspiration.

Hancock could see the formation shift as each soldier stood a little straighter, with a new sense of determination. Some cried, and some cheered, as the names Hancock and Meagher sounded through the ranks.

When the brigade commander finished speaking to all five of his regiments, he turned to Hancock, "Sir, we are at your command."

Hancock appreciated a well-delivered speech to soldiers. He was aware of Thomas' oratory ability. Witnessing it was heartening, even to Hancock. When the guns sounded in front of Franklin's position signaling Meade's advance, Hancock and his soldiers knew the fight was finally here.

"Samuel, move your division forward!"

Couch and Hancock watched as French's brigades, one after another, moved through the city and were enveloped by the waiting Confederate artillery fire as soon as they emerged.

Army of Northern Virginia

The late morning sun burned the fog away and illuminated Nathan Kimball's brigade as it moved forward, with three regiments as skirmishers leading, into the open space sloping uphill towards Marye's Heights. The Confederates waited for some time, and the hour had finally come on their portion of the line. They watched the Federals emerge from the town and form their lines. The artillery continued its deadly work, firing into the oncoming blue lines and beyond. Sections of the advancing infantry were cut down as a farmer downs wheat with a scythe. The determined ranks closed on one another, filling the gaps.

Cobb understood the advantage he held. His three Georgia regiments stood behind the stone wall near the base of Marye's Heights. The wall bordered a sunken road and stood only three feet high, but the infantrymen cut into the bank, lowering their stand and providing more cover and nearly impossible targets for the advancing Federals. His infantry, four ranks deep, waited patiently. Excitement, fear, and determination all mixed within each man, in both forces, as the blue line steadily moved toward the waiting Confederates.

"Fire!" Cobb's brigade let loose their deadly projectiles.

The front rank was firing, and those behind loading and passing charged weapons forward. The intensity of the fire, never having been witnessed before, appeared to Hancock as a constant volume of fire.

Officers led the lines forward, and they fell like in groups. The fortunate soldiers unscathed by the withering fire were ordered to drop to the ground taking cover behind anything available, including dead comrades. Longstreet's frenzied infantry regiments were screaming as they poured their fire into the lines, halting brigade after brigade, regiment after regiment.

"Sweet Jesus!" a soldier yelled, as bullets from the first volley hit the soldier next to him, taking the poor man's body apart. The dismembered parts were sprayed over those next to the unfortunate young soldier and those behind. Even veterans reeled at the sight, while others were frozen in mid-step and pushed along by their comrades.

Army of the Potomac

Hancock lowered his head for a second. He expected as much and understood that Lee had weeks to prepare the defense. Watching from the outskirts of town, he saw the Confederate regiment placed in reserve behind the first line. He noted the earthworks that covered the heights were filled with infantry, firing over the heads of the lines in front and downhill at the oncoming blue line. Artillery spread across Marye's Heights, and each gun pit had its ammunition chests brought from the limbers and stockpiled with the guns, firing round after round into Kimball's brigade.

Darius Couch was alarmed that he could not see the developing situation due to the smoke from the guns and the remaining fog that hung low over the battlefield. French had begun his attack less than 30 minutes before. The volume of fire that met Kimball's brigade was confirmation that the Confederate repulse now underway was of a level heretofore unseen by the Federal soldiers. French understood that he was to press the attack as soon as Hancock joined him, but his casualties were quickly mounting.

Couch, accompanied by Oliver Howard, quickly sought a better observation point and found one in the dome of the courthouse on Princess Anne Street. As they scanned the ground leading to Marye's Heights, Couch was appalled by the chaos displayed before him.

"Oh, great God!" he said to Howard, "The poor men are falling!"

French's division was nearly gone. Remnants of units intermingled as men sought protection from the constant artillery and rifle fire pouring down upon them. Fences, depressions in the sloping ground, and fallen bodies provided cover from the Confederates.

Couch quickly left the courthouse and found Hancock on the edge of Fredericksburg, observing the battle between the corps' lead division and the Confederate regiments.

"Winfield, I need you to move and reinforce French. For God's sake, his division has stalled well before we have reached the wall. I watched them from the courthouse tower. The musketry is unremitting, and volleys come within seconds, one after another."

Yelling over the sounds of battle, Hancock pointed uphill, "I saw that French had trouble getting across the Mill Race. It breaks up the line of battle halfway to the wall, and then you must reform on the other side under fire. I'm aware of it. If we press quickly, one behind the other, we can close on their line. I need Howard right behind me."

Hancock's men were ready. Glancing at Zook and waving him forward, he yelled, "Samuel, go quickly." The sound of battle nearly drowned out the orders of everyone on the field.

Couch raised his voice to his aide.

"Get to French and tell him to renew the fight as soon as Hancock's forces join him."

Hancock knew the mission had changed from a demonstration, as Burnside had envisioned, to an assault that would sweep Longstreet off Marye's Heights.

On the left, Franklin heard the sounds of the battle raging against the heights as he pulled Reynolds' corps back. Jackson's Confederates counter-attacked, and Hunt's artillery opened ferociously, stopping the Confederate advance across the low plain.

Hancock galloped in front of his line following French's division. He could see the bloody path to Marye's Heights, just as he forewarned. The lead regiments emerged from the town, and what lay before them shook even the most battled hardened veterans – a chaotic scene of the fire, smoke, and blue uniforms strewn across the sloping fields; some gripping the ground, some crawling back, many helped by their comrades. Many more lay still in their surrender to death. The intense fire sounded more like a stirred hornet's nest. The ground erupted from the thunderous artillery fire, the cannon not yet suppressed by Hunt's guns. Case shot and canister, explosive shells, and solid shots were fired into the city and the regiments as they entered the field, forming lines of battle.

Hancock's brave boys marched forward to the astonishment of Longstreet's men.

"Look at them. Magnificent, like on parade," the Georgian artilleryman said as the cannoneers loaded another round. He attached the lanyard to the friction primer and placed it in the cannon's vent.

"Fire!" The artilleryman yanked the lanyard, and the gun roared. Smoke surrounded the gun crew, temporarily blocking their view of the round. The spherical case shot took seconds to traverse the sloping ground and exploded over Zook's first rank. Six men went down, their bodies riddled with iron balls.

"Good Christ! Let's kill those sonsofbitches. Turnabout and join me, and we'll take this ground!"

Hancock rode forward with Zook's brigade and was enraged as he fought to bolster the confidence of the retreating soldiers.

"We can beat these bastards. The day will be ours."

His division entered the fray as soon as they cleared Fredericksburg. The thought of one more route of this Army at the hands of the Confederates was abhorrent to him and the men of the division whom he led. French had lost confidence and ordered his men to withdraw. Hancock could see the look of defeat on soldiers' faces as they streamed back into Fredericksburg, and it served as a harbinger of what was to come. The self-assured Hancock was prepared to enter the fray, as ordered, and carry the heights. He was in full battle-mode, senses sharpened, agile, and ready to adapt to change anywhere he found an opportunity to close on the wall.

Hancock's powerful voice screamed at the retreating soldiers.

"In the name of good Christ, what are you doing? Turn, you bastards, turn around. We'll take the wall. The sonsofbitches will not beat us."

Some rallied at the sight of the general, mounted in the face of a murderous fire, and every bit the inspiring officer he had become. They fell into line beside Zook's brigade, moving across the field and closing on what was the rear of French's division, once again taking up the fight. Others ignored Hancock's abusive language, as well as Zook and his subordinate regimental commanders, moving back towards Fredericksburg to distance themselves from this dangerous ground.

They had done their part, and French was content to let Hancock's division take up the fight. Hancock seemed to be everywhere, riding among the troops, pushing them onward, and ordering what remained of French's brigade to join Zook, who were a few yards from the wall. Zook's men felt the combined artillery and musketry that raked the field, increasing their number of dead and wounded. Still, they pressed on. Their line of battle reformed, they stood in front of the enemy within close musket range, trading fire. Men were taken apart when the sheer volume of fire guaranteed that many rounds would hit a single man during a volley. The large-caliber lead balls changed shape once they found flesh, dismembering a soldier as his horrified comrades moved forward in the battle line. If one were lucky, perhaps a single round would find its mark, and the soldier would be wounded. Still, they pressed on. Zook's men were overcoming the same obstacles that plagued French – the fences across the field. Cobb's infantrymen welcomed each interruption of the enemy advance as they took careful aim and shot the unfortunate Union soldiers. Swinging around to bring up the trailing regiments, Zook felt his horse shake beneath him as it was struck with solid shot, missing him, but passing cleanly through his mount. The horse went down hard, startling Zook. He quickly regained his senses and moved to cover in the swale packed with soldiers.

"Get back to Hancock and tell him we need Meagher," Zook called to his aide.

The mass of blue, throwing itself against Longstreet's stone wall, one brigade after another, was becoming a mixture of regiments. Each attempt to seize the heights failed in the face of overwhelming Rebel fire. Hancock rode past the wave of wounded soldiers making their way back from the open ground, as he surveyed the expanding chaos before him. French's division lay prone upon the field, every shot of the cannon on Marye's Heights finding its mark and sending human debris into the air. Screams of men and animals being ripped apart by the crack of thousands of muskets reverberated with loud sound and continuous walls of smoke. He had seen war and already knew it intimately, but this was something foreign, something unnerving.

"Take the hits and get moving," was foremost in each man's mind, as they crouched down in a futile effort to avoid the exploding metal. French's division had already spent itself on the approach to the stone wall, and Zook was stalling. Hancock knew the intent was a massive wave of Union soldiers, taking their losses and moving forward. The Commanding General's "plan" sent brigade after brigade against the entrenched Rebel regiments faster than the Confederates could kill them.

In a moment, he steadied himself and instinctively began barking orders, full of language that had made him famous, or infamous, he could not tell which. No matter, they moved at the sound of Hancock's voice. His aide went down; the horse shot from under him. A bullet made a sharp crack as it whizzed past his ear and thought nothing of it. Over the sound of battle, he called to Meagher.

"Move General. French has taken the blow and we roll forward."

Meagher's regiments had marched up Caroline and Princess Anne Streets, and turning on George Street, the Irishmen halted just before Hanover, the bloody pathway to the heights. The low area where George Street and Hanover Street intersected became a new killing ground for the Confederate artillerymen, targeting the area whenever they saw a blue formation. The artillery, at times, bouncing off the road and into the quick marching Irishmen. The men tried to disperse, but there were few places to seek cover effectively.

Hancock's calm demeanor, in the face of the danger, steeled the waiting soldiers. The Irish, steady in their movement and confident in the leadership of their Irish hero and commander, Meagher, surged forward. The brigade turned onto Hanover Street and moved up the hill, their colors a bright emerald green, a golden harp, and

"Faugh A Ballagh" emblazoned on the banner. Each regiment carried similar colors with their regimental designation. Boxwood sprigs in their caps and marching towards their enemy behind the wall.

Hancock rode down the street, moving the men forward. Once clear of the city, the regiments moved forward across the open area to the makeshift canal crossings. Formations broke apart as they headed for the cover of scattered buildings, remnants of border fences, or a gentle swale that hid them from enemy observation, at least for a time.

Reforming the brigade, Meagher ordered "Fix bayonets!" The officers ensured the regiments were ready, and the Irishmen rose out of the swale towards the wall. The men moved over the ground, covered with French and Zook's soldiers. Like Zook, they discovered the thousands of muskets rising from behind the stone wall. Regiments were going down in groups as the men crossed the remaining field. Bodies marked the path to the wall as if to say, "come join us in the final rest," while the ranks stepped over and around the blue-coated soldiers. Officers attempted to maintain cohesion, nearly impossible under fire. The emerald green Irish Brigade's colors flew with the National colors as Meagher, mounted and at the center of the brigade, directed his men forward. Within 30 minutes, the brigade's advance collapsed, and the Irish went to ground as well.

Cobb's 24th Georgia Infantry was as Irish as Meagher's Brigade. The Rebel "Sons of Ireland" stood behind their wall and, rising, took careful aim and let loose a volley on their countrymen, followed by near-continuous independent firing. Meagher's soldiers went down like raindrops hitting the ground, and still, they moved forward. The Georgians marveled at the sight of their splendid Northern lads, battle lines and bayonets perfect, colors waving in the wind, stopping to fire a volley then moving ahead. As if they were braving rain or a hailstorm, the men leaned forward, heads low, and bodies slightly turned against the storm with shoulders hunched. The

Confederate Irish did their deadly work, at times through tears, as they wept for their countrymen being slaughtered in front of the stone wall. In half an hour, Meagher's brave Irishmen had gone to ground, less than 50 paces from the wall, expended all of their ammunition and began to withdraw.

Caldwell left the city just behind Meagher moving forward across the mill race. Hancock calmly rode along the crest with his courageous staff members trailing. John knew his brother was acutely aware of the risks but focused on the battle at hand. Hancock had even directed his brigade and regiment commanders to proceed on foot, but he remained mounted, if for no other reason than to be visible to the men. It came as no surprise to those who knew him personally. If he were shot from his horse, then he would do so commanding his soldiers. Hancock rode among the battle lines, stirring all who could see him, appearing to disregard the unbelievable amount of lead passing through the air, but fully aware of every bullet that came too close. They seemed to be everywhere, striking those on the ground, those who rode with him, and those who were trying to leave this dangerous place. The smoke enveloped him with its acrid, powder smell. Instead of recoiling from the sights, sounds, and smells of war, he was invigorated by it.

Caldwell's men had taken cover in the low ground beyond the mill race, providing enough protection from the Confederate fire, but crowded with men from five earlier brigades. The brigade commander readied his men; then, bayonets charged, and, on order, the entire line scrambled up and out of the swale. Regimental commanders repositioned their lines in the face of the enemy.

As he rode, Hancock saw the faces of the men formed and prepared to make their mark on the bloody field.

"Will you carry the enemy works?" Hancock yelled, and the collective cheer drowned out even the continuous firing, but for a moment.

Nelson Miles' trailing regiments, the 61st and 64th New York moved behind Caldwell's front line, barely able to see the forward lines from the smoke that covered the field. The brigade passed around structures that dotted the battlefield between the city and the heights, breaking up formations as men sought protection from the Confederate fire. Cross' 5th New Hampshire surged across the muddied field, churned up from thousands of boots who had passed before, wet from weather and blood, finally reaching the Stratton House; the remnants of all who had come before them prone and scattered around the house.

A deep guttural sound and the sudden rush of air left Cross' lungs as the explosive shell hit just in front of him. He felt the sensation of being swept off his feet and being propelled backward, then hitting the ground hard. Immediately, he tried to get up as the regiment continued forward.

"Colonel, we've got you, and we'll get you off the field," Major Edward Sturtevant said, as he yelled for his New Hampshire men to move forward. Shrapnel peppered Cross' upper body and head, blood covered his face and chest, and he teetered on the edge of unconsciousness, but aware enough that he waved to Sturtevant with a signal that indicated the Major was in command. The regiment continued to move, even as Cross went down from an explosion. The remaining regiments marched behind the New Hampshire men, soldiers falling, some hesitating, with lines breaking apart. The formation was getting smaller with each step towards the wall. They finally reached Zook and Meagher's brigades, prone and intermixed with French's division. Unit cohesion evaporated as soldiers and their officers took positions behind even the slightest rise in the ground from which they could fire.

Hundreds of soldiers continued to fire at the wall, creating a new threat for Caldwell's advancing regiments moving between the prone Union soldiers and the Confederates. It was just as easy to be shot in the back as it was in the chest. Commands changed three and four times as officers became casualties.

Hancock moved behind the lines, as Caldwell's brigade began to stall and go to ground. He waved his aide, Mitchell, over to him.

"Get to Colonel Miles and tell him I wish his two regiments to move to the right. I want him in a position to block any counter-attack."

Mitchell galloped off and relayed the directive to Miles, whose New Yorkers ran across the field through the enemy fire, crossed Hanover Street, and positioned themselves near a small house. Miles could see the enemy line forty yards past the fence that his soldiers used as cover. He estimated his men could be upon the Confederates before the artillery could range the onrushing line or fire their muskets more than one or two times. There was artillery farther up the hill, and Miles directed his infantrymen to fire on the cannons. Convinced that a final surge with bayonets could get over the wall and turn the line, Miles rode to Caldwell.

"We can close the remaining distance quickly from my position," Miles explained.

"I need additional troops from the rest of the brigade to move with me."

Zook joined Caldwell as they looked beyond the house at the wall.

"We have lost cohesion and are a mixture of two divisions. It would be difficult to form up and move across the field to you."

Zook agreed, "I no longer have the brigade that moved forward less than an hour ago."

"Then I will move my regiments alone," Miles yelled over the firing.

"There are no reinforcements until the next division comes up," Caldwell said, "and I cannot order the assault by you alone."

Miles nodded at his superior's decision. Staying low to avoid the Rebel fire, he ran to rejoin his command. When Miles reached his regiment, a mini-ball struck him in the throat. He dropped to the ground grasping the wound and spitting blood. Miles passed the command to Brooks with instructions to "hold at all hazards."

Caldwell had just returned to the brigade after the battlefield council and received word that Miles was wounded. He moved quickly to rejoin his regimental commander on the right when he felt the sharp pain in his side.

"Damn it all! I'm shot!" Caldwell dropped to his knees, holding his side to stem the flow of blood. His aide turned to see the general. "I'm not leaving the field," Caldwell yelled. That decision changed when he was knocked to the ground as another round entered his shoulder. "Find von Schack! He'll command."

Hancock rode to Caldwell, who was being evacuated from the field and saw Colonel George von Schack, 7th New York, who had just arrived.

"George, you command this brigade! Hold here. Oliver Howard is coming up."

"We'll hold, General. I hope Howard is quick about it."

"I'll see what we can do about that, Colonel."

Hancock turned and headed down the line.

Army of Northern Virginia

Cobb's brigade, behind the wall, continued to savage the Union lines. He stood behind the Stephens home when an artillery round found its mark on the house and the sharpshooters inside. The blast, only feet from the general, sent shrapnel in a circular pattern that decapitated a soldier dragging ammunition forward, and bringing down three infantrymen in front of Cobb.

"Pour it on, boys," Cobb yelled.

As his words left him, his leg buckled from the impact, tearing a large hole in his upper thigh and severing the femoral artery. Soldiers moved quickly to their colonel and were cut down by Hancock's sharpshooters. Cobb calmly raised himself on his elbow, continuing to give direction to the infantrymen. Their colonel was their hero, and seeing him carried from the field sank the hearts of many of the Georgians.

"I'm just wounded, boys. Hold your ground!"

Encouraged, the infantrymen would hear later that Cobb slipped into shock, and the surgeons were unable to stem the flow of blood and lost the commander of the wall. Lee and Longstreet stood near the crest of Marye's Heights, observing the slaughter unfold before them. The continuous boom of the artillery and musket volleys hammered Hancock's lines of battle. The field was already carpeted with blue uniforms, and the screams of men and animals dying before the wall had their effect on the Confederate commanders. Characteristically stoic, as he often was in battle, Lee was moved by the scene before him.

"It is good that war is so terrible. It keeps us from growing too fond of it."

Longstreet nodded, realizing that the courageous Federal lines being wasted on the wall could only end this carnage by retiring.

"What was Burnside's plan? He could never dislodge this corps from the heights."

Lee agreed. "Remember, we were late in arriving here. Had the Federal crossings taken place ten days earlier, this would undoubtedly be a different engagement. Burnside was not wholly wrong in planning, just late."

CHAPTER 22
FIGHTING TO A STANDSTILL

Army of the Potomac

Hancock moved among the men; all three brigades now stalled. All three of his aides were down, and his enlisted orderlies trailed behind him, trying their best to ignore the bullets.

"We will not leave this field. If we go to ground, we will stay and give battle."

The soldiers of his division were joined by others who only wanted to be with Hancock in this fight. They fired at the lines behind the wall over and over until their ammunition and that of the dead and dying was gone. They would have risen as one and assaulted the wall with bayonets if Hancock ordered such a thing.

"Steady gentlemen. There are more who will pass through our lines and make for the wall. Howard is right behind."

Hancock spun around searching for Miller, then Parker. Realizing both were shot from their saddles, he turned to his escort sergeant.

"Are you ready, Mackenzie? We're not finished yet!"

The cavalry corporal smiled at the general and spurred his horse just as a round whizzed past his head.

"Shit, that was the widow maker," Mackenzie yelled. Hancock laughed, and the two galloped behind the division, heading for Couch, who was bringing up the next brigade.

The general remained with the front line, moving the regiments forward, reinforcing the lines and directing fire – being visible to the hundreds of soldiers on the field.

He watched as the Confederates positioned on the face of Marye's Heights began to break.

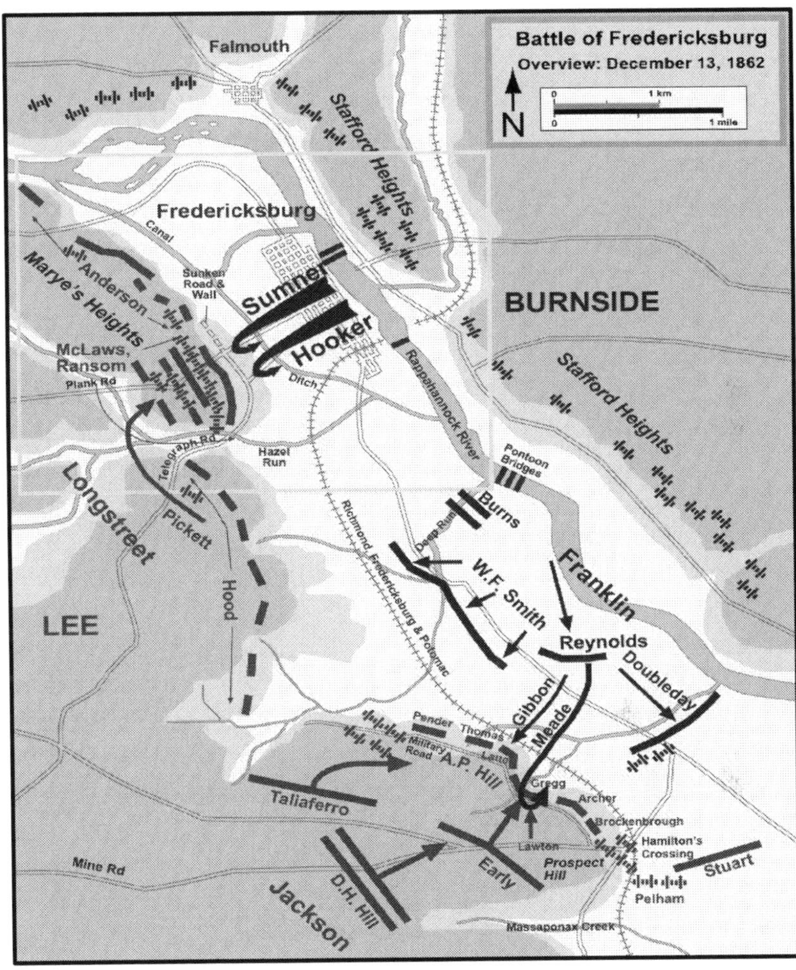

"Goddamn, they are giving way."

"Corporal Mackenzie, get to General Howard and tell him I see the Rebels breaking on the hill. We are paces from the enemy and can move no further without additional forces. He needs to come up and quickly. We may still carry the wall."

The young cavalryman slapped his mount's hindquarter with his hat was off with a shout.

"This is far from over," Hancock said to French as the two generals looked for an opportunity to resurrect the advance.

After two hours of fighting, the Confederates brought the assault to a standstill. Hancock seemed to be everywhere on the field; his soldiers and what remained of French's brigades trading fire with General Ransom's men on the hill. The remnants of units formed a long battle line as they challenged the wall.

"Couch is behind us, and I think Howard is moving."

Mackenzie returned with word that Couch requested his general's presence.

The two rode back to the edge of the city to meet the corps commander. Couch and his division commanders, French, Hancock, and Howard, watched the lines trade fire.

"If you come up behind my division with a brigade, we can then extend the line to the right and flank the wall. I would come straight up Hanover Street," Hancock recommended to Howard.

Howard's brigades were moving out of the city and began taking artillery fire as soon as they entered Hanover Street. The Philadelphia Brigade soldiers made their way to the canal, as every formation before them, crossing on the stingers or through the waist-deep water, and reforming their lines just beyond. The soldiers began to stack up at the canal, and the Confederate artillery fired into the mass of blue. The generals watched as Owen, the successful river crossing commander, turned and waved as his lines moved forward. Almost immediately, his horse went down. The agile commander leaped from the horse, rolled and sprang to his feet. On foot, he raised his sword and led the brigade. Most of the fences were partially down but still slowed the movement. The lethal artillery crossfire never abated, sending case shot and canister down the hill and cutting holes in Howard's regiments.

"If we conduct a supporting attack using Hanover Street on the right, we may yet turn the Confederates."

Couch considered Hancock's suggestion as they crossed Hanover Street and into the field behind the canal. Completely aware of the brigades already on the battlefield, he added, "Sumner has Wilcox's IX Corps uncommitted."

Couch could see the advantage.

"I agree and will notify Sumner immediately."

He passed the information to his aide, Captain Schultze, who quickly galloped toward the city and across the Rappahannock to Sumner's headquarters. Burnside had requested Sumner remain at Stafford Heights while the battle progressed. The old warrior detested being separated from his men and found the occasional venture into Fredericksburg kept him in closer touch with the assaulting II Corps.

Schultze found Sumner along Princess Anne Street. After reading Couch's message, Sumner responded, "Tell Couch he should maneuver as he sees the battle developing and an advantage presents itself."

Sumner watched Hancock's premonition come true, as Couch's corps met Longstreet's divisions.

"It is difficult to see through the smoke, but it appears the enemy is shifting to their left and could counter-attack."

One after another, Howard maneuvered his brigades to the right, and Ransom's determined Confederates fought each to a standstill. The remnants of Couch's corps were in line on the field, waiting for Wilcox's corps to follow.

It took much longer for the IX Corps to prepare. When Wilcox was ready, he ordered Brigadier General Samuel Sturgis' Second Division into the assault from the left of the killing field. The division achieved the same result and pulled back before their casualties equaled that of the II Corps.

Burnside called his Chief-of-Staff, Major General Parke. "Send this to Franklin. 'General, I extend my compliments to you and direct that you attack Lee's right flank with your entire force. We are hard-pressed on the right. Please advise me when your two corps are underway. Signed, Burnside.'"

Franklin's soldiers were bloodied from Jackson's earlier counter-attack forward of Prospect Hill. The order seemed to be ill-timed and too late to make an impact on the assault.

"This is pointless," Franklin thought, and, unbelievably, the Left Grand Division Commander chose instead to disregard the order.

Calling his aide over, Franklin said, "Tell the Commanding General we are engaged on the left with both corps against Jackson. The Confederates have counter-attacked, and our artillery has been successful in halting their advance so far. I have no uncommitted force with which to assault Lee's right. Signed, Franklin.'"

General Hooker watched from Stafford Heights as Sumner's corps went forward. Division after division, brigade after brigade, were throwing themselves at the Confederates. Hooker could see the enemy fire devouring the lines of men. Burnside had ordered him to follow Sumner into the fight. He galloped across the bridge, through the city, and on to the killing field.

Finding Couch and Hancock, he said, "Gentlemen, I am delighted to see you are well. It seems you have had a close call."

Hancock glanced down at the patch of blood at his side. "That was very close. We are still moving on the enemy works. You can't move up the hill without stepping on a soldier, dead or otherwise."

Hooker looked towards the heights and could see, by this time, the approach to Marye's Heights appeared blue. He conveyed Burnside's latest order and discussed its effectiveness with Couch and Hancock.

"IX Corps will follow and, if you bring your Grand Division to the fight, we may finally overwhelm the defense. One would have to climb over the casualties to do so," Hancock offered.

Galloping back across the bridge to Burnside, who also stood near the Lacy House observing the assault, Hooker approached the general.

"General, we have thrown the II Corps against the heights without success. Couch is moving Howard in behind Hancock. Lee is well-positioned there, and it is simply a killing ground. We are no closer than 100 feet. If you look closely, the field is blue from the city's edge to the stone wall." Burnside was unmoved. He knew Hooker was recommending a change of orders, but the Army commander was not finished with his plan, just yet.

"Sumner is following up this initial assault with his IX Corps divisions, Sturgis and Getty. I will follow their assault with your Center Grand Division." Hooker at first thought he misunderstood Burnside, then, to his astonishment, realized the general was planning to bring four more divisions against Longstreet's entrenched Confederates.

"Sir, should we not move that size force against the right of Lee's line and reinforce Franklin?"

"I think not. If we press we can carry the heights." Hooker read the order and left to prepare his force to move. "When this is over," he thought, "I will ensure someone at the top hears that this is Burnside's fault alone." He detested Burnside.

It was mid-afternoon, and Howard, followed by Sturgis' division, had thrown their weight against the heights without success. Three more divisions under Generals Charles Griffin, Andrew Humphreys, and George Washington Getty, one after another, were ordered into the fight with their divisions, each gallantly going forward without success, and they retired. Burnside still believed the Army's strength would move, like a wave, up and over the wall while absorbing the fire. Soldiers gave their lives, never getting closer to the wall than had Hancock's brigades, who stood 25 paces from the Confederate muskets. The field was a sea of Union dead and wounded, in grotesque positions where they fell, making it nearly impossible to move forward.

Hancock made his way back to the city and past his headquarters on the corner of Hanover and George Streets looking for the Irishmen. Meagher had withdrawn the remnants of his brigade from the field. Hancock had ordered they resupply their ammunition and prepare to continue the fight.

"Meagher, what the hell have you done? The orders were for your brigade to pull back once Caldwell's brigade reached you, and to refill your cartridge boxes. I'm told you've moved the brigade to the rear and crossed the river! I need you to return immediately, General. This action is not over."

The general remained mounted to observe the exchange of fire between his division on the hill and the Rebels, his temper rising the longer he spoke with Meagher. Hancock completely understood the "fog of war," and in the chaotic situation before the wall, miscommunication of orders was entirely possible.

"Is it possible that you misunderstood my directions, General?"

Hancock was very aware of the Irish Brigade's honorable and gallant service and wanted to ensure he said nothing to discredit the unit. However, Meagher had pulled the remnants of the brigade, with their wounded, out of the line when Caldwell arrived.

"General Hancock, I cannot explain whether it was a miscommunication in the orders being relayed under great fire, as you were aware, or my misunderstanding. I believed your orders were to disengage and recross the river out of the enemy's range."

"You heard my direction, Sir! You are to return with all of your men who are fit for duty."

The evening was approaching, and Meagher departed to reform the unit immediately, but the Irish Brigade would not return until early the following morning with only 240 men. They had lost half of their men and the majority of the officers in front of the wall.

Soldiers were ordered to lay down. The lucky ones hid behind dead horses, those less fortunate asking for forgiveness as they used their fallen comrades for cover. There was a sickening thud of bullets hitting the dead bodies, but saving lives. The killing was ebbing as the night closed over them. Men were moving, crawling back to the rear, some dragging wounded comrades, others wrapping themselves against the dropping temperature and the terror of battle. The December night had finally fallen on the Army of the Potomac.

The soldiers who had assaulted the heights over the last four to five hours formed a long line of battle from Hanover Street on the right, running parallel to the wall and extending to the railroad cut on the left. Into the evening and through the night, the line held. They lay there, on the slope, hoping the end of the fight had finally arrived, the stillness of the cold December night occasionally broken by the sound of a musket firing as a Confederate tried to make out movement along the ground. It would be the next day, on the morning of 14 December, before regiments began to withdraw from the killing ground, all ammunition expended, the battle lost.

"Mitchell, I'm damn glad that you've been seen to by the medical personnel. What is the report?" the general asked as he walked into the headquarters.

His classic white shirt now tinged with powder residue, sweat, and blood; his uniform, riding gloves, and boots spattered with mud; and his face stained with a mixture of sweat and soot from the battle smoke from thousands of guns. The battle-worn general still had a look about him that said he was ready to do it all once more, and the soldiers would most assuredly follow their general into the breach.

Mitchell was worn after the horrendous hours on the slope, keeping up with the energetic Hancock, losing two horses, and finally being ordered from the field due to his wounds. Hancock needed Mitchell, but not more than he needed to have the aide's injuries attended to so he could accompany Hancock on a future battlefield. Hancock had selected men like Mitchell as aides and hated the thought of possibly losing them in battle, but that was the nature of the fight. He would ask them to do no more than he would do himself.

"Sir, first let me say that Isaac Parker and James Rorty are both well and have had their wounds seen to by Doctor Dougherty. They will recover fully."

"And what of the division?" Hancock asked.

"The division went forward with 5,000 men, and our losses were around 2,000, but the exact figure will be determined as we check with the brigades and regiments. That, in itself, is creating a problem. We lost approximately 150 officers. Colonel Cross' 5th New Hampshire had five separate commanders once the colonel went down. His wounds are severe, but he will recover."

"You could see the ditch and the fences break the momentum of the brigades, one after another, as they went forward. The enemy barely had to aim to strike one of our soldiers."

Hancock anticipated the problem when he tried to persuade Burnside and Sumner days earlier. His demeanor had not changed, and the staff watched as their commander calmly received the information.

"Gentlemen, we did not carry the heights this day, but we retain our honor. We still hold the ground and will do so until relieved."

CHAPTER 23
ONCE MORE ACROSS THE RAPPAHANNOCK

Couch entered Hancock's Hanover Street headquarters. Hancock seemed to be energized by the excitement and terror of battle, while others appeared battle-worn.

"Winfield, you are directed to support Orlando Wilcox's IX Corps tomorrow. They will assault the heights by the direction of the Commanding General."

Hancock stared at Couch in disbelief. Then, realizing Burnside's commitment to his original plan, reread the directive.

"Darius, forty percent of my division is either dead or wounded. My best commanders are down, some regiments are merely companies, but I will do as ordered. When you direct, I will begin to consolidate my division and prepare for the next assault."

Couch was already aware of the considerable losses in the II Corps and thought, "Howard is in better shape, but Hancock is more aggressive and the rational choice to support Wilcox's assault."

"I will provide additional orders after I see Sumner."

In Burnside's headquarters, having comprehended all too late the impact of his assault, the distraught Army commander swore to make ready the IX Corps, his old unit. He would personally lead them in a final attack on the hill.

"Sir, you can't possibly consider the assault with one more corps will have any different effect than that which we have experienced today? We shall adjust our plans and meet Lee again." Sumner tried calmly to convince Burnside that his emotional reaction to the day's debacle should not be pursued.

"We must be rational in our next move. Your desire to lead a corps will result in an unnecessary loss. Lee was determined and had established the defensive line that was unassailable. We have hundreds, if not thousands, dead on the field and must make arrangements for them."

Burnside was near tears, inconsolable.

"Why didn't I listen days ago? What were our losses today?"

"Over 13,000, mostly on the heights." Burnside hung his head while the generals gathered.

"We must withdraw and take our dead and wounded from the field. Send a message to General Lee under a truce flag."

Sumner and Franklin looked questioningly at one another, then back at Burnside. The gravity of what Burnside had just said signified the finality of the day's slaughter.

"Sir, General Couch sent this message," Mitchell said, handing the paper to Hancock.

"It says we are no longer going to follow up with the IX Corps against the heights. Rational thought prevails, gentlemen. I'll see the brigade commanders when I return from Couch's headquarters. Fredericksburg is over for this Army, and I expect we will withdraw back over the Rappahannock within the next 24 hours."

Hancock walked out of the headquarters, mounted his horse, and, with Mackenzie and his small group of cavalry aides, headed back to receive further orders.

Hancock's men spent the next day retrieving their casualties from the field, under a flag of truce, and the watchful eyes of Longstreet's soldiers behind the wall. Winfield sat quietly at the Mill Race, watching the long lines of ambulances and support wagons making their way to and from the battle-torn field that sloped up to the wall. They held human cargo four and five deep. To him, they appeared very much like the long columns of engineer wagons and boats that had made their way to the river four days earlier. Hancock raised his field glasses to scan the heights, and he could see Longstreet and McLaws, also mounted, as they watched the Union wagons traveling up and down Hanover Street.

"That's Hancock just beyond the canal," McLaws said to Longstreet.

Pete Longstreet brought his glasses up and could see Winfield with a few members of his staff.

"I remember when I first heard his name at West Point. I was the Cadet Sergeant tasked with moving the newly-arrived conditionals to their company barracks."

"His boys are laying at the foot of this wall," Longstreet sighed. "He'll be back, and we should take note where he deploys on the next field each time. Winfield will not take this battle lightly."

The following night, Burnside's Army retired across the Rappahannock, so quietly and effectively, even Lee was surprised that they were gone. Burnside sought another opportunity to turn Fredericksburg's misfortune into a victory for the Union.

A Matter of Culpability

The Army of the Potomac tried and failed to flank the Army of Northern Virginia in January. The rainy weather was uncooperative and dangerous, creating a swamp on the routes Burnside's grand divisions must transit to cross the Rappahannock farther up the river. The roads became worse with each passing division.

Winfield stood in the Lacy House and, lost in thought, glanced out of the window at the chilling rain. He thanked the war gods that his division was positioned as the rear guard, while the Army made their sweeping move north. The Confederates were in Fredericksburg and along the high ground outside of the city. Whether it was due to his actions in December or the luck of the draw, it didn't matter. His soldiers were not going to endure the march through the sea of mud that was grinding the Army to a halt.

The "Mud March" ended what was to be redemption for the debacle at Fredericksburg. Burnside ordered the Army back into camp along the Rappahannock. His officers and men were dispirited, and, in some cases, officers were actively plotting against their commander.

Unable to absolve himself from Fredericksburg with a decisive win against Lee, Burnside wanted to shift the blame for the loss on his officers and their failure to carry out the orders he had given them during the battle. He, therefore, published a general order that would relieve many of the senior officers from command. The recriminations were sent to Halleck and passed to both Stanton and the President. When word of Burnside's action reached Generals Franklin and Smith, they knew a face-to-face meeting with Halleck was required. If for nothing else, the session would provide additional facts about Fredericksburg.

"Seems Burnside is deflecting the blame for Fredericksburg," Couch said as he and Hancock relaxed in the parlor of the Lacy House, once again.

"What could he possibly say? We crashed against that damn wall over and over again while executing his orders. There was much uncertainty in his direction, such as moving to support Franklin, then rescinding the order, or the directive to support the IX Corps in a follow-on assault, and then he canceled once again. There may be more then we see on the surface."

Hancock puffed on the cigar and, letting the smoke out slowly, watched as it drifted upward.

Couch agreed. "Talked to Franklin when he and Sumner were together earlier. Franklin and Smith want to see Halleck."

If nothing else, Hancock was a professional and believed skirting the Army's Commanding General was detrimental to one's career, but in this politically-connected Army, generals were always seeking an advantage to assignments and promotion. Franklin and

Smith were Academy graduates, and Hancock became concerned for his former commanders and friends.

"I think I'll go to see Baldy Smith."

Couch trusted Hancock's judgment and liked his style, in and out of battle.

Early the next day, Hancock rode to Baldy Smith's headquarters. He understood that Franklin and Smith, and likely others, were very dissatisfied with Burnside's ability to command the Army, and they intended to discuss with Halleck the missteps Burnside had made at Fredericksburg. Most of the senior officers were aware of the rumored trip, and Winfield believed that he should spend some time with Baldy if the rumors were true.

"Winfield, how the hell are you? Come, take a seat with me and have lunch. My staff has prepared everything, and you are my welcomed guest."

"I am damn glad to see that you are well," Hancock replied.

"How is the II Corps? Is Darius alright? He has some medical issues that take their toll every once in a while, but I hear he remained on the field at Fredericksburg."

"He certainly did and, to his credit, moved as many men forward as he could in a short amount of time. A real fighter! The II Corps was bloodied and badly. I lost nearly half of my division."

The two made small talk of home, the march, the next turn for the Army of the Potomac, and, of course, Fredericksburg.

"Never saw anything like the firepower Longstreet had on that hill and behind that damned wall," Hancock offered."

"We could have rolled up the left, but Jackson reacted quickly," Baldy countered. "I'm always glad to see you, my friend, but what brings a former member of the VI Corps back here?"

"Baldy, what the hell are you doing? This move against Burnside may be seen as rebellious by the leadership in Washington. I feel it is my obligation as a friend to at least make you aware of what the general officers in this Army are saying. Shit, when Burnside gets wind of this, there will be hell to pay! Remember what he thought of me before we assaulted, and I only wanted him to consider other possibilities."

"Franklin and I are not going to Washington. John Newton, my Third Division commander, is going. He's traveling with one of his brigade commanders. They intend to see Halleck and provide all the facts about Fredericksburg. We certainly were pressed, and Meade took the brunt of the assault on the left, no thanks to Burnside's vague orders. Instead of pushing forward, Franklin pulled Reynolds back before Jackson could build enough strength to push us to the river. Henry Hunt's artillery was a lifesaver."

"I must remind you that Ambrose has a problem with confidence. He'll come after you and Franklin, and I'm sure anyone else, starting with Newton when this is over. Hooker is already sending signals to his political connections. There's no love lost between Hooker and Burnside."

"Thanks, but we must do what we can to enlighten the higher command."

"Take care, my friend. The generals should watch their backs in Washington."

Hancock thanked Smith for lunch and catching up, but could not help feeling that he was saying a final goodbye to his friend once the impact of the officer's Washington trip was history.

He had already written Allie and penned a letter to Hilary, as his soldiers settled down for another wintery night along the Rappahannock. He took a sip of the whiskey and water on the desk and set the glass down next to the oil lamp. Outside, the wind became stronger, and the tent canvas shuttered. He thought for a moment, then began the letter wishing Hilary and his family blessings for the new year. Hancock then focused on the recent proclamation from Lincoln's White House that he knew his brother would find interesting.

"When the President proclaimed emancipation at the beginning of the year, the reason for this conflict became clouded, for I had always believed it was the preservation of the Union as the singular objective. I have been a professional soldier for nearly two decades, and if ending slavery is a major objective, I shall accept it fully. The Confederacy is fighting for its survival; however, in the wake of the terrible beating we've taken in Fredericksburg, I believe we shall ultimately prevail. A major victory eludes us, and this struggle could go on for some time, but the freedom promised in the proclamation is dependent upon Union victory."

Hancock dipped the pen in the small ink bottle and wrote, "Confederate soldiers and their leaders are just as determined in their struggle, no matter how wrong I believe their goal to be. Such is the case with Harry Heth, who I believe is still in Tennessee. He mentioned his great friend and West Point roommate Ambrose Burnside many times. The impression I had of the man based on Harry's many stories is vastly different from the one I now have after this terrible loss in Fredericksburg. I wonder what is in store for this Army as spring arrives?"

He paused and read the words slowly, then continued Hilary's letter.

"Believe me when I say we will succeed, but I fear another change in command of this Army is on the horizon. For the present, I shall stay far removed from that process and hope we find the right commander. McClellan may have been cautious, but he was well-suited for high command. Only God and Mr. Stanton know who is on the President's list for consideration."

Washington, D.C.

Lincoln was once more facing the decision to change the command of the Army. Newton saw Secretary Seward, and he, in turn, escorted them to Lincoln. The President listened, as did Secretary Stanton and General Halleck, to the generals and their explanation of Burnside's shortfalls in December. Lincoln listened intently to their report of vague orders, lack of confidence on the part of the commander, and the failure to alter the plan in the face of Lee's hardening his defense, while the Army of the Potomac was delayed in crossing the Rappahannock.

The generals were unaware that Burnside intended to level charges against senior officers, Hooker and Franklin included, through a General Order that would eventually find its way to the President. Hancock warned Smith that once Newton returned, and word of their session with the President reached Burnside, they would be on the list for breaching the Army's security. Given his earlier "run in" with Burnside over the delay in crossing into Fredericksburg, Hancock was not singled out in the order, nor were Sumner and Couch. Burnside's wrath fell on Franklin and Smith's command, and on Hooker, personally. Lincoln alone could order the relief of so many general officers, so Burnside went to the White House.

"General Burnside, I am glad to see you once more. We are alone, so you may speak openly about the Army of the Potomac," Lincoln offered quickly, trying to determine the real reason Burnside requested the meeting.

"Mr. President, I have a General Order for your review and decision. I know you have already spoken with two of my generals regarding Fredericksburg and my command."

"You are correct. Secretary Seward brought General Newton to see me. They had several concerns."

"Sir, the Army of the Potomac is suffering. The fact that two of my generals thought it best to bypass me and bring their grievances personally to Washington speaks volumes about the misplaced loyalty of some officers. I cannot lead the Army under such conditions."

"I believe that to be true, but I would like to discuss this with Stanton and Halleck. I would ask that you remain here in Washington tonight, and I'll have an answer for you in the morning. Am I correct in seeing your letter of resignation also here attached?"

"Yes, Mr. President. If you feel that I am unfit for a command, I will resign and return home. Remember, Sir, that I did not seek this command, but was directed to replace McClellan a little over two months ago."

The President thanked the general and escorted him to the door. Burnside knew Stanton and Halleck would likely talk Lincoln back from the wholesale reliefs he demanded. That left one alternative, the general would not see another week in command.

Burnside returned the following morning, as Lincoln requested.

"General Burnside, I have decided that you shall be relieved of command; however, I cannot accept your resignation. We need you. This nation and I highly value your service. Major General Hooker will relieve you as Commanding General of the Army of the Potomac, effective immediately."

Hancock's concern became a reality, with Franklin and Smith reassigned and no longer with the Army of the Potomac.

Hooker was a West Point graduate and decorated soldier. However, he was a narcissist who never shied away from an opportunity to criticize his superiors, and that included Burnside. He knew the political game and learned to play it to his advantage. He was a champion of the radical Republicans in Washington, and their influence played heavily in Lincoln's decision to make him the next Army commander. The press had picked up the sobriquet "Fighting Joe" Hooker previously, and it seemed to fit the hard-drinking and egotistical general, but he was genuinely courageous and a battle-tested leader. He, like Burnside before him, sought the opportunity to bring Lee to battle.

When, in early April, Lincoln arrived at Hooker's headquarters, they discussed the plans for the Army of the Potomac. More importantly, Lincoln wanted to know when Hooker would move. Lincoln had similar discussions with McClellan and Burnside. Hooker was yet another commander whom the President felt should hear from his Commander-in-Chief. When the meeting was at an end, the President rose and, while heading to the door, turned to Hooker and Couch, also in attendance.

"I want to impress upon you two gentlemen in your next fight, put in all of your men. I have said this before, and I have little patience remaining."

In Lincoln's mind, the conservative approach to fighting Lee had never worked. Union generals continued to husband their forces and acceded to the Confederates leader what would otherwise have been a victory for the Union.

Army of Northern Virginia

Lee had conducted a brilliant campaign, defeating the Federal Army time after time throughout the previous year. He still sought a decisive victory, and if he could achieve that, then there existed the possibility that the Northern population would lose faith and end the war. Similarly, if Lincoln lost his re-election bid as a result of successive military failures, the North, again growing weary of the conflict, would sue for peace. The election was still a year off, in 1864; however, this was the spring of 1863, and President Davis and General Lee needed to capitalize on their victory in Fredericksburg.

CHAPTER 24
FIGHTING JOE

"It is unfortunate that we lost the 7th New York Volunteers. That was truly a veteran's infantry regiment." Hancock reviewed the latest reports of regiments mustering out of the Army. Volunteer regiments often had specific terms of service, and generals, Hancock included, all dealt with the constant shifting of units into and out of service. Winfield's brother John held the latest unit list.

"We have two newly-arrived Pennsylvania regiments joining us; the 140th and 148th Pennsylvania."

"Have the brigade commanders report the current status of their regiments. I'm interested in their initial assessment of readiness," Hancock directed, adding, "What about the new staff officers?"

Mitchell responded.

"Yes, Sir. The staff officers you've identified have started to report to the headquarters. I will send them in as you have time."

Pausing to ensure his request would be received positively, William added, "Sir, do I get to comment on them?"

"Of course you can comment, most certainly. If there's something that escapes me that you have picked up on during your casual conversations, I need to hear it. I want officers who can keep up with me, who are intelligent and able to operate with the minimum of supervision. God Almighty! I'll have enough direction for them. I can train them to be excellent staff officers, but we need a foundation from which to build. If they displayed gallantry in the face of the enemy, all the better, for they grasp what is expected on the battlefield. That is not a prerequisite, though."

Mitchell smiled at his commander, knowing what was required to keep up with Hancock. He was still recovering from his wounds at Fredericksburg, as were Rorty and Parker, and all three were present for duty.

"How does he ignore all those bullets, each intended to take him from the saddle?" Mitchell wondered.

"Any new officers must also learn to control their fear in time, for there is still more battle on the horizon, that is certain."

"Alright, who am I to see first?" Hancock asked.

"It looks like Captain Henry H. Bingham of the 140th Pennsylvania. He's from the newly-arrived regiment."

"Lieutenant Miller?" Miller stuck his head into the tent. "I want to check the training of the regiments. The reorganization is complete, and the four brigades should be in better shape. I don't want to lose the necessary skills while our headquarters determines the next step, and we wait to move yet again. We can take this time to enhance our skills. Bobby Lee will make quick work of us if we are not ready. First, let me see Bingham."

Bingham entered Hancock's headquarters, reporting to the general.

"Sir, Captain Henry Bingham is reporting as ordered."

Hancock stood, returned the salute, and came forward to shake Bingham's hand. The young officer was slight of build, not much more than 100 pounds, but Hancock appreciated the firm grip and energy of the man.

"Welcome to the First Division, Captain. Please, take a seat. I have selected you, among others, to be part of my staff."

"Sir, I am honored to be considered, but I've only been with the regiment since August, about eight months."

"Your time in service is not an issue. It's your legal training, for I see that you are a Philadelphia lawyer?"

"Yes, Sir. However, shortly after graduation, I joined the regiment."

Bingham had not met many generals in his short time in uniform, but there was something unique about General Hancock. The connection between the general and each of his staff officers, or Hancock's friendly nature, instilled in each officer the desire to excel at his duties in support of this general. They spoke of Pennsylvania, and the formation of the regiment, of Bingham's company command, and training the regiment had undergone before arrival. He could sense from the conversation that the general was exacting in his direction to his staff and commanders and that details were of no small consequence. Bingham would provide everything Hancock needed from a staff officer.

"Sir, if I am selected, I have my personal effects with me, and can begin at your discretion."

"Selected? Captain, that's already behind us. You are my Judge Advocate and will serve as an aide, from time to time. Miller will get you settled."

Bingham and Miller turned and walked out as Mitchell entered.

"Are we complete in our selections, William?"

"Yes, Sir. With Bingham's addition, you now have Lieutenants Parker, George Scott, and William Wilson as aides-de-camp. Of course, Lieutenant Hancock is assigned as is Batchelder."

"Although not fully recovered from their wounds, all are present for duty?"

"That is correct, and all are ready to ride with you immediately."

Hancock was proud of each one, courageous to a man when under fire, and able to anticipate his requirements.

"Give them all you can, William. They are a fine group of men."

Newly-promoted Sergeant Mackenzie held the reins of the general's horse while waiting for Hancock to finish interviewing Bingham. The general energetically burst out of the tent while putting on his gloves, and Mackenzie could tell his ride through the brigades would be filled with more stories for the enlisted orderlies when they retired around the fire that evening. He had been with Hancock long enough, both in and out of danger, and knew the general would make each day enjoyable. The personal staff, officers, and enlisted men alike wanted nothing more than to be by Hancock's side.

"Zook, old sonofabitch that you are, I heard your infantry training was less than Goddamned adequate, so I wanted to see for myself what your bastards are up to."

Zook was surprised at the remark, then realized, once more, that it was Hancock's way. He refused to take the bait.

"I'm surprised you found time to get away from that shithole you call a headquarters. The assholes you have working on your staff are a daily nuisance, but I see you've finally found time to see some real soldiers, didn't you? Well, it's about fucking time!"

The soldiers within earshot strained to listen to the latest colorful exchange between the two warriors, the air starting to turn blue around them. Officers not accustomed to Hancock's manner of speech on a campaign were somewhat chagrined, but quickly settled in to await the next barb between the two generals.

"What in hell are you saying? Those bastards in grey who want to shoot us keep searching for my headquarters. If I made it appear like yours, I felt I could blend in better with the likes of this brigade."

The soldiers and Zook howled, and Hancock tipped his hat.

The exchange complete, the two rode off to see the 140th Pennsylvania Volunteers. Zook knew the exacting standards Hancock demanded of his infantry regiments. That was on full display as they held the line before Marye's Heights. His brigade would not disappoint their Commanding General.

It did not take long for General Hooker to put his mark on the Army of the Potomac. Within 90 days, he had dispensed with the "Grand Divisions" and placed all seven infantry corps under his direct command. The Army had suffered from low morale since Fredericksburg and the "Mud March." Hooker began the process of rebuilding the Army and their confidence, granting leaves, resupplying the units, enhancing subsistence, and bringing the soldiers back to the fighting force that had arrived along the Rappahannock back in December.

"Approved! The designation is just what I ordered."

Hooker was animated as he reviewed the final list of corps symbols. He was instituting a system of unit designations with symbols unique to each corps, and their subordinate divisions by color. Soldiers almost immediately identified with their "badge" and, for the leadership, it was quite easy to locate a soldier's unit of assignment, at least to division level.

General Hancock studied the II Corps' designation, a Trefoil, and his division color, red.

"Not bad. Wish I the hell I had come up with it."

Mitchell and Batchelder laughed, but they agreed.

"Let's get this distributed throughout the division, immediately."

The Trefoil and the motto "Clubs are Trump!" became a way to single out specific unit accomplishments and enhance the esprit de corps throughout the II Corps. The soldiers wore their designations, their "unit patch" with honor.

Hooker set aside the growing pile of reports from the various divisions on the state of readiness. His focus was on the next turn for his Army.

"Dan, get in here!"

The Chief of Staff, Major General Daniel Butterfield, entered the room where Hooker was planning his next move.

"I need your opinion of this plan before I call the corps commanders in to discuss it. Lee still has forces in the Fredericksburg area and along a line on the heights. If I leave a part of the Army there, I can fix the Confederates in position. I can swing the larger part of the force farther up the Rappahannock, conduct another crossing, and come in on Lee's flank and behind him. Ambrose was correct in his assessment. His plan was sound in January. The weather beat the shit out of everyone, but swinging around Lee was just as sound then as it is today."

Hooker paused briefly, then continued. "Halleck and I spoke. Lee and the destruction of his Army is the objective. We'll handle Richmond later."

"It's spring, and we should be aware of the condition of the fords upstream. Also, who do you believe should command the Fredericksburg force?"

"I believe Sedgwick is right for the task. He'll have John Reynolds' I Corps, as well. We must identify the necessary fords, so find General Stoneman. His cavalry should be able to handle that for me."

"I agree. When do we move?"

"I don't want Lee to get wind of this, so we'll move the corps farthest from the Confederate picket's sight first, and those closest, Falmouth to the Rappahannock, will remain in place to hide the movement in their rear. We'll move the V, XI, and XII Corps first, then consolidate the Army near the Chancellor house."

"I'll start drafting the orders. Should we include your plan to attack Lee?"

"Hell, no! The fewer people who see this plan, the less chance it can be compromised. The corps commanders will receive a second order when they are in position across the river. Once I get the reconnaissance report, we can draft the order. I believe the 26th or 27th will be soon enough."

Hooker's plan was in motion. "My plans are perfect," Hooker boasted to Butterfield, "and when I start to carry them out, may God have mercy on General Lee, for I will have none."

Couch laid the map out before his division commanders.

"Winfield, tomorrow you and General French will move to the United States Ford, just south of the where the Rappahannock and Rapidan come together. Let us secure Bank's Ford, as well. General Gibbon, your division will remain here under Sedgwick, who will have the left-wing of the Army with about 50,000 men positioned near Fredericksburg. All I have from Hooker is a movement order."

"That's great, but what the hell is the plan for five separate corps once we cross the river, besides attack Lee's flank?" French asked.

"I believe the intent is to fix Lee's Army in place across the Rappahannock. Then Hooker plans to come in behind Lee on multiple avenues of approach, and, when each corps is in position, he'll hammer Lee against Sedgwick's anvil."

"The Army is moving all at once? Are we following, as I see our fords are less than twelve miles away," Hancock inquired.

"Hooker has ordered Oliver Howard and Henry Slocum to Kelly's Ford, about 25 miles north on the Rappahannock. They are preparing for the move. George Meade will follow tomorrow with his V Corps, and Sickles will remain on this side of the river unless called forward by Hooker. The II Corps will move after Meade. Prepare for the march!"

Darius Couch looked around the room. "Are there questions?"

French spoke up. "Finally, we are moving. This time we'll catch Lee facing the other way."

"Keep in mind who we are facing. Lee will always do the unexpected, regardless of the odds. He is an agile bastard. If he catches wind of our movement, he'll quickly adjust and find a way to come at us," Hancock replied.

Couch agreed. "I like the advantage in numbers, but that never troubled the Confederate command. Just be ready once we are in position. We shall consolidate in the vicinity of the Chancellor House intersection. Hooker is sending Stoneman's cavalry well to the rear of Lee, cutting off the supply line from Richmond."

The generals looked at one another with a renewed air of confidence that the battle was but a few days away. It had been five months since the slaughter. A new commander, with a solid plan, was once again bringing the battle to the Rebels.

Assured that his brigades had prepared for the next engagement, Hancock gathered his commanders to hear Hooker's plan and receive orders. He directed Meagher to secure two crossing sites on the Rappahannock River. Within hours, Meagher split the Irish Brigade and taking two regiments, marched to United States Ford; Colonel Patrick Kelly, the 88th New York commander, took the remaining two regiments to Bank's Ford.

Hooker's move against Fredericksburg began with Reynold's I Corps crossing the Rappahannock. Confederate General Jubal Early was spread out from Marye's Heights to Prospect Hill to counter the Union advance.

"The Army has crossed south of Fredericksburg, providing the opportunity for us to move quickly up the river and cross ourselves. You may commence your move to United States Crossing. Signed, Couch."

Hancock scanned the message. The division started its move north away from Fredericksburg with the memory of the December loss still fresh in the veterans' minds. Hancock's division moved forward and encamped near United States Ford in late April, awaiting completion of the engineers' bridging operation. The corps camped short of the ford, and Hancock was uneasy with the delay caused by the completion of the pontoon bridges. His division crossed, and a short time later reached Chancellorsville, less than three miles away. Picking up Patrick Kelly's regiments along the way, Hancock was opposed to leaving Bank's Ford wide open and unsecured, so he left a single company at the ford. Meagher's regiments continued securing the ford and remained there until 3 May, when they rejoined Hancock. The men were exuberant at crossing the river without a fight, unlike the contested crossing in Fredericksburg months earlier.

Miller rode up to Hancock and handed him a message from Couch's headquarters, one that originated with Hooker. Hancock read it aloud to the staff gathered around him.

"The operations of the last three days have determined that our enemy must ingloriously fly, or give us battle on our ground, where we will destroy him."

Hancock read it once more to himself.

"It appears the general is well pleased with our unrestricted movement to this location. Let's hope Lee has somehow missed us and is not aware, at least for the next few hours. Get a message to the brigade commanders that includes Hooker's accolades and my instructions – to wit, get pickets forward, and prepare for battle!"

Miller headed for the brigades, and Hancock moved forward of the crossroads to search for the best ground. Chancellorsville was just a clearing in the wooded area, commonly referred to as "the Wilderness."

"This is impossible ground on which to fight," Hancock said to Caldwell, as the two generals rode slowly along the main road that cut through the woods – the Wilderness.

"The denseness of the trees and the underbrush would break up any formations and severely restrict visibility as one force closed on another."

"Let's go a bit further and see if this lightens up."

Moving with his cavalry escort and Mitchell, Hancock rode down the Orange Turnpike more than a mile and emerged from the Wilderness to open ground that looked like it stretched east to Fredericksburg. Hancock quickly took in all that he could see and visualized the forward positions of infantry and artillery, noting that he must control the high ground to his front.

"Why are we holding at Chancellorsville? Howard and Slocum are holding there, and the rest of the Army will soon be in position. I need to see Darius promptly and discuss what we have seen here. After my experience with Burnside, I may take a different approach. I will be more tactful this time before I make any recommendations on the current plan. Already caused a shit storm before the Fredericksburg assault. I'm uncertain whether Couch or

Hooker will accept my recommendations, but we'll see. Time is critical."

The small detachment cantered back to the division positions at Chancellorsville. Entering his tent, Hancock removed his coat and hat, unbuttoned his vest, and sat at the field desk to write his letter to Allie. The orderly arrived and brought with him the next day's white shirt and a box of cigars, just sent from Hilary.

"Corporal Mahan, did you open this box?"

"Not completely, my General, Sir."

The Irish accent unmistakable.

"I was curious and wondered as to the contents guessing they were cigars. I knew you would not mind if I opened it and placed the box on your field table. I knew you'd offer one to me. Your generous nature well compliments your warrior persona."

Hancock faced his orderly with amusement.

"Eamon, you impress me with your daily ruminations, bordering on full of shit."

Mahan laughed as Hancock handed him a cigar and waved him out of the tent. He had already grown used to the young Irishman's quirks, and he thought them insignificant in a battle setting, and, therefore, not worth mentioning.

"I should check the whiskey, as well. That son of Ireland is probably sampling it every time we set up this damn tent."

He beheld his glass and, turning it around in his hand, studied the pale brown liquor it held. The thought of Hilary having experienced trouble with drinking bothered him. His personal life and law practice suffered significantly. John told him of Hilary's problem after receiving a letter from their father.

"I guess Father thought I had enough on my mind. I should ask Hilary directly in my next letter. Perhaps another time. You know he has asked for money in the past."

Winfield set aside personal issues for the more important ones on his desk; however, this was family and required attention soon. Settling back in his chair, he thought about Father and Mother, and of Allie and the children. "One more engagement, once more within the sights of some hidden sharpshooter. I'll be as safe as a general can be in this continuous deadly match." He took pen in hand and wrote to his dear Allie.

CHAPTER 25
CHANCELLORSVILLE

Army of Northern Virginia

Jackson dismounted, and, removing his gloves, entered Brompton Mansion, on Marye's Heights. The stately home was impressive in its construction and beautiful, even in Jackson's eyes, but it carried the scars of December's battle. The surrounding grounds still held artillery pieces in defilade, ready to repel the Union divisions should they decide to try to take the heights once again. General A.P. Hill was waiting inside the doorway and greeted Jackson.

"Looks like the Yankees have found their way to this side of the river in the west."

"Good evening, General Hill. I expect that is true! Then we shall kill them on the ground that we will choose," the acerbic Jackson replied, the inactivity of the previous four months making him uneasy. Although replacements had arrived since the Fredericksburg battle, supplies were scarce. Longstreet was trying to solve that for Lee.

Jackson was a professional, the best corps commander in the Army, and sought action. He thoroughly hated sitting across the river, waiting on the Union to make a move. It would appear that he had found the opportunity to bring the fight to the Federals, yet again. Hopefully, his commander felt the same.

The room included things one would expect in a Virginia mansion. Jackson was pleasantly surprised and impressed that everything had weathered the action after all the musket and artillery rounds fired by the Yankees in December. Longstreet had used the mansion as his headquarters previously. McLaws and Anderson, of Longstreet's Corps, were standing together discussing possible Union Army intent, and its new commander, Major General Joseph Hooker. Lee entered the room with General Stuart and everyone stood.

While the Federal Army held their positions across the river, the Commanding General believed the timing was right to conduct such an operation. He had sent Longstreet, with his two divisions under Pickett and Hood, to Southern Virginia to forage. With Jackson's Corps, Stuart, McClaws' and Anderson's divisions, Lee knew he had less than 60,000 soldiers in the field.

"I'm glad to see everyone is well. General Stuart has informed me that the Federal Army crossed the Rappahannock in the west and is deploying near the crossroads around the Chancellor house. We did not foresee his move across the river, but he is here, and we must look to his strategy. There are, at least, two Union Corps who have crossed and are in the plain before Prospect Hill, on the right of our line. I believe Hooker to be more aggressive than Burnside and McClellan were before him. 'Fighting Joe' Hooker, they call him! He has also held a portion of his force farther north of the river in Falmouth."

"Sir, the force on Prospect Hill has not moved. They may be there to hold us in position while the bulk of their army moves north." A.P. Hill was as anxious as Jackson to begin operations. It had been a long winter since December's victory.

"True, the force facing Prospect Hill has not moved forward, but we must address both of these crossings, as he appears to be attempting to challenge us from the front and rear. General Longstreet is away from this Army, but I intend to split this force further and meet the Federals approaching from the west. I believe this to be a greater threat."

The generals each strained to see the map. Stuart's cavalry estimated the position of the Union line near Chancellor House, extending from the Orange Turnpike to the Rappahannock. Jackson thought for a moment and was the first to speak. The generals were deferring to him.

"If he moves forward, as we all expect he will, and given Stuart's surveillance, then we should move quickly to drive him from the ground east of the Chancellor House. I am not familiar with the ground there, but the wooded area surrounding the crossroads is called the Wilderness, and for a good reason. Perhaps we could use that to our advantage?"

"I thought the same thing, General. I want General Anderson to move west to see if the Federals are along the Orange Turnpike. General Jackson, turn a large portion of your corps back to the west and prepare to meet the Federals, should they be there."

Stuart added, "They are around Chancellorsville, and they appear to be moving forward to the low ridgeline to the east."

"If, as you say, we can drive him from the high ground, we would be in a better position. We must, however, continue to hold our position here along the Fredericksburg line."

Jackson pointed to the map.

"General Early's division is at Fredericksburg with additional support. The defensive positions are excellent, and Jubal will be able to hold. I am concerned that we will split our force, yet again. I'm not overly concerned, but aware that Hooker could bring the larger part of the Army against our rear and Marye's Heights at the same time."

"I believe we are in a solid position here and will hold if he comes against the heights, as he did before," Early said firmly.

"We can move quickly down the Orange Turnpike or use the parallel Plank Road," Jackson said, looking around the room. The generals agreed with his observation.

"Then, we can seize the initiative. We must prepare ourselves to repulse the enemy. Are there any questions?"

They each concurred with the planned maneuver without comment and departed for their respective commands. Anderson immediately ordered his brigades to march forward along the turnpike to comply with Lee's direction, and his division left within hours.

"We should seek a way to take the fight out of Hooker. Perhaps a move to turn his flank. The woods are quite heavy and severely impact infantry movement, but that may be to our advantage." Lee nodded in agreement. He thought through the next move and expected Jackson would have a recommendation.

Army of the Potomac

Hancock strode into Couch's headquarters in the morning on the first day of May.

"Glad you are here, Winfield. General Hooker plans to move on Fredericksburg, immediately using three avenues of approach: the Orange Turnpike; the Orange Plank Road, which connects with the turnpike about five miles from here; and a road that runs along the river past Banks Ford."

Couch indicated the routes on a less than an adequate map, but the only one his staff could procure.

"The XI and XII Corps will use the Plank Road, and Meade's V Corps will move along the river road. He is sending Sykes' division straight down the turnpike. Frankly, I don't believe General Lee knows we are across the river and about five miles from his force. We've been sitting for months, and everyone is ready for this fight."

"Fine! Where is the II Corps' position?"

Hancock started to formulate his battle plan as he recalled the ground east of the Wilderness.

"I've been ordered to send one division to support Sykes' regulars when he moves. That's you, Winfield, but stay within striking distance astride the turnpike. Lee will turn our way soon enough, and Sykes is only one division."

"The rest of Meade's force is just north and could support Sykes as well."

"You see the high ground to our front? We should take and hold it."

Hancock explained about the commanding terrain and requested Couch take a look for himself.

"Hooker sees it, and Hunt, especially Hunt!"

Hancock was confident that Couch understood, and his reference to General Hunt and his artillery would drive the point home. Couch was interested in placing his reserve artillery batteries on the best ground, and the ridgeline offered an excellent position.

"You will move tomorrow morning."

Hancock smiled and headed for the division. Battle was on the horizon.

Hooker issued orders for the Army to move eastward against Lee's flank and rear. Sykes' division, of Meade's V Corps, marched east on the Orange Turnpike, with Hancock's division positioned in support, a mile behind at the wood line.

Meade secured Banks Ford, where Hancock had stationed a single company in anticipation of the mission.

Slocum's XII Corps, followed by Howard's XI, marched along the Orange Plank Road, south of the turnpike, securing the Tabernacle Church along the way, where Hooker planned to make his new headquarters.

Dan Sickle's III Corps was ordered forward as a reserve and positioned itself near the Chancellor House. Everything was going as planned, and Hooker was elated.

"I will destroy Robert Lee and make up for the failure at Fredericksburg. I will save the Union!" Hooker thought as he watched Sykes' division move along the Orange Turnpike.

"I can catch the Rebels by surprise while Lee focuses on General Sedgwick. That's enough force to capture his attention."

His mind raced as he turned alternatives over, trying desperately to outthink Lee.

Hancock's division was designated the II Corps reserve. Couch had a follow-on mission from headquarters to move a division to Todd's Tavern, five miles south, and secure Hooker's right flank, on order.

"The thickly wooded area surrounding Chancellorsville needs to be behind us quickly. Then we can maneuver large elements freely and destroy Lee's Army."

Couch continued to review the map. Hancock thought the same thing; a hundred related issues were rushing through his mind as they often did before a fight. Nothing in his outward appearance betrayed the tactical chess moves played out in his mind. He calmly sat on his horse, and soldiers called his name as they passed along the road. He responded to each with some greeting, usually peppered with spicy language. He was their commander, always inspiring, motivating, and leading – he was Hancock! All seemed to be well and the plan solid, he thought, as his division moved behind Sykes. Perhaps it was going too well, as his battle sense told him they ought to have seen Confederate pickets or skirmishers already, as Sykes closed on Lee's left flank.

Army of Northern Virginia

Emboldened by Lee's guidance to "make arrangements to repulse the enemy," Jackson planned to meet the Federal force head-on. Long before the sun rose, Jackson left Fredericksburg with his staff and moved along the turnpike to the Confederate line, arriving at Zoan Church after daylight. He found Lafayette McLaws' headquarters and was directed to the division commander's location, currently overseeing the building of earthworks along the ridgeline. McLaws greeted Jackson.

"Lafayette, stop fortifying this position. We will move west into the attack."

McLaws had alerted his commanders for the possible change based on Lee's war council and sent his aides to inform them to march west.

"We have already prepared for the move, General Jackson. It will take minutes to move the boys onto the road."

"Excellent. I shall see you along the route of march and be prepared to form a line of battle from the march as soon as you see the Federals."

He headed for Anderson's location farther down the ridgeline. The men were also fortifying their positions against the anticipated attack from the west when Jackson ordered them forward into the attack. Anderson's lead skirmishers met Sykes' advancing dismounted cavalry before noon, just west of Zoan Church. The skirmishers scattered as two of Sykes' brigades formed a line of battle and surged ahead. The Battle of Chancellorsville had begun.

"Sir, General McLaws sends his compliments and reports a large number of Union infantry are to his front," the aide reported.

Jackson brought his field glasses and turned towards the officer. "Thank you, lieutenant. Tell General McLaws he must hold his position and assume the fight. I will move to the left with Anderson and Rodes."

Sykes had emerged from the wooded area east of Chancellorsville with his aides and Colonel Patrick O'Rorke, his Third Brigade Commander.

"Sir, it would appear that the Confederates have positioned across the turnpike," O'Rorke observed. McLaws' Confederates were now in front of them.

"We can still move them off that ground. Get this message to Meade: Enemy to our front. It could be Lee's rear guard or a blocking force, as Lee may be aware of our plan. We still have the advantage. I will move forward, but would be greatly assisted by an attack into the Confederate right flank from the river road."

Jackson galloped ahead to observe the Union force. McLaws' first brigade, sitting directly in the Union's path, had slowed the advance. Jackson could hear the tempo of the battle increasing as the remainder of McLaws' division entered the fight, bringing the Union to a standstill and threatening Sykes as the Confederates spread north and south of the turnpike. The Rebel artillery found Sykes' line and began taking its toll. The explosions and impact of the case shot slowed the Union advance, but the regiments moved forward. Rounds hit among the lines, in many cases taking groups of men in a single blast. The sounds of war were everywhere. McLaws' infantrymen were visible on the slope and firing volleys into the oncoming Union brigades.

Jackson rode up to McLaws, moving with his brigades forward of the high ground.

"General, hold your ground. I will move my divisions to the left and strike their right flank."

He turned to his aide. "Get to General Rodes and tell him to meet me at Anderson's location."

The bullet whizzed past McLaws, who gave Jackson an expression that said this was nothing unusual. Jackson remained stoic but thought it quite amusing that McLaws, like most generals, shrugged off the close calls as annoying. Jackson immediately rode to Anderson, only a half-mile behind and on the turnpike, and Rodes joined them within minutes.

"I want to move at the double-quick down the Orange Plank Road. McLaws will hold the Federals along the turnpike. General Anderson, you move first, followed by General Rodes. I'll move with you."

Anderson's brigades moved more than a mile forward of McLaws' position on the turnpike as they tried to maneuver around the right of Sykes' division. Jackson could see his lead division halted as they slammed against the XII Corps and six brigades in the line of battle across the Orange Plank Road.

Army of the Potomac

Hancock watched from his front line, anxious to get into the fight. He moved nervously in the saddle. Couch had ridden forward and watched as Sykes' division came under fire. Union artillery sounded from behind their position and could be heard from Meade's location well to the left of the line. The rounds had their intended effect on the Rebels along the ridge, giving Sykes precious seconds to move forward.

"He's in trouble. It appears the Confederates are moving more infantry into the fight. If they get their guns on that ridge, Sykes could have more trouble."

"We are not ordered in yet, Winfield."

Hancock's blood was rising, battle senses reaching their peak, and he wanted to surge forward in support of Sykes, as initially ordered. Confederate artillery was finding its way between Sykes and Hancock's division with effect.

Hooker was in the Chancellor House listening to the fight that had begun to the east. The rider reined in his horse and handed the message to Butterfield, who stood at the bottom of the stairs leading up to the veranda and Hooker. Saluting, the rider held in place for a response he could return to Sykes.

"We have made contact with the enemy, and he is reinforcing in our front. We can carry the ridge and move forward down the turnpike with support. Signed, Sykes."

The battle's tempo increased, and Hooker began to question his earlier plan. The Confederates had reacted much quicker than he had anticipated. Hooker paused for a moment.

"Send this to all the corps. You are to withdraw to the vicinity of the Chancellor House and assume your original positions of 30 April. Effective immediately."

Butterfield was stunned and began to question the directive, but Hooker cut him off.

"I'll not risk the Army here. I expected to meet Lee much closer to Fredericksburg, not this far west. We will consolidate and strengthen our defenses here and entice Lee to attack us."

Hancock would not wait longer and moved his force to the left of Sykes. Riding with his aides, Hancock personally scouted the position and, a mile from Chancellorsville came upon Mott's Run, a ravine in which Nelson Miles and his New York regiments were posted as skirmishers.

"How are you, Miles? Everything is well in hand, I see."

Hancock rode to the edge of the position. Miles was as aggressive and fearless as Hancock, and the general knew well he could depend upon the infantry officer.

"Sir, we are in a strong place. The Confederates keep pressing us and have been since morning. It may be A.P. Hill's men under Heth. Might still be McLaws, but we continue to give them hell and roll them back with each assault."

The occasional musket round zipped past them as an enemy sharpshooter sought mounted Federals, most often officers.

Hancock shrugged. "I expect this will go on all day. They are reforming. You are the center of the line and the rock, Miles. Hold here; these sonsofbitches will keep coming. If you need support, send a runner to me, and I'll handle it personally. I'm damn glad it's you holding this ground."

The artillery shell screamed past the two officers and exploded not more than twenty yards away. Hancock immediately felt the shrapnel hit his back, and his horse shuddered as the small metal fragments entered his hindquarter.

"Close, but insignificant this time," Hancock chuckled. Miles well understood. He had not fully recovered from his Fredericksburg wounds.

"Sir, perhaps you should check the regiments farther back," Miles joked, a broad grin on his face.

"It is bastards like you that keep me coming to the forward lines, Nelson. Take care of yourself."

Hancock signaled his aides and rode back along the line to the right.

Couch, like Hancock, had an overwhelming desire to be at the front in a fight. Riding with Hancock, he had just gotten the latter's division into position and moved forward towards Sykes when General Gouverneur Warren, the Army's chief engineer, rode up to the turnpike with a small escort.

"I hope to God this isn't bad news. Here comes Warren, and I expect he wants to survey the ground and report back to Hooker."

Warren personally brought Hooker's order to Couch and handed the circular to him without comment.

"Something was very wrong when G.K. had nothing to say," Hancock thought to himself. Couch read the order to the officers, who were dumbfounded.

"The battlefield was one that the Army of the Potomac had always been crying out for – one on which they could see the enemy they were called to fight and destroy him," Couch said.

"Withdraw?" Hancock was louder and more animated than usual. Sykes had joined the generals, and they were unanimous in their opinion – do not yield the position.

"We have just arrived and received orders to withdraw all the troops."

Hancock repeated to the small group, trying hard to keep his temper from rising.

"This is a costly and Goddamned mistake. Are we sure we understood correctly?"

"There is no mistake, but I will go to Hooker and recommend we push forward."

The Commanding General had abandoned Banks Ford, vacated the position Meade had gained on Lee's flank, conceded the high ground out in the open won by Sykes, and pulled all his troops back to the Wilderness, to take their positions around Chancellorsville. Hancock could see a replay of Burnside's missteps at Fredericksburg, and the force would, unfortunately, pay the price. This time it was even more perplexing.

Couch and Hancock headed back to the headquarters at the Chancellor House. Along the turnpike, they met General Slocum, who was equally angry and confused over the order.

"Darius, what in the hell does he mean by this? We've just made contact and he is running! I'm heading his way."

There was anger in each of Slocum's words.

Couch could not explain the order.

"I'm on the way myself. I'll ride with you to find Hooker. For God's sake, Meade is well along the river road and could easily support action on the turnpike. He had seven corps!"

The three arrived at the headquarters and were intercepted by Butterfield.

"I understand why you are here, and the Commanding General is looking to bring Lee in close."

"Well, he can't get any closer than being in contact and fighting. I just made contact with a force trying to maneuver around to the right. We're giving up ground that we must have to maneuver. Where is Hooker?"

The Commanding General walked into the room and said, "I want the Army to assume a defensive posture near this area. I believe Lee will take the opportunity to attack."

"Joe, the Army pushed forward on all three avenues and is in a commanding position. We can maneuver. Moving back into the wooded area, although clear for a short distance around this house, gives the initiative to Lee."

Hooker was adamant and repeated his directive to defend rather than attack.

"We expected to meet Lee's rear guard somewhere. It appears to be a division, and we can sweep them from the field if we support Sykes' division. My division is already in position and tasked with that mission." Hancock was fully aware that he need not repeat what happened with Burnside.

"You will comply with my orders and pull back into a defensive line around the Chancellor House."

Hooker raised his voice more forceful.

"If we have a solid defense, we can force Lee to attack us in the same manners as that we crashed against the wall in Fredericksburg. Let him come! Do I make myself clear?"

"Sir, we can win here. However, we will execute your orders as given," Slocum replied. The three generals saluted and departed the headquarters.

Mounting up, Couch turned to Butterfield, who had walked out with them.

"Dan, this could end badly for us. I don't know what happened, but I believe Hooker's confidence is shaken."

The three generals departed for their respective commands. As they rode, Hancock said, "Hooker is a whipped man, and we've just started this fight."

CHAPTER 26
JACKSON'S SWEEP

Army of Northern Virginia

Lee and Jackson sat on camp chairs beside a fire, only steps from the Plank Road. Behind them were their staffs, all accustomed to listening to their Commanding General and prepared to respond when he asked for their opinion on the developing plan. With Longstreet and two of his divisions in the south, Lee discussed the possibility of maneuvering around the large Union force. Audacity had always marked Lee's planning, and this would be no different. Jackson was of the same breed.

"When they pulled back, I was not far from the Chancellor House, perhaps a mile. Their defense had hardened, so I didn't push the assault any farther," Jackson said with resignation, almost uncharacteristically, and Lee took immediate notice.

"Stuart reported that Hooker's right flank is 'in the air.' I estimate the enemy strength to be at least double of ours," Lee said, "but they leave us an opening I cannot ignore."

Jackson paused for a moment.

"If that is correct, and I do not doubt it is so, then we must come up with a plan to maneuver around that force and surprise him on either flank."

"We have both watched Hooker move his many corps back, and he is in a defensive position around Chancellorsville."

"I believe we can get around them on the right and strike both the flank and rear, as he had planned to do to us. The wooded area is thick and likely treacherous at night, and I am not familiar with the small roads that would help us negotiate the ground. I would recommend we try the flanking movement, regardless. With the right size force, I could roll up his regiments."

"I agree; his right is the best option. What do you propose?"

"I will take my entire command around the Union right. I would leave McLaws' and Anderson's divisions here with you to counter the Union force on the right, should they finally move from the plain in front of Prospect Hill."

"That will leave about 15,000 soldiers behind, and that is adequate. I approve of your recommendation. You should make plans to move as early as possible."

"Sir, Reverend Lacy knew of a local man who could help with the route of march. His name is Wellford, and he has marked out a route."

Jackson reviewed the map, calling for his division commanders. It would be daylight before the large force began its move. They pulled back from the Union lines and, using Furnace Road, started their long sweep around Hooker. Wellford knew the roads and trails very well, and the route allowed the 30,000-man column to move through the dense underbrush.

Army of the Potomac

With Sykes withdrawing, Hancock stretched his division to the right and connected with Geary's left flank. Enemy artillery occupied the eastern ridgeline and opened fire on the Federals from a position abandoned when Hooker ordered the withdrawal. The ground sloped down to the wood line where Zook, Caldwell, and Brooke's brigades dug in. Miles' New York Volunteers, with four new regiments, held the forward line of rifle pits and continued to turn back all Rebel assaults sent against them.

Sickles called up from Fredericksburg, positioned a division forward, near Hazel Grove. His pickets watched as part of Jackson's force became visible at the edge of the clearing. Hooker was notified and recognized the move as a flanking maneuver against his right and alerted his corps commanders. Sickles personally observed the column turning south and headed for Hooker's headquarters.

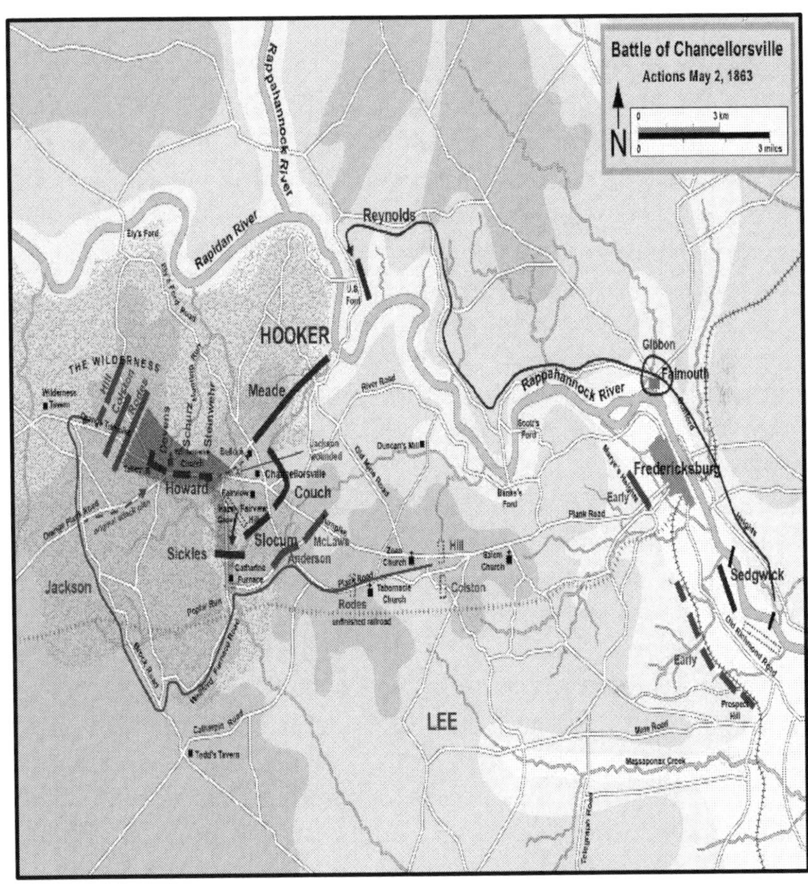

"Time is critical here, Joe. Let me get after them before they get away."

Sickles didn't want to miss the opportunity to engage the Confederates before they escaped to the west. Hooker was unsure, but the persuasive New York politician-turned-combat-general convinced him to, at least, let him attack the rear of the Rebel column.

"They are moving away from Chancellorsville. Shit, Joe, let's make them hurt a bit more. Lee is running away."

Hooker relented, approving the action and shifted brigades in support of Sickles. He unintentionally created a gap in his line between Howard's far-right corps and the main body near Chancellorsville.

Army of Northern Virginia

Jackson's men marched twelve-miles to the south arriving at the intersection of the Brock Road and Orange Turnpike in mid-afternoon. Turning east, the Confederates moved closer to the right flank of the Federals. The ground proved difficult as Jackson's division and brigade commanders tried to form into a line of battle. Oliver Howard's Corps was thinly spread westward along the turnpike with their flank unsecured, and daylight was fading. In response to Hooker's earlier warning that the Confederates may be moving to flank the Army, Howard assigned his two rightmost regiments to face west. Little had been done to prepare for what was about to happen. The battle senses faded as Union soldiers relaxed, believing that Lee was further east, likely facing the other corps.

The long march did little to drain the anticipation and excitement as Jackson's force reached the old turnpike near 4:00 p.m., about three miles behind Chancellorsville. Quietly, slowly, the corps deployed into three echelons over the next two hours. When each division arrived, they formed at right angles to the road – Rodes in front; Trimble's division, commanded by Colston, in the second line; and A. P. Hill's in the third. The line stretched more than a mile. Stonewall was satisfied that he would take Hooker by surprise and cut a swath through the blue formations. "I'll bring an end to the Army of the Potomac, God willing."

With a chilling Rebel yell early in the evening, hundreds of men crashed into the two surprised Union regiments two miles west of Chancellor house. The initial volley tore into Howard's infantrymen, bringing down scores. Men scrambled for their stacked weapons and died before they could reach them. More were killed as they brought their weapons up in a vain attempt to return volley fire. Some men ran, and company officers attempted to form lines and stem the advance of Jackson's infantry. They quickly swept over the Union lines.

The soldiers ran back, attempted to form a line, fired sporadically, then ran again. Each time, they left a line of soldiers as evidence of their attempt. Always aggressive, Jackson followed with two more divisions, and for 90 minutes, the lines pushed so hard that the Federals were unable to create enough distance to mount an effective defense. Soldiers melted away from the Confederate volleys, and the line began to roll up. Resistance was piecemeal. Howard personally rode into the fray to rally his retreating line and sent word to redirect the artillery to engage the Confederate wave.

Army of the Potomac

Hancock could hear the battle on the right flank and rear of the Army. It was drawing closer as Jackson's divisions pressed the Eleventh Corps.

"Get the damned second line turned. We'll take the enemy on right here. We can break this advance."

Hancock rode along the rear of the division, his first line of battle repelling McLaws' assaulting infantry from the east. Colonel Nelson Miles emplaced his New York Infantry on the line facing east towards Fredericksburg. Hancock was aware of the danger of fighting across the lines of communication and the confusion it would inevitably create.

Hancock and Caldwell rode along the line and had observed McLaws' regiments marching up to the abatis, then beaten back by Miles' New Yorkers. Couch had arrived at the same time.

"Hancock, move your division to the left and take a position along the road from the Chancellor House to United States Ford. I want you in a position to advance against the enemy sweeping across our rear. Our line of communication is vulnerable. I'm moving a battery near the house to assist Geary. He's hard-pressed."

Couch spurred his horse, and the animal started to go down, a large piece of shrapnel missing the general and tearing into the horse's neck, killing it instantly. The agile corps commander was up and over the front of the horse as it went down, rolling quickly and upon his feet again. Finding his aide, Major Burt, the general waved that he was alright. Burt found a new mount for the general, and they were off within minutes.

Hancock prepared to issue the orders when General Hooker galloped up with his escort of cavalry.

"Hancock! Damn glad it's you in this position. Leave a brigade here and keep your line of battle focused on the turnpike. We'll handle the Confederate assault in the rear, but I need your division to command the turnpike road."

Army of Northern Virginia

Through the sound of battle in his immediate front, Lafayette McLaws could hear the intense fighting much farther to the west and knew Jackson caught Hooker by surprise and was moving this way.

"This fight may force Hooker back across the river," McLaws thought to himself. They all knew "Stonewall" very well. McLaws would not be surprised if Jackson did not try and kill them all as he passed through the Army of the Potomac. To him, crossing the river would mean a new fight later, and Jackson would prefer to break the back of the Union.

Jackson had driven Howard's corps back, but the Army had finally reacted with a solid defense. The Confederate artillery fired from both the rear and front continuing to find Hancock's infantrymen. The brigades held firmly to their ground, refusing McLaws' and Anderson's day-long series of attack, retire, regroup, and attack again, but never reaching the main line of defense.

Miles was right. He could hold as long as needed. The Confederates never dislodged him, partly because his position was a strong one and, as Hancock knew well, mainly to the tenacity of Miles as the forward commander.

Hancock listened to the action in the rear until after midnight, and to the sporadic firing on his right, where Geary's line fought throughout the day. Darkness enveloped the battlefield, even darker in the tangled woods of the Wilderness. The Confederates had swarmed over the XI Corps, driven them back two miles, but the rest of the Army remained firm.

The rapid thrust of three divisions, moving through the tangled woods, and the approaching darkness combined to break all unit cohesion of Jackson's force. Commanders tried to bring order to the chaos, without success. Jackson, aware of the problem, rode forward of the line and prepared to continue the advance. One forward element, mistaking their commander and his party for Union soldiers, opened fire and wounded Jackson.

"Sir, General Jackson is down." Lee heard the words, but his mind would not accept them. Taylor waited for the questions that may follow, but Lee remained quiet.

"General Jackson, when?"

"A few hours ago, while he was surveying the line."

"How serious is the wound? Is it mortal? Please find out from the doctors, if you will, Major Taylor. I will see him when we settle here. Please keep me informed."

Lee called for Stuart. "General Stuart. We have lost General Jackson's services. You will assume command of the corps."

Army of the Potomac

Throughout the day and into the evening, there were periodic attacks on Hancock's lines, and Miles continued to repel each one. Hancock observed Miles throwing back one of McLaws' attempts.

"Isaac, ride down there and tell Miles I said he is worth his weight in gold."

With a yell, Parker spurred his horse and headed for Nelson Miles' regiment. Hancock recognized a true leader when he saw one. Miles was a warrior with no formal military training nor education, who had distinguished himself at Antietam and Fredericksburg. Hancock thoughtfully planned his moves regarding his division and wanted to ensure nothing would interrupt Miles' command position.

"If he can stay out of the way of a bullet or artillery round, and that is nearly impossible given Miles' propensity to be in the thick of things, then I'll make sure the regiments I send to him have colonels who are junior. I don't need any seniority arguments when I see that Nelson Miles is the right man."

The Confederates were pressing hard on his line, and Hancock wondered if these were merely supporting attacks.

"What the hell is Lee doing? Just how many Confederates are behind us?"

Hancock could hear the sound of the battle in the rear starting to die down, but his aides were about to find out. The enemy, commanded by his old friend, Henry Heth, was advancing in line of battle, having emerged from the wooded area into the open plain. Hancock ordered his line to face about taking a position on the Plank Road in line with Colonel Cross' 5th New Hampshire, anchoring his right flank on the turnpike, and securing the supporting artillery batteries deployed around the Chancellor House. The artillery opened and held Heth's advance back. The Confederate artillery moved forward and bombarded Hancock's brigades from multiple directions.

Hooker stood on the veranda of the Chancellor house, leaning with his back against one of the many columns. With the number of artillery rounds, both Union and Confederate, passing through the area, no one could warn the general of the round that struck the column just opposite him. The impact of the shot and the resulting explosion threw Hooker from the veranda as if he were a toy. The staff, some standing and some mounted, watched in horror as Hooker was propelled into the air, landing hard about 10 feet from the house.

"Christ, they've killed him," an orderly yelled.

The aide jumped from his horse and ran to Hooker. Butterfield was stunned.

"You may be right," said the aide-de-camp anxiously.

Butterfield leaped from the veranda to the yard below in one large bound, as the unconscious Hooker lay face down on the lawn. The staff approached Hooker and noticed little, if any, blood, but hesitated for a second to turn the general over. He stirred, and, to their amazement, rolled over and rose to a kneeling position.

"What the hell happened?"

"Sir, we've called for the doctor. You were blown off the veranda by artillery," Butterfield responded, kneeling beside Hooker, who then rose to his feet and, waving the officers away, said, "I'm Goddamned alright. I must see to the corps." Before they could stop him, the general was off but halted before he entered the wood line. Dismounting again, he called for Butterfield, "I need to see Couch. He is to assume control, but I still command."

Couch received word that the Hooker needed to see him.

"Winfield, take care of things here. I see you are covering a large front on your own, and I will get you as much help as I can."

Couch departed Hancock's line and headed for the open field in the rear of Chancellorsville. The small section of tents was the new headquarters of the Army of the Potomac. As he rode into the area, Couch saw Meade, still mounted and accompanied by his aide and son, George. Greeting Meade, Couch dismounted and was approached by Dan Butterfield.

"I am not sure whether the general has all of his faculties," Butterfield said to Couch.

Hooker was resting inside one of the tents.

"Darius, you have control of the Army, but I want you to withdraw the Army to a new position north of here with the ford at your back. We must be prepared to cross to the other side of the Rappahannock. Sedgwick should already be on the move against Lee in Fredericksburg."

"Hooker has lost his nerve," Couch thought as he listened to the directions.

The hard-fought Army was in his hands. He'd see how the general was upon his return.

"Major Burt, take the order to the commanders to retire."

Along the front lines, Hancock rode to his left and came upon Sykes' right flank regiment countering another Rebel assault. They were slowly giving way. Sickles was on Hancock's right and had started to withdraw.

"Sonofabitch, will no one hold their positions? Very soon, we'll have to face the enemy from both directions. The line must hold. Get back to Couch and tell him I can stay here only a short time without support."

Riding to the sound of the guns, Hancock directed alternating fire from one direction to another. He was facing Lee's Army alone and fighting on two fronts – one facing Fredericksburg, the other towards Gordonsville with the lines about a half-mile apart. The Confederate artillery fired continuously, and rounds passed over Hancock's lines from front and rear, while more guns were positioned to support deadly enfilading fire. The infantry regiments were suffering heavy losses.

Riding with Bingham, Wilson, and Mackenzie, he returned to the Chancellor House and could see Rebel battle flags less than 500 yards away. His 14 pieces of supporting artillery, positioned close by, fired round after round as the Union cannoneers halted the Confederate advance. The counter-battery fire took a deadly toll on the cannoneers. Hot metal from exploding shells also struck the house being used as a hospital, creating a fire that threatened scores of wounded soldiers inside.

Hancock immediately turned to Wilson.

"Lieutenant Wilson, get over to Colonel Brooke and tell him I need soldiers to help pull the wounded out of that building. Then come find me along the line."

The aide was off at a gallop and returned to the Chancellor House within minutes with a detail. Brooke had anticipated the same requirement and had already directed a detachment to go to the aid of the medical staff. Dismounting short of the house, Wilson yelled at Brooke's infantrymen, "Follow me."

Without hesitation, the squads of men rushed in and began carrying wounded out. Sergeant Yergey and Corporal Rahn, with privates Detwiler and Rhoads, of the 53rd Pennsylvania Volunteers, rushed to the second floor. Flames darted across the ceiling, and the screams of men unable walk echoed through the house. Yergey turned right and saw one unfortunate, already being consumed by the fire. He saw another soldier, legs amputated, attempting to crawl away from the building's flames. He picked the man up, threw him over his shoulder, and moved down the stairs. Privates Detwiler and Rhoads were just clearing the bottom stair with a litter when an artillery round struck just beyond the veranda. The two men and their litter patient pitched forward, all three hitting the ground hard, the pillar of the house to their left shielding them from the blast and taking the shrapnel instead of them. Lieutenant Wilson ran over to assist and, getting the two men up, continued to the wood line to leave their charge. They turned and raced back into the building for another helpless soldier.

"Get the hell up here," Rahn yelled when the two privates re-entered the building.

"On the way, Corporal."

Detwiler bounded up the stairs. Smoke filled the house, making it almost impossible to see and breathe. The room filled with soldiers, many of whom were amputees. Each man picked up a fellow soldier and headed for the stairs. Lieutenant Wilson was inside on the first floor directing traffic out the main door of the house and into the surrounding yard. There was no safe place on the battlefield, but at least they were away from the fire.

Infantrymen carried wounded on litters, tables, chairs, and in many cases, in their arms to bring them safely out and away from the fire. The lieutenant had the wounded soldiers placed just short of the clearing, towards the edge of the woods, to provide some measure of cover afforded by the trees. Confederate artillery was still having its deadly effect on the battle lines, and the occasional round found its way to the exposed groups of wounded men.

Couch found Hancock along the battle line to the east.

"Winfield, your position is strong. I need your division to cover the line as Sickles and Slocum pass through and establish their positions near the Bullock house, behind Chancellorsville. Withdraw the division once Sickles has retired."

Hancock turned to Wilson, who had just returned.

"Wilson, go to the batteries near the Chancellor House and tell them to move back along the road leading to the ford. I'll place them when they arrive." Wilson spurred his horse and was gone.

"Bingham," he said, "go back to Brooke and tell him I wish him to withdraw towards United States Ford about one-half mile. I will tell Zook and Caldwell. The commanders should meet me along the road, and I'll place them on a new line."

Within an hour, the division moved. Hancock found Meagher's brigade along the route of march posted in a wooded area securing an artillery battery. Caldwell's brigade was to the right of Meagher. Hancock pulled the artillery pieces and the regiments forming a new front line of battle. He occupied the left of a salient created as the Army withdrew the corps towards the ford. The soldiers quickly went to work to strengthen their line with rifle pits and abatis. Hancock was confident his regiments would hold as long as Couch required.

The Confederate artillery rained down from all sides, but Hancock's division held as the III and XII Corps withdrew to the rear. Casualties started to mount as Lee continued to push the Union corps, collapsing their line and forcing the Army of the Potomac into a tighter defensive perimeter. Stuart's force pressed onward and by mid-morning linked the wings of the Army.

Army of Northern Virginia

Lee and his small staff galloped along the Plank Road to McLaws' headquarters.

"My compliments to the General. You have done well. The Federals appear to be moving into a tighter perimeter. You've, no doubt, heard the sounds of battle in the east around Fredericksburg. The Federals have attacked and gained the heights. General Early's soldiers fought gallantly, but have withdrawn and are close to Salem Church. I don't understand the Federals' caution after seizing the heights, but it is no less appreciated and affords us an opportunity. I want you to turn your division about and move east, joining General Early. We will attack towards Fredericksburg and take back the ground."

Searching east, McLaws said, "I will resupply along the way and should arrive at Salem Church by early afternoon. I must disengage from this line. Anderson's flank will be in the air."

"I believe Hooker has lost his taste for the offense, although I cannot say the same for some of his subordinate generals. Sickles and Hancock come to mind. However, I feel that pulling your division back from the line will not cause a problem for General Anderson. I have plans for his division, as well."

McLaws saluted, and Lee rode off along the line to the south headed for Anderson's division. He could see success in his grasp on both fronts but knew he must move. The risk was something that he accepted, but his confidence in the soldiers and his commanders always compensated for it. Chancellorsville reinforced that feeling. Anderson waited for Lee behind the line on the Plank Road.

"Good morning, Sir. We have them with their backs to the river. My only regret is General Jackson is not here to conduct the final strike. He surprised them when he struck from the west."

"I'm pleased to see you, Richard. General Jackson's loss equally saddens me."

His comment hid the deep sense of loss Lee had felt over Jackson, and the impact his loss would have on the Army.

"Your soldiers have performed superbly. The enemy reeled back, and I'll not question the fact that they possessed twice our number. I have a new task for you and your men."

"We are ready, and the morale is high, Sir."

"General Stuart will continue to press the Union line. I need you to pull back from that line and move to the east. General McLaws is also moving east to Salem Church. You will join him and General Early, who was forced to withdraw from Fredericksburg. I will join you there, and we will move against the Federals coming from the east."

In the early evening, Lee struck Sedgwick from three sides. The Federals collapsed and were forced into a perimeter with their backs to the Rappahannock. Before Lee could destroy Sedgwick's corps, they withdrew across the river.

CHAPTER 27
HOOKER'S DAY IS OVER

Army of the Potomac

Hooker read the communications Butterfield handed him; the expression on the Chief of Staff's face indicating lousy news.

"Goddamn it! Am I just getting this information? Sedgwick says he was fought to a standstill about five miles west of Fredericksburg. He is being pressed on three sides, and plans to cross back over the river."

"Sir, he must use Scotts Ford. We gave up Banks Ford when we pulled Meade. Sedgwick left Gibbon to secure Fredericksburg, and John is withdrawing to Stafford Heights," Butterfield added.

"We were going to crush Lee here. We still have a considerable force available. What if we strike out from this perimeter? Must Lee be limited in forces arrayed against us here? I want to see the corps commanders; get them here!"

The commanders gathered in the early morning hours of 5 May. Many recommended attacking Lee, but Hooker decided to withdraw across the Rappahannock.

Hancock could see that Chancellorsville was lost. His brigades remained in position awaiting the assault from three divisions, proving they could hold their own in a fight. The soldiers were ready.

The lieutenant rode into the headquarters area as if visiting, with little urgency in his gait, and handed the message to Bingham.

"Sir, we have a message from General Couch."

Hancock took the paper and read it silently. Deep within, he expected orders that his division would lead a strike against the Confederates, but the fight was over, and the Army would leave the field. The win was once again in their grasp, and questionable decisions were the bane of the Army of the Potomac.

"We are ordered across United States Ford back to our original position in Falmouth." The new orders disheartened the commanders. Hancock read it in the way his men stood and in their eyes as he quickly scanned each face.

"Our time is coming. We have fought hard and will continue to move forward. We will ultimately succeed in this struggle, and Lee's Army will be defeated, I assure you. I'll not try and explain what has happened here in Chancellorsville. I will continue to do as ordered, and you will all do the same. Look to your brigades. They must withdraw in the face of the enemy and move back across the river. We shall accomplish that mission better than any other division in this Army."

Hancock finished and told Bingham to draft a reply to Couch saying he acknowledged the order, and the division would move at 3:30 a.m. for the bridges. Couch and Hooker were confident that Hancock would protect the withdrawal. Facing off against Stuart's three divisions, Hancock rode along his line, encouraging, motivating, and leading. The division had been in the thick of the fighting for three days and lost over 1,100 men. They would be the last to cross the river.

Army of Northern Virginia

Lee received the news of Lieutenant General Jackson's death as a soldier would, not in disbelief, but with silence and solemnity. He closed his eyes and slowly lowered himself into the chair, trying to understand the impact of so significant a loss to the Army of Northern Virginia, and him personally.

"Major Taylor, have the divisions reported?"

"Indeed they have, Sir. It appears the Federals have suffered severe losses, and their dead and wounded are still on the field, although the dense woods may have had much to do with locating their casualties. We have taken about 5,000 prisoners, 13 cannons, 20,000 stand of arms, and 17 unit colors."

He had severely beaten the Army of the Potomac once again.

Army of the Potomac

Hancock sat quietly in the saddle while his mount grazed in the pasture, absent the ear-shattering sounds of artillery and musketry that marked the area only a few hours before. The evening sun was beginning to set beyond the trees to the west, and he listened to the sounds of one of the regiments settling in for the night, as they secured the flank of the Army. He loved this time of the day as he moved throughout the division area, exchanging words with the officers and enlisted soldiers, inquiring as to their welfare, especially after the battle. It was essential to Hancock that soldiers see their leaders before, during, and after an engagement. He would eventually read the necessary reports furnished to his headquarters from across the division, but spending time with the regiments and companies provided insights fresh in the minds of lieutenants and captains not possible in any correspondence.

Stopping to speak to Caldwell about the day's action, they considered what had happened to the Army in Chancellorsville. Hancock felt downhearted; however, he refused to show feelings of doubt to the thousands who would follow them into battle, seeking direction and inspiration. Although his division did not experience the severe casualties of Fredericksburg, the Army continued to suffer loss at the hands of good officers. Each general had a solid plan, but their inability to execute it with a high degree of agility and adaptability came at a price – in lives.

Winfield chose to confide in Allie, as he had so many times before. He entered his tent and listened to the muffled sounds of his subordinate leaders, giving orders, and settling soldiers in position. The sounds of an Army going about its warfighting business drifted on the spring breeze. He could not help the sinking feeling of yet another engagement lost due to the latest miscalculation by one more Army Commander. Mahan stepped into the tent and set a whiskey and water down on the writing-table. Nodding appreciatively and, taking pen in hand, Winfield began to express his inner-most thoughts to his dear Allie in St. Louis.

"My Dear Wife. I am well, but I must apologize for not writing these last few days. We have been fighting at a crossroads west of Fredericksburg. My division has performed well, but our losses and those of the enemy are heavy. Take comfort that neither John nor I were hurt. I will not be able to come home as we planned. No general officer will be allowed a leave of absence."

His concern for the Army of the Potomac after Antietam, Fredericksburg, and Chancellorsville weighed heavily upon Winfield.

"I am uncertain what will be next for this unfortunate Army. I believe Hooker's day is over. Some periodicals are partial to certain generals among whom I believe Sickles belongs. God help us. If he were to command, it would be too much for me. I would ask to be relieved at once."

He sat back in his chair, taking another sip of the drink.

"I am unsure if I can abide more disappointments like this one. We should have been the victors due to our advantage in numbers, but Hooker refused to commit. I believe Providence intended our defeat on this ground. Earlier, Hooker was heard to say, 'God Almighty could not prevent him from winning tomorrow.' He also told Mr. Lincoln that he would either win or be in hell. The President told him to carry plenty of water."

He and Allie had spoken many times of command positions and selection for promotion, and in her 13th year as an army wife, she understood better than most the political maneuverings that accompanied advancement; and, more to the point, promotion during this turmoil.

"There is much discussion concerning interviews for the Army of the Potomac's Commanding General position. These officers, in their current staff positions, serve as sounding boards for their commanding generals. I have been approached again in connection with the command of the Army. Rest easy; I cannot see a scenario in which I would accept the command. That is a different class of general officers. Besides, the Republicans would not support the decision to place me in command. I refuse to suffer the same criticism as McClellan. Please kiss my dear children for me, and believe me to be, as ever, your fond husband, Winfield."

The II Corps Commander, Darius Couch, was distressed and angered by the failed actions at Chancellorsville. Hancock, accompanied by his brother, John, arrived at the Corps headquarters in the late evening when the stillness of the night provided a welcomed break, and soldiers throughout the force settled down for a short respite. Reporting to Couch, all Hancock could think of was follow-on action and the pursuit of Lee's Army. He started to speak when Couch held up his hand and quietly interrupted.

"Winfield, I am happy that you are safe, and we have some time to talk. Your division fought magnificently, holding off Lee while this Army withdrew across the river, and I am grateful for the effort. I have the pleasure of promoting Captain Hancock to the rank of major."

John appeared startled at the news, while Winfield slapped his brother on the back. Winfield turned to his newly-promoted brother.

"You have a knack for staff and campaign work, brother. I fear your competence portends a shift away from my staff in the future."

Winfield cared deeply for John. He knew that his brother would continue to place himself at his commander's side on the battlefield. Although Winfield was uncomfortable with his brother's decision, he was incredibly proud of John. His brother was courageous and daring – words Winfield could appreciate but words that caused their parents' concern.

Hancock could see the toll these past few months had taken on Couch. The confidence he usually displayed was starting to fade. Hancock was not surprised and thought, "What an untenable position for a corps commander? Couch is a courageous officer who has lost faith in Hooker. No matter, Hooker is on the way out."

Couch confirmed what Winfield was thinking.

"A change is coming. I had to speak with the President during his trip a few weeks ago. I recommended a change in leadership. There are many, no doubt, who see themselves as the Army Commander and would jump at the chance. I would also expect some will be maneuvering their political support for nomination to the position. Then there's George Gordon Meade."

Hancock thought for a moment, and then it struck him that Meade was an excellent choice.

Couch continued, "I believe he is the right officer, and he'll likely say that he isn't suited to command the Army. I have a different opinion and said so to the President. Whether Lincoln takes that recommendation or not is to be seen; however, this Army needs a change."

He paused, weighing his words carefully, knowing that Winfield would be supportive.

"I have asked Halleck to transfer me from this Army. My thoughts of Hooker I will keep to myself. I cannot believe we have squandered yet another opportunity. I feel I can no longer continue under Hooker's command. Headquarters endorsed my request when I was in Washington. I fully expect that command of this Corps will go to you. At least that was my recommendation, once approved."

Hancock, who was equally exasperated with the operation orchestrated by Hooker's minions, studied his commander's face. Couch was a combat veteran of the highest caliber and would not have come to this decision lightly. Hancock was also aware of the constant medical issues that plagued Couch.

"If Halleck follows through with my transfer soon, and I fully expect that he will, you will take command of this Corps within the next couple of weeks. There was never any doubt as to my successor in the II Corps."

"You are aware that I've been asked to command a cavalry corp. If ordered, I will certainly do so; however, my preference would be to stay with the infantry. I do appreciate your recommendation on my behalf. I have been with the II Corps since Antietam, and am well acquainted with these men."

One thing was clear to Hancock that Couch held firmly to the position he was unwilling to lead a corps under Joe Hooker. He was reluctant to wait for the change in Army command that Winfield felt was sure to come, and very soon.

"I would ask you to please reconsider or hold off on your move until Washington makes a decision."

"Hooker may not move for some time. Even though I recommended Meade for the job, Lincoln could take some time deciding."

"I assume I am not the only one who will be called by Stanton and Halleck for an 'interview.' Let's move on to better things. How is the division resupply going? Oh, yes, how is Nelson Miles?"

"He was wounded as the Army withdrew and taken from the field. I watched that young colonel, and, if he survives this war, I fully expect we shall all be working for him one day. He has a marvelous career ahead of him. Miles certainly is gallant and courageous, and is one of the best regimental commanders."

The conversation shifted to the more mundane things associated with readiness and soldiers encamped.

CHAPTER 28
PURSUIT

Washington, D.C.

It was well into the evening at the White House, and Lincoln called for Secretary Stanton and General Halleck to review the latest reports from the field. Mary had come earlier and collected young Tad who loved to play in the rooms adjacent to his father's office. Lincoln favored the boy since his brother, Willie, died only a year before. The late hour made for a tranquil building, a distinct change from the lines of people who, throughout the day, tried to gain access to the President. The stillness magnified the sounds of his senior staff and advisors discussing issues focused on the Army of the Potomac.

"I would do well to hold my temper or the night will carry my voice to the capitol building," he thought to himself.

Lincoln was frustrated with the lack of success by the Army. In many instances, planning for a specific campaign excelled, but the execution always lagged. Since the Rebellion began, there were five general officers appointed to command the Army in the eastern theater alone.

"I'm besieged on all sides, which I don't necessarily mind, but Lord, give me one success that sends the Confederates reeling. This situation is tiresome. It appears to people that command of the Army is a revolving door. I am faced, once again, with managing the Army."

Halleck shifted uncomfortably in his chair. Management of the Army was his job. The President liked Hooker; however, Stanton and Halleck agreed that Hooker should go.

"We must create the conditions where Hooker asks to be relieved or submits his resignation. That way, it would be at the general's request and not my firing, as we've experienced over the last two years," the politically-astute Stanton offered.

Lincoln stopped pacing.

"I cannot believe Hooker held back more than two corps at Chancellorsville. Did he not hear me when I said hold nothing back? As God is my witness, I will find a general who can match Robert Lee."

Halleck rose and walked across the room. "Lee is surely a brilliant tactician, and we continue to play to his strengths."

"Our commanding generals, through delays, miscommunication, hesitation, and disagreements, continue to cede the advantage to Lee," Lincoln added.

"We begin again. The man we seek probably believes he isn't right for the job. Burnside felt that way, but his confidence was shaken. Hooker executed a marvelous plan initially, but gave the initiative to Lee, even though he had thousands of troops uncommitted. Almost to a man, the corps commanders have served gallantly. I have a list of generals for you to consider, and Hay will set up interviews," Stanton replied.

"We must do this quickly and quietly. I've read your report that 30,000 soldiers are completing their term of service in May and June. Let's get on with it."

Lincoln went back to his desk and Hay's daily stack of papers. Over the next few weeks, they quietly spoke with other corps commanders that Halleck and Stanton believed were qualified to command the Army of the Potomac.

"Mr. Secretary, we have spoken with Darius Couch, Henry Slocum, John Sedgewick, and John Reynolds. Perhaps we should consider Winfield Hancock?" Halleck said as Stanton raised his head at the mention of Hancock's name.

"Hancock? He has continued to shine throughout the various engagements. As far as I can determine, the general is well-respected by seniors and subordinates. Hancock is the leader to whom they look in the heat of battle. Why haven't we spoken to him?"

"I have, and Hancock believes he is best suited for command of a division. He also said we have a better selection among the existing list of corps commanders and even recommended we consider someone in the western theater."

Winfield Hancock's service was familiar to the President. Stanton agreed that his name should be forwarded to the President, as well. Each officer was aware that this command position, in particular, had become a bulls-eye for political criticism. Congress already mistrusted the Army's top-level commanders and created a joint committee to review battlefield command decisions. There were few senior officers eager to operate under such oversight – Hancock foremost among them.

Winfield rejected any move to succeed Hooker. Halleck had spoken with him on the possibility of command the day before. He could always confide in Allie, and he missed being able to sit over coffee and lay his inner feelings on the table before her. Allie would naturally ask why he hadn't been selected or at least considered.

"Then, we are agreed?" Halleck said to Stanton.

"We are! Interestingly, we did not consider him initially. Even more interesting, others on the list recommended him."

Stanton rose from behind his desk.

"I will take our recommendation to the President today. Colonel Hardie will carry the orders if the President concurs."

"I fervently hope the new Commanding General takes on Robert Lee as soon as possible," Halleck offered, as he departed Stanton's office.

It took only minutes for Lincoln to decide.

Army of Northern Virginia

The generals relaxed in the parlor of a home along the Orange Turnpike, just outside of Fredericksburg.

There was little action since May, and the Confederate Army was shifting westward from Fredericksburg. Hill's corps still held the ground, keeping Hooker's force in place north of the Rappahannock River.

Lee was supremely confident in the ability of his men. The soldiers had proven themselves time and again over the last two years. Their trust in Lee's leadership bordered on reverence. They held in Antietam, had won in Fredericksburg and Chancellorsville, but each victory bled the Army of its strength, which required replacements. The Union could easily replace its losses in short order. Provisioning the two armies across the Virginia countryside was becoming difficult.

Lee knew well the Army he commanded and its leaders even more so. Longstreet was his steadfast commander. Richard Ewell and Ambrose Hill, Jackson's former division commanders, were battle-hardened. Lee carefully considered each man before selecting them as corps commanders. It was time to move against the Union Army once more, and Lee sought the opinion of the commanders on his proposed plan. They stood over a map spread out before them, Longstreet and Hill, on either side of Lee and Ewell standing to the left of Hill. Each corps commander brought various members of their respective staffs and was accompanied by their division commanders, standing opposite Lee and facing the senior officers. Lee wanted each officer to hear, and more importantly, to comment on the proposed plan. He took a moment to greet the commanders and inquired of each as to their status on the march, so far.

"I wish to take the fight away from Virginia soil. The state has endured much over the last year, and I, as well as President Davis, believe it is time to carry the fight once more to Union ground in Pennsylvania."

Fresh from its victory, Lee believed it was time for the Army of Northern Virginia to campaign in the North. He had lost his most exceptional corps commander, "Stonewall" Jackson. His loss only highlighted the fact that attrition, resulting from defensive battle in Virginia, would ultimately rob the Confederates of some of their best leaders and men.

"The battle must be carried to Union soil. Winning there and destroying the Army of the Potomac north of Maryland would cause public opinion in the Union to change by the fall. People will be disheartened enough to quit, and an independent Confederacy would prevail."

Heth added, "I have read that Lincoln's administration is under renewed attack by Congress and the press for the continued loss they suffer at the hands of this Army."

"I have written to Secretary of War, and I proposed there is nothing to be gained by this Army remaining quietly on the defensive. I am aware that there are difficulties in taking aggressive action with so large an Army in its front. However, a new offensive aimed at the North is worth a trial. All our preparations should be pressed forward with greater vigor."

Hill nodded approvingly. "The bounty available in Pennsylvania would also allow us to provide for our troops while depriving the enemy of a portion of his resources."

Longstreet thoughtfully added, "I believe, Sir, that if we can find the truly advantageous ground and bring the Federals to battle, we can defeat them on their soil. Washington and Baltimore would be within our grasp."

"I wonder how long it will take Hooker to move. I expect he'll continue to screen Washington and keep his force between us and the capital. We could get a jump on him and be halfway up the Shenandoah before they are aware we are on the move," Hill replied.

"General, I believe this is certainly true, and may, once we succeed, cause the North to lose their taste for war and seek peace. They are already war-weary, and the administration can ill afford to suffer another defeat. What is the status of your corps?"

"I believe that if we can identify favorable ground in the North as we have planned, and present ourselves in a manner where General Hooker believes we will threaten

Harrisburg, or possibly south to Washington, we can draw Hooker out to battle and defeat him."

In the very late spring, Lee moved with as much speed as marching infantry would allow, sometimes even to the amazement of their commanders. The Army withdrew from the Fredericksburg and Chancellorsville area, mostly undetected by Hooker. The success in Fredericksburg and, more importantly, Chancellorsville, cleared the way for Davis' approval to move north once again. The Army was transiting the Shenandoah Valley of western Virginia through Maryland. They kept the Blue Ridge between them and the Federals, farther to the east and just north of the Rappahannock River.

Hill's Corps moved along an eastern route from Culpeper to Hagerstown. In the west, beyond the Blue Ridge, Longstreet's Corps and Ewell's Corps moved through Winchester and Martinsburg, crossing the Potomac at Williamsport.

Army of the Potomac

General Butterfield read the communication.

"He may be on the move, but his objective remains unclear."

"I'm skeptical that some major campaign is underway. I need more information on the Confederates. One thing is certain, Lee was lucky at Chancellorsville, and that will not happen again. I'll not risk this Army until I determine his intentions."

Brigadier General John Buford, commanding the First Cavalry Division, was notified that a large portion of the Confederate force was no longer to their front. Buford's troopers scouted forward to report any movement. The Army sat idle for days while they desperately tried to determine Lee's intent. Uncertainty plagued the headquarters as conflicting reports filtered into the staff and to Hooker. The cavalry finally found the enemy.

"Damn it all. Longstreet and Ewell are in the Shenandoah. The Army must move, and Lee has a two-week head start."

Hooker was fuming. Butterfield had already started to prepare the movement order.

Hancock and his brigade commanders were gathered in the division headquarters in Falmouth, discussing the possible shift in position and the Army's dilemma, trying to determine Lee's location and intended objective. Lieutenant Colonel Charles H. Morgan, Couch's Chief of Staff, quickly strode into the makeshift headquarters of the First Division. Smiling, he handed orders to Hancock, who read his assumption of command of the II Corps, dated 10 June 1863. Dismissing the commanders, Hancock pointed towards the field desk and chairs.

"Please sit, Charles, and take a glass with me."

"Thank you, Sir. I believe I will. General Couch sends his regards. He conveyed that you were already aware of the possible change in command."

Corporal Mahan entered and placed the glasses on the desk between the two officers, nodding to Morgan.

Morgan appreciated the respite and an opportunity to talk to his new corps commander. Although Hancock knew Morgan from his many dealings with the headquarters, he also had seen the colonel on the battlefield in Fredericksburg and Chancellorsville. Morgan was brilliant, courageous, and likely the premier chief of staff in the Army of the Potomac.

"Tell me about yourself, Charles."

Hancock was always amiable when relaxing and making conversation with his officers.

"Sir, I graduated from West Point in 1857, and served as General Sumner's chief of artillery, at least initially. When General Couch assumed command, he selected me as his chief of staff."

"Well, you will certainly continue in that role for me. However, I will bring my aides with me. Become acquainted with these outstanding officers quickly. They have been at my side in the thickest of the fighting and are fearless. Every one of them was wounded in Fredericksburg, some multiple times, and have recovered.

I must say you are very familiar. Have we served together before?"

"I was with General Albert Johnson's Utah expedition."

"Excellent! I was a captain serving as quartermaster on that trek across the west." Recognition was clearly showing in his expression.

"General Couch and I have spoken, and he mentioned his pending request for transfer to Halleck. Where is he reassigned?"

"He initially planned on resigning, but it appears the Washington headquarters has plans for him in Harrisburg."

"That is a great decision and one that will benefit the Army. If the command of the First Division falls to me, I recommend General Caldwell for the post. The brigades all are acquainted with him, and he will do well in command."

Hancock had four excellent brigade commanders from which to choose: Zook, Meagher, Brooke, and Caldwell. Halleck's decision and Hooker's endorsement was not a complete surprise and would prove to be significant for the Army of the Potomac.

"Corporal Mahan, pack up, we're moving," Hancock said to his valet positioned only feet away.

"Morgan, tell me about the staff."

When the unexpected vacancy in the II Corps' command developed, Hancock was the logical choice. There was no question about it. He was the outstanding division commander in the II Corps and Army-wide. In less than a year, he gained the admiration and confidence of the soldiers whom he had commanded. Hancock was also a very astute leader who aspired to greater heights, but his focus would be on whatever position he currently held. He relished being at the forefront in battle, inspiring and motivating his soldiers.

Those who knew him understood that Hancock's mere presence instilled confidence. He was excellent in tactical maneuver, cold in his approach, and always composed in battle. Although it pained him to see Couch depart, he could not suppress the feeling that he had prepared for this opportunity all of his life. Hancock was ambitious, confident in his abilities, and fully aware of the responsibility that was inherent in any command.

When he began his correspondence to Allie telling her of the pending command, he was overwhelmed with a desire to see her. "If the men I command have their full confidence in me, then that is all the esteem I would hope for."

"She'd likely read this after I am in command of the corps," he thought. News and the mail always ran a bit slowly, given the circumstances.

"Fighting Joe" was on the move by mid-June and marching the Army northward. The cavalry serves as the eyes of their commander, and Stuart's ride around the right of the Federals failed to provide Lee the necessary information as to the Hooker's correct position and strength. Lee learned, in late June, that Hooker was farther north than he anticipated. The absence of intelligence from Stuart irritated Lee. Hooker suffered from the same affliction – Pleasanton's cavalry and its inability to provide accurate and timely information on Lee's Army.

To effectively move nearly 120,000 soldiers, seven corps, and their supporting units through Virginia, the Army used three separate groups. The I, III, and XI Corps moved through Manassas, then Leesburg, crossing the Potomac River at Edward's Ferry. The V Corps would pass through Manassas Junction, following the first group across the Potomac at Leesburg. The II, VI, and XII Corps would go through Dumfries and Fairfax Court House while covering the displacement of the supplies at Aquia Harbor.

Hancock sat with his three division commanders: General Caldwell, who commanded the First Division, Gibbon the Second, and French the Third.

"Gentlemen, Lee has moved north from Culpeper and is reported in the Shenandoah Valley as we speak. Hooker has ordered the Army to move quickly and stay in between the Army of Northern Virginia and Washington. We are the right flank of the Army and will move through Manassas Junction. We march tomorrow, so ready your divisions."

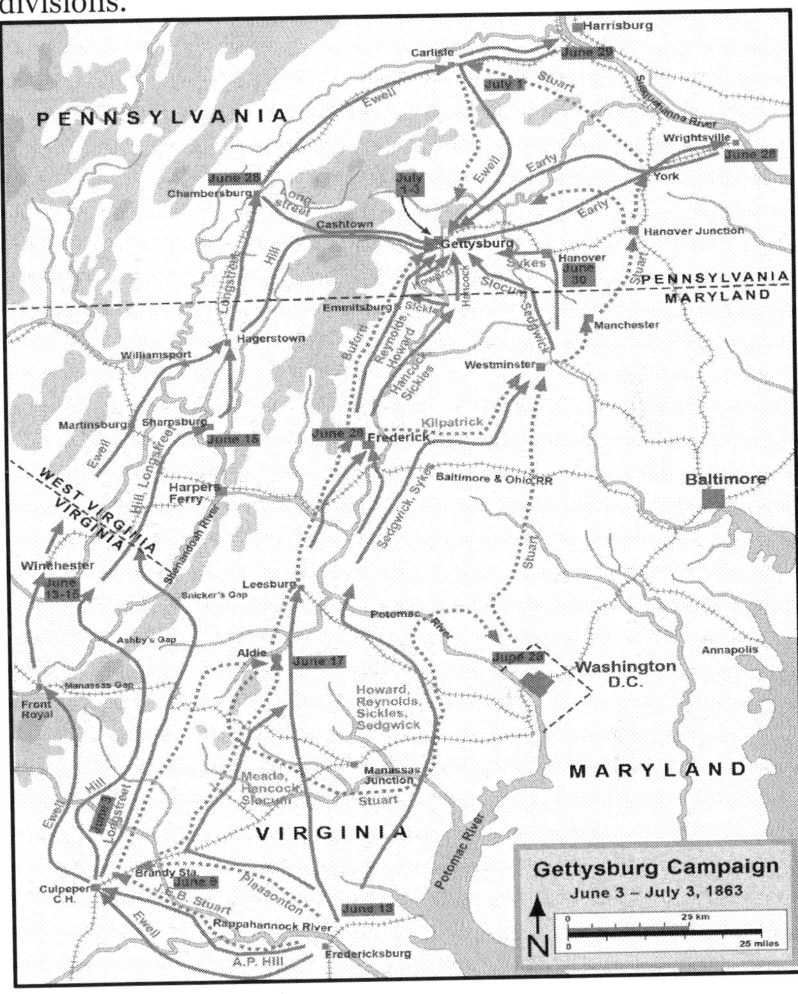

The heat was stifling, and the dust so thick that soldiers had trouble breathing, yet they increased their pace to catch the Rebel Army. The general wiped the sweat away that was running down his face and could feel the soaking wet shirt clinging to his back and arms, the wool uniform jacket adding to the discomfort. If he was uncomfortable, he knew that the rate of march and lack of sleep would combine to exact their toll on the infantrymen. Exhausted troops fell out of the movement, far more than the officers saw in previously forced marches. Hancock was always aware and planned for this contingency. He understood the number would likely increase, and he directed that ambulances assigned to the corps be brought up to the rear of the units and pick up stragglers.

Hancock moved with his troops. Morgan, Parker, and Bingham rode with him and slightly behind. The staff was surprised that the general, in command only eleven days, elicited cheers and greetings from nearly all of the soldiers he passed. The confidence he instilled by his presence became something his staff became accustomed to wherever Hancock went.

"They are pleased the general is in command of the II Corps," Parker said to Morgan.

"I've come to know Hancock as a division commander," Morgan replied, "and Couch was also highly thought of by the men. However, General Hancock's rapport with the soldiers is something to behold."

Hancock turned to his staff, "Charles, send a message to General Hooker that we have secured Thoroughfare Gap. It will not present a problem for the Army. Signed, Hancock."

Morgan handed the note to Bingham, who departed for the headquarters. Both armies moved northward between 15 to 25 miles each day and headed for the Potomac River within the week.

"Sir, General Hays has arrived," Morgan said from outside the tent.

"Alex, get your ass in here."

General Alexander Hays started to walk towards the tent, and Hancock met him just outside. The two generals grasped one another's hand firmly, with Hays putting his hand on Hancock's shoulder.

"What the hell, Alex, are you just getting into this fight?"

"Been here, but I have four New York regiments in my brigade coming to you. We were delayed a bit after we were caught up in the surrender at Harpers Ferry last year."

"It is good to see you. I already have a new position for you. William French is assigned to command Harpers Ferry. I need a division commander, and you are just the right man! We'll cut the orders, and Hooker will approve this without comment. Who is next in seniority to command your brigade?"

"Willard, Colonel George Willard. A good man and someone we both can depend upon without question."

"Very well. Let's talk of times long past, and how you got me started drinking at Benny Haven's."

Hays laughed heartily, and the two friends spent part of the morning over breakfast, coffee, and the occasional lie.

Winfield made his rounds to the regiments along the route of march. It provided time to reflect on his corps, the Army, and the enemy. He could not believe the fates had smiled on him so, and that Alex Hays had joined the II Corps. Later that day, Hancock had just completed his inspection and settled back into his tent to catch up on correspondence when Lieutenant Colonel Morgan reappeared.

"General Alexander Webb has just arrived to speak with you. Oh yes, he is currently unassigned."

"Send him in."

Webb entered the makeshift field office, and they spoke for a short time. Winfield was well-pleased with the new brigadier and assigned him to John Gibbon's division to command the Philadelphia Brigade.

The Corps crossed the Potomac and moved forward another twenty-five miles, arriving at Monocracy Junction a day later. Lee had long since crossed, and Ewell was well into Pennsylvania and heading towards Harrisburg. Couch readied his force in Harrisburg and anxiously waited for the Army of the Potomac to find Lee before he crossed the Susquehanna.

AFTERWORD

Army of the Potomac

Captain George Meade was up and seated at a desk in the headquarters. He greeted Hardie and pulled the pocket watch from his vest – it was nearly 3:00 a.m. and quiet. The air was still warm from the heat of the previous day. The occasional sounds of soldiers rustling about and horses stirring carried through the fields where the corps headquarters sat.

The march had been hard on everyone. General Meade had just settled down himself for what he hoped would be a good three hours of restful sleep. His staff was instructed to wake him before dawn. Captain Meade was hesitant to disturb his father, but even the captain understood the gravity of having a colonel from Washington within the headquarters at this hour.

"Thank you, Captain. I must see General Meade immediately." The tone of his voice indicated that the delay was out of the question.

"Sir, the general is in his tent asleep. If you accompany me, I will wake him."

George peered inside the tent and could see his father sleeping on the cot.

"General Meade, Colonel James Hardie is here from Washington."

Meade stirred. He immediately swung his legs around to the side of the cot and sat upright. Pausing to clear his head, he acknowledged his son's announcement with a nod. It took only a second for the name to register.

"Hardie, yes, from Washington. Send him in. What the hell time is it?" Meade asked as he cleared his head of the deep sleep.

The colonel entered and said, "It's 3:00 a.m., and I've come to give you trouble."

Hardie then apologized for the late hour but reassured Meade that he was directed by Lincoln to handle an urgent matter.

Meade asked, "What could be so critical at this hour."

Hardie paused and, opening his leather satchel, removed the two documents Halleck and Stanton had given him. Handing them to General Meade, he requested the general open the President's first.

"... Hooker is relieved of command of the Army of the Potomac. Major General George G. Meade is appointed to command.... Signed, A. Lincoln, 28 June 1863."

George Gordon Meade was the new Commanding General of the Army of the Potomac.

Late in the evening, Hancock, Morgan, and Mitchell sat near the small fire as Mahan placed another log. Sparks rose slowly in the night air as the three men watched, lost in thought about home, the exhausting march, and Robert Lee. The messenger walked forward, breaking the silence, and handed Morgan the paper.

"It seems we have a new commander. George Meade now commands the Army."

Hancock turned slowly, nodding approval.

"I thought Reynolds or perhaps Sedgwick, but I had not considered George Meade."

"Sir, do you expect our plans will change?" Mitchell asked quietly.

"Gentlemen, under George Meade, our next meeting with Lee will be a turning point for this Army. God knows we are ready for it."

Army of Northern Virginia

General Lee and Major Taylor rode through Messersmith Woods, near Chambersburg, and halted before the small house his Chief of Staff, Colonel Chilton, identified as Lee's new headquarters. Seeing the senior officers only added to Lee's frustration by the absence of his cavalry commander, Major General Stuart. Had he not been clear, or, perhaps he had given the false impression that Stuart was free to move through the Maryland and Pennsylvania countryside setting his objectives.

"We have very little information on the enemy," he began. "I am aware the Federals are near Frederick, Maryland. I want to choose the ground where we will meet them and, given our dispersion throughout this area, we may be open to attack. Therefore, we must consolidate."

Longstreet remarked, "It appears that Joe Hooker no longer commands the Yankee Army. Yesterday he was relieved and replaced by George Meade. Good soldier, a real fighter."

Lee was familiar with most of the Union officers' corps and his chief opponents, the former Army of the Potomac commanders. Meade was the latest of four within the past twelve months.

Lee searched for the right words as he considered this latest information regarding yet another change in Union command, but no less confident that the Army of Northern Virginia would succeed, regardless. Always the professional, who had likely served with many of these officers, both blue and grey, Lee nodded thoughtfully and, glancing at his commanders, acknowledged the new Union Army commander's innate capability.

"In Fredericksburg, Meade had nearly broken the right of our line on Prospect Hill against General Jackson. If reinforced in time, it might have been a different fight," Lee observed. "He will commit no mistakes on my front," he continued, "and should I make one, he will be quick to seize upon it."

More for himself than the others, the assembled leadership of the Army still took Lee's words to heart.

Gettysburg was close. With its convergence of roads and a rail line, General Lee ordered his force to concentrate there as soon as possible. Major General Stuart had yet to provide his commander with information on the Army of the Potomac's location and strength. Lee reasoned there are times when an Army moves on incomplete information, and the best intelligence one has, given the circumstances. He disliked decisions made on such limited information. Taylor and Chilton knew that well, but noted uncertainty was almost foreign to their commander, who continuously exuded an air of confidence in anything the Army would attempt. If there were doubts, Lee would not show it.

* * *

In 72 hours, the Army of the Potomac would find Lee, and Winfield Hancock would become George Meade's most trusted field commander. The tide would finally turn for Meade, the Army of the Potomac, and President Lincoln in a Pennsylvania town named Gettysburg.

ACKNOWLEDGMENTS

General Hancock's story would not have been possible without the factual information detailing the chronology of his life and career, and the very detailed accounts of major military engagements in which Winfield Hancock played a prominent role. The list of various works by historians, academics and authors are listed herein. I wish to thank the authors, archivists, and subject matter experts who provided encouragement, support, and assistance in the preparation of this book. In particular:

Nancy Sullivan, Archivist, Historical Society of Montgomery County

Bruce Stocking, Historian, *The Winfield Scott Hancock Society*

Francis Augustine O'Reilly, Ranger/Historian, Fredericksburg National Military Park, Fredericksburg, Virginia; Author: *The Fredericksburg Campaign*

Greg Mertz, Ranger Supervisor, Fredericksburg/Chancellorsville/Spotsylvania National Military Park, Fredericksburg, Virginia

The Rangers of the Gettysburg National Military Park Ranger Program

Dr. Perry Jamieson, Author: *Hancock at Gettysburg*

U.S. Army Historical Education Center (USAHEC), Carlisle, Pennsylvania

United State Military Academy (USMA) Library, West Point, New York

Sarasota Public Reference Library, Venice, Florida

United States Library of Congress, Manuscript Division, Washington, D.C.

James H. Kelly

Maps

Civil War Maps provided with permission of Hal Jespersen, www.cwmaps.com, (Creative Commons Attribution 3.0 license; http://www.cwmaps.com/freemaps.html).

Center for Military History Publications

Carney, Stephan A., *The Occupation of Mexico May 1846-July 1848, The U. S. Army Campaigns of the Mexican War; CMH Publication 73-3.*

Jamieson, Perry D., and Wineman, Bradford A., *The Maryland and Fredericksburg Campaigns 1862-1863; CMH* Publication 75-6.

Kolakowski, Christopher L., *The Virginia Campaigns, March-August 1862; CMH Publication 75-5.*

Newell, Clayton R., *The Regular Army Before the Civil War, 1845-1860*; *CMH Publication 75-1.*

Wineman, Bradford A., *The Chancellorsville Campaign, January – May 1863; CMH Publication 75-9.*

Articles

O'Reilly, Francis A. *"The Real Battle of Fredericksburg: Stonewall Jackson, Prospect Hill, and the Slaughter Pen"* Blue & Gray Magazine; Volume XXV, Issue 5; 2009.

Tucker, Glenn. "*Winfield S. Hancock*" Civil War Times Illustrated; August 1968.

Official Reports

Hancock, Winfield S., *Official Reports of the Military Operations of Major General Winfield Scott Hancock, 1861-1865*; Volume One. (1882).

Hancock, Winfield S., *Civil Record of Major General Winfield S. Hancock During His Administration in Louisiana and Texas.*

Ohio State University; *The War of Rebellion: A Compilation of the Official Records of the Union and Confederate Armies*;

Academic Papers

GeRue, Gerald G. *"Generals Chamberlain, Hancock, and Thomas: A Leadership Study for the Modern Leader."*

Letters and Addresses

Lambert, William H. *"Major General Winfield Scott Hancock: Oration at the National Cemetery,"* Gettysburg, May 29, 1886.

Library of Congress, *Henry Hunt Letters: Official Reports and Correspondence.*

Military Service Institute of the United States. *Letters and Addresses Contributed at a General Meeting of the Military Service Institute, Held at Governor's Island, New York City, New York, February 25, 1886, in Memory of Winfield Scott Hancock*

Military Order of the Loyal Legion of the United States (MOLLUS). *In Memoriam: Major General Winfield Scott Hancock, United States Army*

Memoirs and Autobiographies

Early, Jubal. *Lieutenant General Jubal A. Early, Confederate States of America.*

Grant, Ulysses Simpson. *Personal Memoirs of U. S. Grant (Two Volumes).*

Gordon, John B. *Reminiscences of the Civil War;*

Hancock, Almira Russell, *Reminiscences of Winfield Scott Hancock.*

Heth, Henry. *The Memoirs of Henry Heth*

Hood, John B. *Advance and Retreat: Personal Experiences in the United States & Confederate States Armies.*

Lee, Robert E. *Recollections and Letters of General Robert E. Lee.*

Longstreet, James. *From Manassas to Appomattox: Memoirs of the Civil War in America.*

McClellan, George Brinton, *McClellan's Own Story*

Meade, George. *The Life and Letters of George Gordon Meade, Major General United States Army*

James H. Kelly

Sorrel, G. Moxley. *Recollections of a Confederate Staff Officer.*

Books

Alexander, Edward Porter. *Military Memoirs of a Confederate: A Critical Narrative.*

Axelrod, Alan. *Generals South, Generals North: The Commanders of the Civil War Reconsidered.*

Bearss, Edwin C. *Field of Honor, Pivotal Battles of the Civil War.*

Buell, Thomas B. *The Warrior Generals: Combat Leadership in the Civil War.*

Dennison, Charles Wheeler. *Winfield: The Lawyer's Son and How He Became a Major General (Public Doman Reprint).*

Foote, Shelby. *The Civil War: A Narrative, Volume 2-Fredericksburg to Meridian Volume 3-Red River to Appomattox.*

Forney, John W. *The Life and Military Career of Winfield Scott Hancock.*

Goodrich, Frederick E. *Life and Public Service of Winfield Scott Hancock, Major-General.*

Gottfried, Bradley M., *The Maps of Antietam.*

Guelzo, Allen C. *Gettysburg-The Last Invasion.*

Historical Society of Montgomery County. *Bulletin of the Historical Society of Montgomery County Pennsylvania: Volume XXXVII.*

Jordan, David M, *Winfield Scott Hancock: A Soldier's Life.*

Junkin, David Xavier & Norton, Frank Henry, *The Life of Winfield Scott Hancock: Personal, Military and Political.*

Kreiser, Lawrence A., Jr. *Defeating Lee: A History of the II Corps Army of the Potomac.*

Lyman, Theodore, (Edited by Lowe, David W.). *Meade's Army, The Private Notebooks of Lt. Col. Theodore Lyman.*

Millard, Candice, *Destiny of the Republic, A Tale of Madness, Medicine and the Murder of a President.*

First and Always: Rebellion

Morrison, James L., *The Best School: West Point 1833-1866.*

O'Reilly, Francis A. *The Fredericksburg Campaign, Winter War on the Rappahannock.*

Quarstein, John V., and Moore, J. Michael. *Yorktown's Civil War Siege, Drums Along the Warwick.*

Robertson, James I. *General A. P. Hill: The Story of a Confederate Warrior.*

Stine, J. H. *History of the Army of the Potomac.*

Stuckenberg, John H. W., *Diary entry, November 12, 1862, "I'm Surrounded by Methodists."*

Styple, William B. *Generals in Bronze: Interviewing the Commanders of the Civil War.*

Walker, Francis Amasa. *History of the Second Army Corps in the Army of the Potomac.*

Made in the USA
Columbia, SC
14 January 2020

86632101R00163